Sarah Mallory grew up in th... England, telling stories. She r... with her young family, but after nearly thirty years of living in a farmhouse on the Pennines she has now moved to live by the sea in Scotland. Sarah is an award-winning novelist, with more than twenty books published by Mills & Boon Historical. She loves to hear from readers, and you can reach her via her website at: sarahmallory.com.

Also by Sarah Mallory

*Cinderella and the Scarred Viscount
The Duke's Family for Christmas
The Night She Met the Duke
The Major and the Scandalous Widow
Snowbound with the Brooding Lord
Wed in Haste to the Duke
The Earl's Marriage Dilemma*

Lairds of Ardvarrick miniseries

*Forbidden to the Highland Laird
Rescued by Her Highland Soldier
The Laird's Runaway Wife*

Discover more at millsandboon.co.uk.

A KISS TO STOP A WEDDING

Sarah Mallory

MILLS & BOON

All rights reserved including the right of reproduction in whole or in part in any form. This edition is published by arrangement with Harlequin Enterprises ULC.

This is a work of fiction. Names, characters, places, locations and incidents are purely fictional and bear no relationship to any real life individuals, living or dead, or to any actual places, business establishments, locations, events or incidents. Any resemblance is entirely coincidental.

Without limiting the author's and publisher's exclusive rights, any unauthorized use of this publication to train generative artificial intelligence (AI) technologies is expressly prohibited. HarperCollins also exercise their rights under Article 4(3) of the Digital Single Market Directive 2019/790 and expressly reserve this publication from the text and data mining exception.

® and TM are trademarks owned and used by the trademark owner and/or its licensee. Trademarks marked with ® are registered with the United Kingdom Patent Office and/or the Office for Harmonisation in the Internal Market and in other countries.

First published in Great Britain 2025
by Mills & Boon, an imprint of HarperCollins*Publishers* Ltd,
1 London Bridge Street, London, SE1 9GF

www.harpercollins.co.uk

HarperCollins*Publishers*, Macken House, 39/40 Mayor Street Upper, Dublin 1, D01 C9W8, Ireland

A Kiss to Stop a Wedding © 2025 Sarah Mallory

ISBN: 978-0-263-34521-6

06/25

This book contains FSC™ certified paper and other controlled sources to ensure responsible forest management.

For more information visit www.harpercollins.co.uk/green.

Printed and Bound in the UK using 100% Renewable Electricity at CPI Group (UK) Ltd, Croydon, CR0 4YY

For the Quayistas—
Jenny, Joanna, Melanie, Liz, Janet and Lesley.

I owe you such a lot!

Chapter One

'Woah, there, Magpie.'

Matt Talacre brought his horse to a stop at the crossroads. He had been travelling along the old Roman road for nearly twenty miles and knew he must be nearing his destination. An old man in a smock was approaching from the north. He was leading an ox cart and Matt eased the horse to the side of the road.

'Good day to you,' he called. 'Can you tell me which is the way to Whilton?'

The old man looked up at him from beneath his battered hat, squinting slightly against the evening sun.

'I'm thinking it should be that road, to the east.' Matt nodded towards one of the tracks.

'Aye, and you'd be thinking right,' agreed the old man, not breaking step. 'Follow that road fer nigh on two mile, past the windmill, and it'll bring ye to Whilton.'

Matt touched his hat and, when the cart had lumbered passed him, he trotted off along the lane. It ran fairly straight, between green fields and hedges white with May blossom. Before long he spotted the round stone tower of the windmill, its sails turning lazily, and not long after he was riding into a small market town.

He made his way along the wide main street until he came upon the Whilton Arms, a large hostelry with a brightly coloured sign hanging over the door. Matt turned and rode through the arch into a large stable yard, where he left Magpie with an ostler, and went into the taproom. After the sunlight it was dark inside and, when his eyes had adjusted, he saw there were very few customers. He ordered a tankard of ale from the landlord and asked, in his cheerful way, if he was far from Whilton Hall.

'No, sir. 'Tis about two miles south of here, by road.'

'And will I find Lord Whilton there?'

The man shrugged. 'I believe not, although His Lordship ain't in the habit of telling me his business.'

The landlord moved off and Matt sipped his ale. It was unfortunate, after coming all this way, if his quarry was not at home, but he would go to the house anyway and enquire.

A couple of hours later, after bespeaking a room for the night, Matt rode off to Whilton Hall. A circuitous, tree-lined drive led to a redbrick stable block, and beyond that a moated manor, complete with a stone bridge and imposing medieval gatehouse.

A stable hand appeared. Matt left the mare and a silver sixpence, for which the man volunteered the information that if he made his way across the bridge and went to the big oak door on the far side of the inner courtyard, he could ask the housekeeper to show him around the house.

It was not Whilton Hall that Matt wanted to see, but he did not enlighten the stable hand. He merely thanked the man and went off to the house, where a footman informed him that Lord Whilton was not at home.

'My enquiries in London gave me to understand that he was coming here,' said Matt. 'Perhaps you could tell me when you are expecting him—in a day, a week?'

'As to that, sir, I couldn't say,' the footman replied woodenly.

Matt extracted a visiting card from a small silver case and handed it to the man. 'Then I will leave this for him. I wish to see Lord Whilton on a matter of business and I shall call again.'

'As you wish, sir.' With a stiff bow the servant stepped back and shut the door, leaving Matt to make his way back to the stables, where he collected his horse and returned to the village.

The Whilton Arms provided him with a very comfortable room and a very tolerable dinner, although Matt did not linger over his meal. Glancing out of the window at the clear sky, he calculated that there was at least another two hours of daylight. Time enough to reconnoitre the ground. Lord Whilton might not be at home, but he might just find what he was looking for.

Flora Warenne stood by the drawing room windows, looking out at the distant woods and hills. She had spent the day shopping in Whilton with her Aunt Farnleigh, but now she was longing to be out of doors again. Not in the garden, with its well-scythed lawn and elegant flower borders, but somewhere wilder, less ordered. Somewhere more in tune with her current restless spirit.

'I think I shall go for a walk,' she announced.

'Really, dear?' Aunt Farnleigh looked up from her embroidery. 'Surely it is too late.'

Flora glanced at the clock; it was not yet seven. Most of their friends would only now be sitting down to dinner, but her aunt and uncle maintained their custom of dining at five whenever they were not entertaining guests. It was something Flora attributed to their age.

Her late father had been the youngest of the family, Aunt Farnleigh the eldest, and it was often supposed by those who had not been introduced that Flora was under the care of grandparents, rather than her aunt and uncle. It had not worried Flora when she was younger, but in recent years she had become aware that they were becoming more fixed in their ways. She smiled fondly at her aunt.

'It is a fine evening and there are a good two hours of daylight yet. Plenty of time for a walk.'

'Very well, my love,' said Aunt Farnleigh. 'As long as you take Betty or one of the other maids with you.'

'I shall not go alone, Aunt,' Flora promised her.

'And be back before sunset,' added her uncle, not looking up from his newspaper.

'I shall make sure of it, sir.'

Flora dropped a light kiss on his head as she passed and ran off to collect her pelisse and bonnet.

Ten minutes later she was walking briskly down the drive. When she reached the gates, she crossed the road and proceeded into Whilton wood. She had every intention of being home again before dark, but as for not going out alone, she had brought Scamp, her uncle's old spaniel, with her. That was surely sufficient protection in these woods, where she had never seen anyone save the woodland creatures and occasionally one of the groundskeepers.

The wooded valley was her favourite walk and this her favourite time of year, with the bluebells in full bloom and even now, so late in the day, the wild garlic was adding its pungent scent to the air. She had not gone far before she realised that the recent rains had saturated the ground, and when Scamp came bounding back with his liver and white flanks a uniform muddy brown, she realised it was too wet to continue walking down into the valley.

Calling the little dog to heel, she made her way upwards until she came to the narrow lane through the woods that led directly to Whilton Hall. Since the grounds there were rather neglected, they would serve her purpose just as well. At this time of the day, with the Viscount away, the gardens would be deserted.

Flora had no idea why she should be so restless. It had been coming upon her gradually all spring and, despite her work with numerous charities and helping Aunt Farnleigh with the running of Birchwood House, she felt she was drifting aimlessly into another summer.

At six-and-twenty, she had few close friends in Whilton. The young ladies making their come-out were little more than schoolgirls, while most of those of her own age were married. Their worlds, and conversation, revolved around home and children and, try as she might, Flora could not enter wholly into their concerns.

She bent and picked up a stick, throwing it as far as she could for Scamp to retrieve.

'The fact is, I am *bored*!' she announced to the air, watching the spaniel coming back towards her with his prize, 'Oh, there are promises of great things, once I am married, but nothing is happening *now*.'

She needed an occupation, something to tax her.

She had reached the edge of the woods and could see the gardens of Whilton Hall ahead of her. The roofs and upper floors of the house were visible beyond the overgrown hedges and everything was bathed in the warm evening sunlight.

'Well, there is no reason why I shouldn't imagine how I might reorganise the gardens,' she said aloud, quickening her pace. 'Scamp, come!'

Before her, on the bend in the track, was a hornbeam hedge with a gate into the formal gardens. She stepped through the gate into the overgrown shrubbery, thinking, not for the first time, that Whilton Hall deserved better care. The Viscount employed only one elderly gardener plus a few assistants who kept the paths free merely by hacking back the bushes, heedless of the way they grew higher in an attempt to reach the sunlight. This resulted in the shrubbery walk being in almost constant shadow and not at all the place to linger. Scamp, clearly not sharing her opinion, went off into the undergrowth to explore new scents while Flora walked on to the Italian garden.

This, too, showed some signs of neglect, but at least here the groundskeepers maintained the lawns and kept everything trimmed to a more manageable height, allowing sunlight to reach the flowerbeds. Flora made her way around the paths, thinking of the improvements she would like to make. The small pool around the fountain should be restocked with goldfish and the colonnade leading to the next part of the gardens would look far better if it was covered by climbing plants.

What should they be? she mused as she reached the end of the colonnade and stepped through the arched opening in the hedge. Honeysuckle, perhaps, or jasmine. Or—

'Oh!'

Flora came to a halt, her pleasant daydreams shattered as she found herself face to face with a stranger.

Chapter Two

'What the devil?'

'Who are you?'

They both spoke at the same time, but the stranger recovered his wits first. He took a pace back, much to Flora's relief.

'I thought the family were from home,' he said.

'They are.'

He frowned. 'You do not look like a servant.'

'I am not. I am walking my dog.'

The stranger's brows rose and he glanced around before fixing her with an enquiring—and slightly disbelieving—eye. She felt a flush rising, but at that very moment there was a bark and Scamp ran up, his tongue lolling.

If Flora hoped for some show of protection from her canine companion, she was disappointed. The spaniel trotted happily up to the stranger, who bent and scratched at the liver-coloured head.

'Well now, who is this?'

'Scamp,' muttered Flora, watching as her pet fawned and sniffed at the glossy top boots.

'Scamp, is it? And a scamp you are, sir, not to take better care of your mistress!'

With a final pat on the dog's head, the man straightened.

He gave a crooked grin which Flora found surprisingly beguiling and she was sorely tempted to smile back. There was no denying the man was attractive, with his dark hair curling out beneath a tall hat and chocolate-brown eyes that glinted with amusement. But he was a stranger and, despite his snowy neckcloth and well-fitting coat, very probably a trespasser, so instead she gave him a haughty look.

He took off his hat and swept her an elegant bow. 'Matthew Talacre, at your service, ma'am. Matt to my friends.'

She ignored his last words, and the glinting smile that accompanied them.

'May I ask again, sir, what you are doing here?'

'I hoped to see Lord Whilton. Having written to him and not received a reply, I thought I would seek him out.'

'But you know the family is not at home, so why are you in His Lordship's garden?'

'I might ask you the same thing.'

That disconcerting smile was still hovering around his mouth and she put up her chin.

'I am Flora Warenne. Lord Whilton's fiancée.'

'His fiancée!'

Flora was not offended by the stranger's obvious astonishment; she often wondered herself what it was that had persuaded Quentin Gask, Viscount Whilton, to propose to her, but she could not deny it rankled.

'And what do you find so strange about that?' she demanded.

Yes, why the devil should that surprise me? Matt asked himself.

The lady was a beauty. Her figure showed to advantage beneath a rust-coloured pelisse and flame-red hair peeped out from beneath a straw bonnet and framed delicate features with the translucent look of fine porcelain. Eyes the colour of hazel nuts, fringed with dark lashes, regarded him fearlessly while a sprinkling of freckles decorated her straight little nose. And as for that generous mouth...

'Well, sir? Has the cat got your tongue?'

He dragged his thoughts away from wondering what it would be like to kiss those rosy lips.

'Why, nothing strange about it at all, ma'am, save that you are unescorted.' He added, before she could protest, 'Although, of course, you do have your guard dog.'

He glanced down at the spaniel, who had lost interest in the humans and was sniffing around the base of the stone statue at the centre of the small lawn. Looking again at the lady, he saw her lips twitch. A smile was forming, but she quickly shut it down.

'I must go.' She turned away and called to her dog.

'I will come with you.'

'There is no need. Scamp, come *here*!'

'But I am staying at the Whilton Arms and therefore going that way. I left my horse at the end of the lane. Did you see her? A piebald mare.'

'No, I did not see her.' Flora was relieved when the spaniel came up and sat at her feet, his flanks heaving. He was unusually relaxed with this stranger and clearly sensed no danger. She added, less sharply, 'I came in through the woods.'

'Ah, yes. I passed a narrow track, about halfway along the path. Would that be it? Please do not be alarmed, ma'am. I am perfectly respectable.'

There it was again, that roguish smile. Flora quickly looked away.

'You are trespassing,' she reminded him.

'But in a good cause. Perhaps you would like to know what it is?' She glanced up at him then, and he continued. 'I came to Warwickshire in search of a statue.'

'Is that why you are here, in this arbour, looking at the sculpture of Mars?'

'Yes, although I know it by its Greek name, Ares, rather than the Roman. It was stolen from me.'

'Stolen!'

'Sold off by someone with no legal right to do so. Would you like me to explain?' He took her silence as assent, and went on. 'I am the co-owner of a pleasure gardens in Gloucestershire. I took charge just over two years ago and shortly before that the manager, a shifty fellow called Hackthorpe, sold off several pieces, including the statue of Ares. It is one of a pair, Ares and Aphrodite, carved from Portland stone and commissioned from Rysbrack by the first owners of the gardens, some sixty years ago. The commission is recorded in an early accounts ledger, which fortunately was never in Hackthorpe's possession.'

'How can you be sure it is the same?'

'I remember seeing the pair, when I first visited the gardens, and I noticed they both had identical markings carved on the back. Ares was gone by the time I took charge.

'There is no record in the accounts of the statue being sold. Hackthorpe denied it and he was careful to cover his tracks, but not quite clever enough. I discovered a letter addressed to him from Lord Whilton, referring to an advertisement in the *Warwickshire Advertiser* and offering him fifty guineas for the sculpture. I found it between the pages of one of the older ledgers, where it had obviously been mislaid.'

As he was speaking Flora moved closer to the statue. She studied the classical face, clean shaven and with curling hair very much like that which was now so fashionable. Very much like that of the stranger, she thought, before brushing the idea aside.

The figure was seated on a rock, sword in one hand and naked save for the stone drapery covering his hips and thighs. It was certainly a very fine piece. She remembered how pleased Lord Whilton had been when he installed it in this garden two years ago. The day he had asked her to marry him.

There might be some truth in the stranger's story, but she could not admit that. It would be like betraying Quentin.

'So, you see,' said the man, coming to stand beside her, 'it is a matter of some delicacy that I need to discuss with the Viscount.'

'And I am sure His Lordship will be pleased to listen to you, when he returns,' she said coolly. 'Good day, Mr Talacre.'

'I am coming with you.'

'I would rather you did not.'

'But I am obliged to go that way, to collect my horse.' His brown eyes gleamed with mischief. 'Or would you prefer me to walk behind you, like a medieval page?'

'Of course not!' It was a ridiculous suggestion and she could not prevent a quiver of laughter in her voice.

He grinned. 'Very well then. Shall we—?'

'Hi, you!' demanded a loud, rough voice. 'What are you doing in here?'

Matt looked up to see a small, thin man limping into sight from behind the hedge. He was wearing an apron over his homespun breeches and holding his garden hoe before him in a menacing fashion, but when he saw the lady he stopped and touched his hat to her.

'Oh, 'tis you, Miss Warenne. I beg your pardon; I didn't see you.'

He was still regarding Matt with a wary eye and she said quickly, 'It is quite all right, Jepps. This is Mr Talacre—he came to see Lord Whilton.'

'He ain't here.'

'So I understand.' Matt regarded the groundsman with a sapient eye. 'Military man, were you?'

'I was, until I was wounded and shipped home from Corunna.'

'Thought so. Even your country clothes and high-low boots can't disguise that straight back. Why, you were even wielding that hoe as if it were a bayonet!'

The man stood a little taller. 'Aye, sir. Rifle Corps. But that aside, you shouldn't be here, what with the Viscount being from home and all.'

He shifted uncomfortably and glanced at Miss Warenne, who said quickly, 'Quite right, Jepps. We were just leaving.'

The man nodded. 'Thank you, miss. Would you like me to come with you?'

Matt saw the lady hesitate. She threw him a glance that held more than a hint of triumph and he shrugged inwardly. Ah well, it had been pleasant talking to her and if she was indeed the Viscount's fiancée then it would have been useful to have her support, but it was not to be. Shame, though, he would have liked to walk back through the woods with her and become better acquainted with Miss Warenne. Flora.

'That will not be necessary, Jepps, thank you,' she said, surprising him. 'What I would like you to do is remove the weeds from the flower beds around the south lawn. They are looking very neglected.'

'Very well, miss.' He touched the brim of his soft hat to them and shuffled off with an ungainly, dragging step.

Matt turned to Flora, but the look she gave him made him change his mind about teasing her.

'Shall we go, ma'am?'

He stepped back, inviting her to precede him through the arch in the hedge. She set off, calling sharply to the spaniel, who abandoned the promising scent he had discovered and bounded ahead. In the colonnade Matt fell into step beside her, but they had not gone far when she slowed and he knew immediately that she had noticed his own uneven stride.

He said quickly, 'Do not change your pace for my benefit.'

'But you are limping.'

'I took a French musket ball in my thigh. It is almost completely healed now.'

She did not look convinced. 'If you are sure...'

'Aye, and I am much better if I don't dawdle.'

Flora risked a slight smile, but turned her head away quickly, lest he think her too forward.

'Were you in the army?' she asked him.

'Yes.'

'That explains how you recognised Jepps as an army man. Lord Whilton told me he found the man begging on the streets and took pity on him. He sent him here to work in the gardens.'

'That makes me think better of His Lordship. We see that a great deal more now, since the men came home from Waterloo.'

They walked on in silence, her companion dropping behind whenever the badly tended plants encroached on the path. They had almost reached the hornbeam hedge and the gate into the woods when Flora's muslin skirts snagged on a stray bramble. She stopped quickly to avoid doing more damage.

'Here, let me.'

Flora stood quite still as he bent and carefully unhooked the fine cloth from the thorns. She watched him, admiring the strong hands that could work so delicately. The thought of his fingers so close to her ankles made her breathe carefully, anticipating his touch on her skin. She told herself it was fear of tearing her skirts that stopped her from moving, but that did not explain the slight frisson of disappointment she experienced when he had freed her.

With a brisk word of thanks Flora set off again, but now she was painfully aware of the man at her side. His face and hands were tanned from working in the sun and his lean body strong and supple, despite that slightly uneven step. She had never been allowed to walk alone with any man save Uncle Farnleigh or her fiancé and she was slightly unnerved as they began to make their way along the shadowy lane through the wood.

'What happened to your leg?' she said, to break the silence. 'How were you wounded?'

'My luck ran out.'

She did not want to pry and waited patiently, hoping he would go on. He did.

'Waterloo, and we had Boney on the run. Most of the Frenchies were in retreat, but some were still putting up a fight.'

She shuddered. 'I cannot imagine what that must be like.'

'Like being in hell. There is the deafening noise of cannon and rifle fire, thick acrid smoke blotting out the sky and the screams of the dying or wounded.' He glanced at her. 'I beg your pardon. You do not need to know that.'

'No, I want to understand,' she told him. 'Was that when you were injured?'

'Yes, a sudden flash of pain followed by blessed unconsciousness. I would have died there, if my commanding officer had not come back to look for me. I was taken to the field hospital, where the sawbones did their worst.'

'But you survived,' she said.

'I was luckier than some.'

She saw his lips tighten and he rubbed his damaged thigh.

'Is that why you left the army, because of your injury?'

'In part, but I had had enough of soldiering. Too much death.' He grimaced. 'It wasn't so much the battles, facing the enemy fair and square, I could take that. But I can never forgive those damned spies and informers whose information led to so many being ambushed, cut down without a chance to defend themselves.'

He was staring straight ahead, his thoughts elsewhere. Somewhere dark.

Flora wanted to pull him back from his morbid thoughts. She said cheerfully, 'And now you are a gardener.'

The sombre look fled and he laughed. 'Not quite, I pay a very knowledgeable man to look after the gardens for me, but I am learning.'

'Tell me about your pleasure gardens,' she invited him, wanting to keep his mind on more cheerful matters.

'I would not bore you with it.'

'No, I am genuinely interested. When we met, I was actually planning what I shall do with the gardens here at Whilton Hall when I am mistress.'

He chuckled. 'They are sadly run down, aren't they?'

'Yes. Lord Whilton first showed me the gardens two years ago, when we became engaged, and I have wanted to improve them ever since. His priority has been improving the interior of the house.'

'In readiness for your wedding, no doubt. Have you set a date?'

'Not yet.'

Flora clasped her hands together, fingers seeking out the diamond ring beneath her thin kid gloves. In the last two years the Viscount had spent most of his time in London, which only added to the mystery of why he should have proposed to her in the first place.

She said, 'Lord Whilton has been extremely busy.'

Matt was about to remark that the fellow was neglecting his fiancée as well as his gardens, but the blush on her cheek and something in the lady's manner stopped him.

It's none of your business, man. She is not your concern.

'You said you are from Gloucestershire?' she asked him, clearly trying to steer the conversation in a safer direction.

'Yes. Very close to Bristol. In fact, Bellemonte has splendid views overlooking the city.'

'Bellemonte. That is a pretty name. And you have pleasure gardens there?'

'Not only gardens but bathing pools, too,' said Matt, warming to his theme. 'I have also opened a hotel for our visitors, which is proving a success.'

'That must be gratifying. I should like to see it all, I have never visited such a place.'

'You have not been to Vauxhall? Too busy dancing at Almack's, I suppose!'

He was teasing her, but she answered him seriously.

'No. I have never been to the capital. I cannot recall travelling more than five miles from Whilton since we moved to Birchwood House, when I was ten years old.'

'Never?' Matt was surprised at that, but he did not know the woman, perhaps there was a reason.

She laughed. 'I am afraid you will think me sadly ignorant of the world, sir, although I regularly read my uncle's journals and news sheets. And I am looking forward to travelling a great deal more, once I am married.'

He thought there was something a little strained about her answer, but the next moment she was waving a hand, dismissing the subject as she said, cheerfully, 'But we are digressing, Mr Talacre. Tell me about more about Bellemonte, if you please.'

Matt was happy to talk about it. As a gentleman's son who had clawed his way back from less than nothing, he was proud of Bellemonte's success. He had worked hard to restore the gardens to their former glory as well as repairing the pavilion in the grounds, where balls and concerts were held throughout the year. His companion appeared genuinely interested, asking pertinent questions which encouraged him to continue until they reached the small track leading off the lane, where he stopped.

'This is where we part, I think,' he remarked.

Chapter Three

Flora was surprised to see they had reached the point where she had joined the lane to Whilton Hall. She was even more surprised when she heard the words that came, unchecked, out of her mouth.

'It is as quick for me to continue this way,' she explained, shocked at her brazen behaviour, 'I shall walk with you back to the road. That is, if you do not object,'

'Not at all,' he replied. 'Let us walk on.'

Flora accompanied him, feeling more than a little dazed. She had only encouraged the man to talk about his gardens as a way to avoid any awkwardness, but she had soon become intrigued by his plans for Bellemonte. His anecdotes of the restoration and his early errors were relayed with a dry humour that made her laugh, but she had fully intended to bid him a polite farewell when they reached the gate. Instead, she had elected to walk on with him. He must think her very forward!

'Then you are wise to take this route,' he said, as if

reading her mind. 'The sun will be setting soon and you will wish to be home before dark.'

'Yes.'

'And where *is* home?'

It was an innocent enough question, but he would not be asking it if she had not shown herself foolishly eager for his company. Flora knew she must show more restraint.

'Birchwood House. I live there with my aunt and uncle. Mr and Mrs Farnleigh.'

'And your parents?'

'My mother and father are both dead.'

'Oh, I am sorry.'

She thought him sincere and went on, 'It was sixteen years ago, a carriage accident. They were on their way to France, during the Treaty of Amiens, when their carriage overturned.'

'You were not with them?'

'No, they had left me with Mr and Mrs Farnleigh. Thankfully, my aunt and uncle were happy to offer me a permanent home after the accident. I am very fortunate; they treat me like their own daughter.'

'Warenne,' he said slowly. 'Is that a French name?'

'No. At least, not for centuries. My father was English and my mother Irish.' She glanced at him. 'Did the war give you a dislike of the French?'

'Only those who tried to kill me. Or the one who

stole my life's savings. Only that happened to be a woman.'

'A woman!'

'Yes.' He shrugged. 'I should have known better. It was in the Peninsula, the widow of a French captain. I found her defending herself from our Spanish allies and I took her under my protection. Damned fool that I was.'

He fell silent, abstracted, as if he had forgotten her.

'Will you tell me what happened?' Flora blushed. 'I beg your pardon, that was very forward of me.'

He hesitated and she went on, 'I am no ingenue, sir. At six-and-twenty I think I have learned something of what goes on in the world.'

'I was about your age when I met her, but it didn't make me any wiser. She was very grateful, or so I thought. I asked her to marry me, she agreed and the next town we came to I bought her a ring. Then I gave her my purse to buy herself some new clothes and a few luxuries for our lodgings. That was the last I saw of her.'

'She ran away?' Flora's anger made her fingers curl into claws.

'Aye, but that wasn't the worst of it. She found her way back to a French regiment and passed on everything she knew about my regiment, our troop numbers, position and the route we were taking. They took us by surprise a few days later. Two dozen good men killed because I was fool enough to trust a treacherous woman.'

'I am so very sorry. Not only for the loss of those men, but for your pain. You cared for her.'

He shrugged. 'Good thing, really. It reminded me that I am not the marrying sort.'

'Not even for love?'

He laughed. 'Definitely not for love!'

'And you never saw her again?'

'I did, just once. Years later, when I was in Paris with the Army of Occupation. She was by then married to a French diplomat in the court of the restored Bourbon King.' He grinned. 'She had done very well for herself and, naturally, I had to congratulate her!'

'Naturally.'

She answered in the same light manner, but despite his laughter, she knew instinctively that this woman had hurt him badly.

They walked on together, the birds singing in the trees and Scamp running back and forth easing away the tension and restoring the companionable silence between them. When they were approaching the end of the lane, Flora spotted a large black and white horse, tethered to a tree, just out of sight of the road.

'That must be your mare,' she remarked.

'Yes. Magpie. I am very pleased to see she is still here.'

'No one in Whilton is likely to steal her, Mr Talacre, particularly since she is such a...distinctive creature.'

'Aye.' He rubbed the mare's bony nose. 'Ugly beast, but she suits me very well.'

Flora looked at Magpie, taking in her flowing mane and huge feathered feet.

'I don't think she is ugly at all.' She laughed as the horse gently butted his master. 'And she is clearly devoted to you!'

'And so she should be, I rescued her from a cruel master. She has a good life now.'

He grinned at Flora, who found herself smiling back. She was shocked at how easily they had slipped into an easy camaraderie.

She said primly, 'Goodbye, sir, and thank you for your escort.'

'Will you not let me accompany you to Birchwood House?'

'No, thank you. It is but a step from here and Whilton lies in the other direction.'

'Very well, but let us say au revoir, not goodbye. I may well see you in Whilton.'

Flora shook her head. 'The Viscount is not expected to return to the Hall for another two weeks at least. You will hardly be wanting to kick your heels here for all that time.'

'Oh, I don't know,' he murmured, his dark eyes glinting. 'I could be persuaded to stay.'

Her cheeks on fire, Flora quickly turned and walked away. Matt Talacre was an unconscionable rogue, trying to flirt with her when he knew she was betrothed!

Whatever his business with Quentin, she hoped it was settled quickly, so she would not be obliged to see the man again.

Matt smiled as he watched Flora Warenne hurry off, then he scrambled up into the saddle and rode back to the Whilton Arms. It had been an amusing encounter, but teasing Lord Whilton's fiancée was probably not the best way to enlist her help. With hindsight, he should have asked her more about the Viscount, what sort of man he was. Instead, he had been far too busy enjoying the company of a pretty woman.

'That's your problem, man,' he berated himself aloud. 'For the past few years it has been all work and no play. You have been giving far too much time and attention to Bellemonte.'

Well, perhaps he could mix business with a little holiday. He had planned to be away from Gloucestershire for a full week, so he would remain here and enjoy the local society. They might be able to give him some insight into the owner of Whilton Hall.

He had no wish to enter into a protracted legal battle to regain the statue. That could seriously dent Bellemonte's finances. He hoped the matter might be settled amicably, if he approached Lord Whilton in the right way.

* * *

Flora made no mention of her meeting with Mr Matt Talacre to her aunt and uncle. They were always so careful of her reputation that they would have been shocked to learn she had encountered a strange man in the Viscount's garden. And they would have been aghast if they knew she had walked back with him through the woods, with only Scamp for a chaperon.

She had lived in Whilton since she was a girl and had never seen the need for an escort, even though her aunt and uncle insisted it was necessary. She took her maid or a footman whenever she walked in the town, knowing word was sure to reach Birchwood House if she did not, but she often slipped away to enjoy a solitary walk within the grounds of Whilton Hall, where she never met anyone, save the odd servant or gardener.

Flora did not to join her aunt on a visit to Whilton the next morning, just in case Mr Talacre had not yet left the town, but for the rest of the day she could not settle to anything. She remembered his final words and the look that had brought a blush to her cheeks: she would not put it past the rogue to come to the house before setting off for Gloucester. However, the day passed uneventfully, and it wasn't until Flora went to bed that she realised how disappointed she was he had not called.

* * *

Matt's casual enquiries in the taproom that first evening turned up little of interest, but fortune favoured him the next day when he ventured out into the town and met Sir Roger Condicote, an old acquaintance. They had met when Matt was in Paris, as aide-de-camp to the Earl of Dallamire, and their meeting again resulted in an invitation to join Sir Roger for a day's fishing on Friday.

Matt's cautious enquiries of the gentlemen in the fishing party elicited the information that Lord Whilton considered himself far superior to his neighbours.

'Breeding is everything to the fellow,' said one. 'He is obsessed with his ancestry.'

'Aye.' another said, laughing. 'Would you believe it? He paid the owner of the other inn on the High Street to change its name from the Golden Lion to the Red Lion. And all because his family originally come from Gascony. That cost him a pretty penny!'

'And now he's anxious to improve his bloodline with a good marriage,' remarked the first.

'Oh?'

Sir Roger, fishing beside Matt, nodded at an elderly gentleman further along the bank, who was currently reeling in a fair-sized trout. 'See Farnleigh over there? Whilton is betrothed to his niece. Flora Warenne only has a small dowry, but she can trace her ancestors back to the Conqueror. The Gasks were nothing until one of the Stuart kings created the first Viscount Whilton.'

'An admirable match on both sides then,' said Matt.

'The Farnleighs are delighted.' Sir Roger replied 'Flora Warenne is a lovely young woman, Talacre, but she is past her first blush, as they say. I think they despaired of her ever marrying.'

'Then local bachelors must be blind,' exclaimed Matt, unable to help himself.

'Oh, 'tis not for want of interest,' said the portly man. 'She's had several admirers over the years, but it never came to anything. Then Lord Whilton offered for her and she accepted.'

'Perhaps she had set her heart on a title,' Matt suggested.

'I am not so sure about that,' replied the portly man. 'She turned him down first time, but her aunt and uncle persuaded her to accept him.'

Matt frowned and was so lost in thought that he did not react quickly enough to the tug on his line and the fish escaped before he could set the hook.

'And will Whilton make her a good husband?' he asked, casting his line again.

'As good as any other great man.' Sir Roger lowered his voice. 'I wouldn't think Farnleigh knows of it, but I heard the Viscount has installed his mistress as housekeeper at Whilton Hall. If it's true, it's a damned shabby thing to do, with his fiancée living so close.' He glanced up. 'But enough now. Here comes Farnleigh and it's not a subject he would want us discussing.'

The gentlemen turned their attention to the fishing and nothing more was said, but when they were all packing up for the day, Matt was surprised to receive an invitation from Mr Farnleigh to come to Birchwood House for dinner. Matt demurred, but Farnleigh brushed aside his reservations.

'Pho, man, I know Sir Roger and his lady have an engagement, so you can't dine with them. And if you've nothing planned other than to eat alone at the Whilton Arms tonight then you must come. My wife loves nothing better than to entertain. She is forever complaining that I do not bring enough friends back to dine with us. And then there's Flora, my niece. She will be glad to have someone younger to converse with.'

Matt suspected that Flora would be anything but pleased to see him and was about to refuse, but some demon of mischief got there first.

'I'd be delighted, sir, if you are sure Mrs Farnleigh will not object?'

'Not at all, man. Nothing she likes more than to show off her housekeeping skills! We dine at seven on fishing days, Mr Talacre, so you have plenty of time to get back to your rooms and change first.'

Chapter Four

By Friday morning Flora had heard nothing more of Matt Talacre and that did much to restore her equilibrium. There was no denying she was at fault for speaking with a stranger, and even more so for accompanying him back through the wood, unchaperoned. The man was even more to blame, of course: he should not have been in the gardens in the first place. Still, no harm had been done, the man must have left Whilton by now and she could put him out of her mind.

It was a shock, therefore, when she entered the drawing room before dinner that evening, to find Mr Matt Talacre conversing with her aunt and uncle. She stopped in the doorway, appalled to realise how pleased she was to see him again. Her heart was beating so hard against her ribs she feared everyone could hear it. This was not right. She had never felt like this at seeing Quentin, had she?

Both gentlemen had risen from their seats, but it was Aunt Farnleigh who greeted her.

'Ah, here is my niece now,' she exclaimed, looking flustered but not displeased. 'Come in, Flora. We have an unexpected guest for dinner tonight.'

'Unexpected, but not unwelcome,' declared Uncle Farnleigh, laughing. 'Flora, my dear, allow me to present Mr Talacre.'

'Good evening, Miss Warenne.'

Flora stared at Matt Talacre as he reached for her nerveless hand and bowed over it.

'We met at Sir Roger Condicote's fishing party today,' explained her uncle. 'And when I heard Talacre was at a loose end this evening I suggested he come and take pot luck with us.'

'Indeed,' she murmured. Was it mere coincidence that he was here? Perhaps the Fates were conspiring to test her loyalty to her fiancé. Or perhaps Matt Talacre was playing some deep game of his own. She would need to be on her guard.

'And very pleased we are to have him join us,' declared Aunt Farnleigh, who prided herself upon keeping a good table. 'Although I have warned you, Mr Talacre, it will only be our usual fare. Just two courses, I'm afraid, but it includes a fricassee of wild rabbit and a haunch of mutton. As well as the trout and barbel Mr Farnleigh caught today.'

'Madam, I can think of nothing finer.'

Aunt Farnleigh's reaction to these words showed quite clearly that she had succumbed to their guest's undoubted charm. A blush warmed her faded cheek and there was an added spring in her step as she moved off to speak with her husband.

Flora rounded on their guest. 'What are you *doing* here?' she hissed.

'Your uncle was kind enough to invite me,' he murmured. 'And as it appeared you hadn't mentioned our meeting, I thought it best to act as if it had not happened.'

This reasonable explanation robbed Flora of any excuse for her anger, but it did nothing for her temper.

'I thought you had left Whilton.'

'I had considered it, but then I bumped into Sir Roger Condicote and his invitation to spend a day fishing was...irresistible.' His crooked smile appeared. 'Are you not just a little pleased to see me?'

'Not in the least!'

'I did not plan this, Miss Warenne, I promise you. Pray, cry pax with me.'

Flora discovered she was no more impervious to the man's charm than Aunt Farnleigh, but she was not quite ready to give him a smile just yet. She indicated by a look that he should move with her towards the window, where they would not be overheard.

'What have you given as your reason for being in Whilton?'

'That I have business with the Viscount, nothing more.' He leaned a little closer. 'So you see, Miss Warenne, your secret is safe with me.'

'*My* secret! I was not the one trespassing.'

He laughed again at that, but as the butler came in at that moment to announce dinner there was no time to utter a rebuke. With an audacious wink he went off to give his arm to Aunt Farnleigh, leaving Flora to accompany her uncle into the dining room.

Flora could not fault Mr Talacre's manners at dinner. He was neither too flattering, praising every dish far beyond its merits, nor too reticent, sitting silently and leaving all the work of conversation to others. He conversed easily and intelligently upon every subject that his hosts introduced and initiated several discussions himself.

She found it impossible to dislike the man and when the ladies went off to the drawing room, leaving the gentlemen to enjoy a glass of brandy together, she was not surprised to hear her aunt describe Mr Talacre as a very amiable gentleman.

'Unmarried, too,' she continued, 'which will set a few hearts a-fluttering at Monday's ball.'

'Goodness, will he be here for that?' asked Flora, startled.

'Why, yes. He is staying until at least Tuesday, because he wants to attend the Antiquarians' lecture that evening.' Aunt Farnleigh's brow furrowed in concentration. 'It is something about Grecian sculptures, I think.'

'Oh, of course,' said Flora, thinking of the statue of Mars. 'That makes sense.'

'It does?'

Flora felt her cheeks grow warm under her aunt's puzzled glance and hastened to say, 'I believe these antiquities are of interest to many gentlemen. Only think of the British Museum, buying the Parthenon Sculptures from Lord Elgin.'

Aunt Farnleigh was unconvinced. 'I must say I cannot see anything of interest in old blocks of carved stone. Very pretty in their way, I am sure, but I believe most of them to be broken beyond repair. Headless gods and goddesses with no arms—why on earth would anyone think that interesting, let alone *valuable*?'

Flora found herself wishing that Mr Talacre was there to share her amusement at that.

'Not that it would do to say as much in Lord Whilton's presence,' her aunt went on. 'He would be quite shocked to hear me speak so disparagingly of the classical world.'

The mention of her fiancé put an abrupt end to Flora's amusement. It was true, Quentin would disapprove of her aunt's views. He had a serious regard for history and he had more than once praised her for her ancient lineage.

'Yes,' she said now, 'we avoid talking of anything contentious with the Viscount, don't we, Aunt?'

She was unable to keep a sigh from her voice and her aunt immediately roused herself to say, bracingly, 'Lord Whilton is perhaps a little set in his ways for such a young man, but he is a *viscount*, my love, and you know how these great men are fêted and, shall we say, a little indulged.' She stopped, lifting her head a little as voices sounded from the hall. 'But hush now, the gentlemen are coming!'

Even as she spoke the door opened. Matt Talacre came in first, laughing at something Mr Farnleigh was saying, and Flora felt her own mood lighten when he smiled at her. He could not be considered classically handsome; his face was too lean, his complexion tanned, a man who spent a great deal of time out of doors. Yet there was something engaging in his smile, and in those dark brown eyes, and Flora could not resist smiling back at him.

That was a mistake, because he immediately came across to sit beside her.

'Your uncle tells me you play the pianoforte, Miss Warenne.'

'Yes, a little.'

'Can I persuade you to play something this evening?'

'Yes, yes, Flora, do play,' cried Mr Farnleigh, overhearing. 'Talacre has been listening to me chatter on for the best part of an hour and I am sure he would like something more entertaining!'

Their guest immediately disclaimed, 'You have entertained me most royally, sir, I have no complaints on that score. But I confess I should very much like to hear Miss Warenne play.'

'You could try out that new piece you have been practising for Lord Whilton's return,' suggested Mrs Farnleigh. She smiled at their guest. 'You might not have heard, Mr Talacre, that my niece is betrothed to the Viscount.'

'Indeed, ma'am?' replied the gentleman, giving Flora an amused glance.

It was a clumsy attempt to warn him off, thought Flora, and Mr Talacre was well aware of it.

'Yes, I know she is our niece, so we are naturally biased, but His Lordship is very fortunate to find such a jewel,' remarked Uncle Farnleigh, with a proud smile. 'But then, we have had the upbringing of her since she was ten years old and, though I say it myself, I do not think there is a more accomplished young lady in the county.'

'Enough, enough,' cried Flora, getting up. 'Such praise is putting me to blush, Uncle. Doubtless I shall confound you now by playing the new piece *very* badly!'

Laughing, she walked over to the piano, trying to ignore her aunt, who was confiding to Mr Talacre that she expected a date to be set for the wedding as soon as Lord Whilton returned.

'Everything was postponed, you see, sir, due to a bereavement in the Viscount's family.'

Flora began sorting through the music, concentrating her attention on her forthcoming performance rather than the conversation in the room. She succeeded so well that she jumped when she heard Matt's voice at her shoulder, just as she was placing the sheet music on the stand.

'Allow me to turn the pages for you.'

'Thank you, but there is no need.'

'If you are not yet proficient, then I am sure there is.'

He was teasing her and she could not help responding.

'My performance shouldn't be that bad!' She narrowed her eyes at him. 'I am more likely to be put off by you hovering over me.'

He pulled up a chair beside her. 'Then I shall sit down.'

His audacity made her laugh and she shook her head at him. 'You are an incorrigible rogue, Mr Talacre.'

'Acquit me, madam, I am only trying to be of service to you.'

Flora resolutely turned her attention to the pianoforte. She was alarmed at how easy it was to bandy words with the man and how much she enjoyed it. She breathed slowly, took a moment to calm herself, then began to play. After a cautious start she began to relax and soon she had forgotten everything except the music.

Sitting beside Flora, Matt's concern that he might distract her faded. Her touch was sure and the performance near perfect. He was alert to every note, making sure he turned each page at the right moment, but at the same time he was enraptured by the pianist.

Flora was simply dressed in a gown of white gauze trimmed with green satin, the high waist and low neckline making the most of an admirable figure. As her fingers flew over the keys Matt had an excellent view of her profile with its straight little nose and dainty chin. Her hair was caught up in a green ribbon and a few red curls had been allowed to fall on to the ivory skin of her neck.

Every time he leaned in to turn a page he caught the faint, fresh scent of her perfume. It teased his senses with thoughts of hot summer nights, the fragrance of jasmine filling the air. While his eyes followed the music, part of his brain imagined planting delicate kisses on the slender column of her throat and his mouth slowly moving down to the soft mounds of those creamy breasts…

He flicked over to the last page and she played the

final bars. As the music died away there was a burst of applause from Mr and Mrs Farnleigh.

Flora folded her hands in her lap. 'Well, Mr Talacre, what did you think?'

'Brava, Miss Warenne.'

'Thank you, but it was not a flawless performance. You know it was not.'

He said, with perfect truth, 'I heard nothing amiss.'

She turned to smile at him and Matt was transfixed by the happy glow in her hazel eyes. Time stopped. He had no idea how long they stayed thus, gazing at one another, perfectly at ease, until Mr Farnleigh broke the spell with an awkward cough.

'Very good, my dear, very good,' he said, in a hearty voice. 'Lord Whilton will be most gratified when he hears it, eh, Talacre?'

'The Viscount is a very lucky man,' said Matt, dragging his thoughts back to the present.

Flora shook her head and looked away, blushing.

'Will you play again?' he asked her, but it was Mrs Farnleigh who came bustling up and answered him.

'No, no, sadly there is no more time. Flora, my dear, pray ring the bell for the tea tray. Well, well, Mr Talacre, you see now how hard Flora has worked on that piece. It is an especial favourite of the Viscount's and she has been at pains to learn it for him. They are quite devoted to one another, you know.'

Matt did not miss the note of warning in Mrs Farnleigh's words and knew he must heed it. Flora Warenne might be a beauty, but she had told him herself she was sadly ignorant of the world and that blush on her cheek confirmed it. He would be a scoundrel indeed to flirt with such an innocent.

Flora moved away from the pianoforte, wondering if Matt would follow her, but Aunt Farnleigh gave him no opportunity to do so.

'Pray come and sit down by me, Mr Talacre, and tell me how you are enjoying your stay in Whilton.'

Flora retired to a chair in the corner and observed her aunt and uncle as they engaged their guest in conversation. It was clear they thought their guest might be a danger. A rival to Lord Whilton for her affections. Their concern was touching, but she knew it was unnecessary. She enjoyed his company, but there was no danger of her falling in love with Matt Talacre. At six-and-twenty she was far too old for girlish fancies of that sort.

There had been a time when she had been susceptible to the charms of a young man, but twice she had been ready to give her heart and her hand to a suitor, only to have them suddenly withdraw, leaving her hurt and bewildered. She knew better than to risk her heart and her happiness on a passing infatuation.

At that moment Matt glanced across at her and she felt again the sudden tug of attraction. She was thankful that she could recognise it and be on her guard against the man's charms. Flora might not love the Viscount, but she liked him well enough and was marrying him for any number of practical reasons. It was an arrangement that suited them both and she had no intention of jeopardising it by indulging in a flirtation with another man.

The party broke up shortly after and Flora could not be sorry, for the evening had become sadly flat. Her aunt and uncle had been at pains to keep Matt Talacre beside them, which she would have found amusing, had she not been so fatigued.

'It was a pleasure to meet you, Miss Warenne,' he said, as he prepared to leave. 'Your performance on the pianoforte was delightful. I hope to hear you play again one day.'

'Thank you. Perhaps you shall.'

He took her hand and Flora's weariness vanished. Her skin burned beneath his grip, tiny arrows of fire darting along her arm. Alarmed at her reaction to his touch, it was all she could do not to snatch her hand away.

To her relief he merely bowed over her fingers before releasing them and she watched him leave the room, listening to his retreating footsteps and the dull thud of the outer door closing. Then she sank back on to her chair with a sigh of relief. She was more vulnerable to his charms than she had thought!

Matt returned to his room at the Whilton Arms and stood for a moment, his back against the door. He had learned precious little about Lord Whilton tonight, but far more than he wanted to know about the man's fiancée. Flora Warenne was beautiful, intelligent, and he found it far too easy to flirt with her, but he could not risk it. Flirting was a dangerous game, even when played by those who understood the rules. Not that he feared for his own heart, but she might mistake his intentions and he did not want to hurt her. Confound it, he *liked* the woman!

He should quit Whilton in the morning and instruct his lawyer to write to the Viscount. After all, he had identified the statue and could prove it belonged to Bellemonte. There was no need for him to get personally involved in its return.

However, after a night's sleep, his mood was far more sanguine. There might be no need for lawyers. He had heard nothing yet to suggest the Viscount was not a reasonable man—if that was the case, then this matter could be settled very quickly and without fuss. And it could do no harm to learn a little more about Lord Whilton.

As for Flora Warenne, if he could make a friend of her, she would be a useful ally. The fact that he found her devilishly attractive was irrelevant.

Or so he told himself.

Chapter Five

It was the Farnleighs' custom, if the weather was fine, to walk to the Sunday morning service at the parish church in Whilton. Flora was therefore surprised when her uncle announced that this particular Sunday they would be using the carriage.

'I have business that will not wait and it will save time if we leave the church directly after the service,' he explained over breakfast.

Flora was not convinced by his airy manner, nor by her aunt's fulsome agreement.

'You are afraid Mr Talacre will be there,' she said, bluntly. 'You want to bundle me into the carriage before he can strike up a conversation.'

'No, no!' exclaimed her uncle, looking most uncomfortable. 'Good heavens, Flora, we would not—that is...'

'My dear sir, I am not in the least in danger of falling in love with Mr Talacre.'

'He is a very charming gentleman,' said Aunt Farnleigh, nervously pleating and un-pleating her napkin. 'It would be quite understandable, with Lord Whilton being away, if you were to find yourself...drawn to him.'

Flora reached across to place her hand over her aunt's restless fingers.

'You need have no fear of that, Aunt. I am aware of Mr Talacre's charms and there is no possibility of my succumbing to them. He is pleasant company, but he poses no threat, I assure you.'

Her uncle harrumphed. 'Well, well. I am very glad to hear that, Flora. However, the carriage is ordered and I think it best that we use it. With His Lordship away we feel responsible for keeping you safe.'

She felt a familiar impatience—irritation at being so hedged about, but at the same time knowing that they were acting like this because they loved her.

She said, 'My dear sir, this is Whilton. I am quite capable of keeping myself *safe* here.'

'Pray now, my dear, do not get on your high ropes,' her aunt begged her. 'We are only thinking of what is best for you. If Lord Whilton should hear that you have been dallying with Mr Talacre, he will not be pleased.'

'Dallying?' Flora laughed. 'What nonsense is this? Why, I have only—'

She stopped. She had been about to say she had only met the man once, and under their roof, but the memory of that first encounter returned and her conscience would not allow her to lie. She stifled her ignoble feelings and smiled.

'Dear Aunt and Uncle, you are always so thoughtful, so considerate. I am a monster to fly up into the boughs when you are only thinking of me. Of course we shall take the carriage and I shall be careful not to…to *dally* with anyone after the service. There, will that do?'

Uncle Farnleigh looked relieved. 'I knew you would understand, my love. Whilton is such a small place and you know how people love to gossip, and drag up old scandals—'

'Not that there is any danger of that!' his wife interrupted him quickly.

'No. No, of course not, my dear.'

'However,' Flora went on, ignoring this interchange, 'Mr Talacre says he has business to discuss with my fiancé and Quentin might be grateful if I could find out just what that business was. It is even possible I could help.'

This made Uncle Farnleigh laugh heartily.

'Whatever the matter may be, I am sure Lord Whilton would not want you to worry your pretty little head about it, my dear!'

She did not reply, but a flicker of rebellion inside Flora had been fanned into a flame by the remark.

By the time she climbed into the carriage after her aunt, she had decided that if she should see Matt

Talacre at church, she would give him her friendliest smile instead of the cool, distant acknowledgement she had originally intended.

In the event, her plans came to nothing. There was no sign of the gentleman at the church. Flora thought that Sir Roger Condicote might mention Mr Talacre when her uncle spoke to him after the service, but he did not, and as they made their way home in the carriage Mrs Farnleigh expressed the hope that perhaps the gentleman had already left Whilton.

'Depend upon it that that is the case,' replied her husband, brightening. 'What would a young fellow do, kicking his heels in Whilton for weeks at a time, waiting for the Viscount to return? I would lay you odds he is gone back to Gloucestershire and will make a proper arrangement to see His Lordship. That would be the sensible thing to do.'

'It would,' said Aunt Farnleigh slowly, 'and yet I think it might be best if we do not attend this month's assembly ball at the Red Lion tomorrow night.'

'What, and miss one of the highlights of Whilton's entertainment?' cried Flora, 'I think not, ma'am. You know how much we both enjoy the dancing.'

'Yes, but Mr Talacre might be there.'

'And what if he is? What possible harm can he do me on the dance floor?'

'A great deal,' replied her aunt, looking anxious.

'We do not know why he wishes to see the Viscount. His Lordship may not be pleased to discover you have been fraternising with the man.'

'I have no intention of fraternising,' she protested. 'Although if he should ask me to dance, I can hardly say no…'

'Oh, heavens, pray do not even think of it,' exclaimed Mrs Farnleigh, fanning herself rapidly.

Flora laughed. 'Pray do not distress yourself, ma'am, I am only teasing you. We do not know for sure if the gentleman has left Whilton, but I am very loath to give up the monthly assembly ball just *in case* he should be present. Besides, all our friends will be there.'

'I confess I do enjoy meeting up with everyone at these events,' admitted Aunt Farnleigh, with a sigh. 'It is not merely the dancing. It is also the only opportunity I have to speak to some of them from one month's end to the next.'

The assembly balls were always lively affairs and were an opportunity for all those in and around Whilton—and who could afford a ticket—to dress up in their finery and enjoy an evening of music and dancing. The assembly rooms also boasted a card room, which was an added incentive for Mr Farnleigh to escort his wife and niece to the ball, and it did not take long for Flora to persuade him they should go.

'There, Aunt,' she said, having won her case. 'We *shall* go to the assembly. After all, why should we deny ourselves the pleasure of an evening's entertainment? Heaven knows we ladies have few enough of them in Whilton!'

It was a warm May evening and the first-floor windows of the Red Lion had been thrown open, allowing the sounds from the assembly rooms to spill out.

'The dancing has already commenced,' remarked Mrs Farnleigh as she stepped down from the carriage. 'Come along, Flora, let us hurry upstairs. You, too, Mr Farnleigh. You know you promised to dance a set with me before you disappear to the card room!'

Ten minutes later they were making their way into the ballroom and Mr Farnleigh was ready to escort his lady on to the dance floor. However, before doing so, he ensured Flora had a suitable partner for the country dance.

Flora was quite happy to stand up with Mr Eddlestone, an old family friend. He was a widower with no thoughts of marrying again, but he had a love of company and dancing and was a regular partner for Flora and the other ladies at the monthly balls. They skipped and tripped through the two dances and afterwards he invited Mrs Farnleigh to stand up with him for the next two. When the lady hesitated, Flora laughed and touched her arm.

'Yes, yes, Aunt, go and enjoy yourself. Jenny Albright and her mother are sitting at the side of the room and I shall join them.'

She watched her aunt walk off with her elderly escort before sitting down beside Jenny. They had been good friends for years and were both accustomed to sitting out some of the dances, since there were never enough gentlemen to partner all the ladies. They were enjoying a lively chat when Mr Makerfield came up.

'Miss Warenne, here is a gentleman most anxious to stand up with you.'

Even before Flora raised her eyes, something told her who was standing beside the Master of Ceremonies. She had liked Matt Talacre in his riding clothes, but now he looked even better, and as he bowed to her she tried not to appear too openly admiring. The snow-white linen of his shirt and neckcloth contrasted with a black tailcoat that clung to his lean frame without a crease and his unruly curls, brushed back into a semblance of order, shone black as a crow's wing.

'I hope you will take pity on a poor traveller and stand up with me for the next two dances, ma'am.'

Flora had fully intended to refuse and introduce him to her friend. Really, she had. Jenny would be delighted to dance with him. But when Matt raised his head and she saw the teasing challenge in his eyes, her resolution wavered. Then he smiled and it melted completely. Without a word, she rose and took his outstretched hand.

'There now,' exclaimed the Master of Ceremonies, beaming at them. 'Plenty of time for the next set, Miss Flora. Off you go now. I vow, Mr Talacre, you could not have a better partner for the Scotch reel! And as for you, Miss Jenny, well now, if Mrs Albright will spare you, there is a young gentleman over here in need of a partner...'

'The man is indefatigable,' remarked Matt, escorting Flora to the dancefloor, 'He is determined everyone will dance.'

'That is his role,' said Flora. She glanced up at her partner. 'Are you telling me you did not ask him to present you to me?'

He laughed. 'I wouldn't dare, since he as good as told you so. Are you flattered or angry with me?'

She shook her head at him.

'Pray do not try to cajole me, Mr Talacre. I am immune to your charms.'

'That is no answer.' He looked down at her. 'Well, ma'am?'

His brown eyes were smiling in a way that sent a delicious shiver running through her. It also set alarm bells ringing in her head and she looked away quickly.

'Neither,' she told him. 'I am content to be dancing.'

'Does the Viscount not dance?'

'Of course. But he is not here.'

And even on the rare occasions when he was in Whilton he could rarely be persuaded to dance, thought Flora as she moved across to take her place in the set. Quentin thought public assemblies beneath him and not all her coaxing could persuade him to dance with her more than once in an evening.

The musicians struck up a lively tune and Flora wondered if Matt's wounded leg would cause him problems in the reel. However, he had no difficulty once the music began.

She was pleased for him, and also relieved that the lively music meant there could be no more conversation. It was all too easy to let down her guard in this man's company. She must keep him at a proper distance. However, by the end of the dance she had enjoyed herself so much that she was happy to leave the floor with him and go in search of refreshments. He procured for her a glass of lemonade and then escorted her to two empty chairs in a deep window embrasure at one end of the ballroom.

She sat down, trying to fan herself and hold her lemonade at the same time.

'Goodness, it is a warm night!'

'Here, let me.' He took the fan from her, wafting the cool air from the open window in her direction. 'Is that better?'

'Blissful.'

She sighed, closing her eyes for a moment, before common sense rushed in and she opened them again quickly. He had turned to face her, plying the fan with one hand while the other rested on the back of her chair. A tiny voice inside warned her she should move away, but she ignored it—she was far too comfortable. It was cooler here by the open window and they were still within view of the dance floor. Well, most of it. There was no impropriety in sitting here, enjoying a glass of lemonade with a gentleman.

Is there not?

That little voice in her head would not be silenced, but she willed herself not to blush.

'We thought you had left Whilton,' she said.

'Oh, why was that?'

'You were not at the service yesterday.'

'I never go near a church, if I can help it. Even being groomsman at my friend Conham's wedding was a trial!'

Something in his voice caught her attention and she glanced up in time to see a shadow cross his face. It was gone in an instant and his eyes were teasing again.

'Was I missed?'

'Not at all. Everyone was engrossed in Mr Johnson's sermon.'

'But *you* noticed.'

This has gone far enough, Flora!

'I will not flirt with you, Mr Talacre.'

'I am not attempting to do so. We are conversing,' he replied, equably. 'Merely passing the time of day. I would not dream of trying to flirt with you.'

He sounded so hurt at the idea that she was obliged to stifle a giggle.

'That's better,' he murmured. 'I like it when you laugh.'

She gave in then and chuckled. 'Are you never serious, sir?'

'Rarely. Life is too short. There is too much to do, too many places to see, ladies to—' he caught her eye again and quickly changed what he was going to say '—to dance with.'

'Then you should go and dance with one of them.' She was finding it more and more difficult to keep the laughter from her voice.

'Later, perhaps. For now, I want to know more about you. How is it you come to be living here, in this quiet backwater?'

'There is nothing to tell. You already know I have lived here very happily since I was a child.'

'No doubt you are looking forward to moving away, when you are married.'

'I shall not be moving very far,' she told him. 'We shall be making our home at Whilton Hall.'

'Is it not a little…small, for a principal residence?'

Flora had thought as much herself, although she would not admit it to anyone.

'The Viscount has a passion for antiquities and Whilton Hall is a fine example of a medieval moated house.' She glanced at him. 'Do you disagree?'

'No, it is a splendid building, but it can hardly be the best of his properties. Is it your choice to live there?'

'He has done a great deal to make it comfortable.'

'Once again you are avoiding my question.'

'You ask too many questions!' Flora retorted, taking her fan back from him.

'I beg your pardon.'

Flora held her tongue and allowed the silence to stretch between them. Until she could bear it no longer.

'I might ask you why you have not returned to Gloucestershire.'

'You know why. I am hopeful of seeing the Viscount.'

'That statue must be very important to you.'

'It is. It belongs at Bellemonte and I want it back.'

Flora remembered how pleased the Viscount had been when he had installed it in his garden. He would not want to part with it.

She said, 'Surely it would be easier, and possibly less costly if it comes to a legal battle, to commission a replacement.'

'Rysbrack has been dead these forty years and a copy would not be the same thing at all. Besides, it is not wholly my property,' he explained. 'I have shareholders to hold me to account, as well as the Earl of Dallamire. He owns the land.'

'One sculpture.' She waved a hand. 'It is very pretty, but is it really worth so much to you?'

'The sculpture is one of a pair and therefore irreplaceable. What I have achieved at Bellemonte has been through honest toil and hard work. I abhor lies and deceit of any kind. It is a point of principle to try to recover my property.'

He sounded very serious and Flora felt a chill of anxiety. If Quentin decided to oppose the statue's return, things could go ill for Matt Talacre.

'Then I wish you good fortune, sir. I hope you will succeed.' She rose. 'The dance has ended. I should go and find my aunt.'

'Yes, of course.'

He took her empty glass and put it with his own on a small side table before leading her away from the window. They had gone only a few steps when she realised how many people were looking at them.

She stopped. 'It might be best if you did not come with me. You should find yourself another partner.'

'Time for that once I have seen you safely restored to your aunt,' was his cheerful response. 'Where are we likely to find her?'

'I would expect her to be with our friends—where I was sitting when Mr Makerfield brought you over. On the far side of the room, by those large windows.'

'Come along, then.'

There was nothing she could do but accompany him as he negotiated a way through the crush of dancers milling around the dance floor. It was so crowded she was not able to see her aunt until they had crossed the room and when she did have a clear view, she saw both her aunt and uncle were talking with the Albrights and Sir Roger and Lady Condicote.

And beside them, watching her approach on Matt Talacre's arm, was Lord Whilton.

Chapter Six

Flora's heart sank. With the Viscount's eyes upon her, she wanted to pull free from her partner, but that would make her look guilty.

'Oh, dear.'

She was hardly aware of speaking until Matt replied, 'I take it that is the fiancé?'

'Yes.' She summoned up a smile and stepped away from her escort, holding out her hands to the Viscount. 'Quentin. What a wonderful surprise!'

'Is it, my dear?' He bowed low over her hand.

'Indeed, it is, My Lord. We had not thought to see you for a se'ennight yet.'

He kept hold of her fingers and pulled them into the crook of his arm, keeping his hand possessively over hers as he turned a haughty gaze upon Matt.

'My servant informed me that someone had called, looking for me,' he drawled. 'Mr Farnleigh now tells me it is you, sir.'

'Yes, it is.' Uncle Farnleigh stepped closer. 'Allow me to present Mr Talacre to you, my lord.'

The Viscount inclined his head in the slightest of greetings. 'You have been here for almost a week, sir. You must be mighty eager to meet with me.'

'Since I have had no response to my letters, I thought I would try my luck at Whilton Hall.'

Flora could almost see the tension swirling around the two men, although they were both at pains to be polite. The Viscount was irritated. He looked at ease and sounded relaxed, but his grip on her hand, where it rested on his sleeve, was vice-like.

'My secretary must have overlooked your correspondence,' he said in a tone of studied indifference. 'I am most sorry you have had to tarry here so long.'

'Oh, it has been no hardship, my lord.'

Matt's eyes flickered towards Flora and she held her breath. He was deliberately taunting the Viscount and that would not help any future meeting between them. She needed to stop this, now.

'Quentin, the next dance is a waltz. Now I have you here, will you stand up with me?' She turned towards him and placed her hand against his coat, smiling up at him and saying playfully, 'If you refuse, I warn you Mr Makerfield will find me another partner. He can be quite a tyrant at these balls, you know.'

'But of course I will dance with you, my dear,' he murmured, his gaze never wavering from Matt

Talacre. 'Call at the Hall tomorrow, sir. At noon. I shall be waiting for you.'

Matt gave a small bow. 'Thank you, my lord. I shall be there.'

With that the Viscount turned and Flora gave a sigh of relief as she accompanied him to the dance floor.

'You were sitting out the dance with Mr Talacre.'

His tone was reproving, but Flora would not be cowed. She responded cheerfully, 'Yes. We were resting after dancing a very lively Scotch reel.'

'What did you talk of?'

'Nothing very much, once I had told him I would not flirt with him.'

The Viscount glanced down at her. 'He tried to flirt with you?'

She laughed. 'Nearly every gentleman tries to flirt with his dance partner, Quentin, you know that. I gave him a set down immediately, there was no harm done.'

The Viscount was silent and she said sharply, 'Whatever the business is between you and Mr Talacre, I will not allow either of you to involve me in your quarrel. Do you understand me, my lord?'

Flora met his gaze and held it, allowing him to see her annoyance, and after what felt like a very long moment he smiled.

'Acquit me of any such intention, my dear. I think perhaps it is Mr Talacre who wishes to cause trouble between us.'

They had taken their places for the waltz and Flora reached out for his hands, ready to begin. She put up her chin and smiled at him.

'He won't do that, Quentin. I promise you.'

The melodic waltz music filled the room. Matt moved back against the wall and watched the dancers as they slowly circled the dance floor. Flora was smiling up at her partner and although Matt was too far away to see her expression clearly, she seemed to be enjoying herself.

He hoped he had not caused any discord between Flora and her fiancé. The Viscount had given Matt a very cool reception, possibly because he was jealous, or maybe he knew why Matt wanted to see him. Flora had said she told no one of their encounter in the garden. If that was so, then the only way Whilton could know of Matt's errand was if he had read his letters.

Matt regretted now that he had baited the Viscount. It might make things more difficult for Flora, although if the man was that jealous, why on earth did he leave his fiancée alone in Whilton for long periods of time?

Ah, well, that was no business of his. Tomorrow he would have an opportunity to put his case to the Viscount about the Rysbrack statue. If things went well and the Viscount agreed to return the statue for the price he had paid for it, then Matt would go back to Gloucestershire and not bother the happy couple again.

* * *

As the last strains of the waltz died away. The Viscount raised Flora from her curtsy and pulled her hand on to his sleeve.

'You do not wish to remain for a second dance?' she asked him as he led her away.

She already knew the answer. His fair hair was ruffled from the dancing and he would want to withdraw and restore its immaculate appearance before disappearing into the card room. In the past she had shrugged and let it pass, but tonight, inexplicably, it annoyed her.

He said, 'I am afraid I do not have your insatiable appetite for the exercise, my dear.'

Flora managed to quell an impatient huff. 'I wonder you should have bothered to attend, if you did not mean to dance with me.'

'Alas, my dear, tonight you were not the main reason I came here. Goole wrote to tell me Talacre had called at Whilton Hall.'

His *housekeeper* wrote to him? she thought, with a flash of resentment. Quentin insisted that all her messages should be included in Uncle Farnleigh's letters, yet a servant was allowed to write!

Flora knew she was being nonsensical and berated herself for her shrewish temper. What was wrong with her tonight? Surely she was not jealous of his housekeeper, just because Mrs Goole was a handsome woman? If so, then she really could not blame Quentin if he objected to her standing up with another gentleman.

'Are you angry with me for dancing with Mr Talacre?'

'Let us say I am…concerned to see you upon such good terms with the man.'

'Good terms?' She laughed and shook her head. 'My uncle brought him to dinner and I danced once with him this evening, that is all.'

'But you also sat out a whole dance with him, in a secluded corner.'

'It was hardly secluded, Quentin. We were sitting in the window because it is cooler.'

'And far more private.'

'Nonsense. We were in plain sight of everyone.' She sighed. 'I am sorry if I have upset you, my lord, but I was trying to be hospitable to a stranger.'

'I would prefer you not to become too friendly with Mr Talacre.'

'Are you in dispute with him?'

His lip curled. 'That would be beneath me. The man is merely an irritation. You are frowning, my dear. Do you disagree?'

'No, but I do not like it when you dismiss people so lightly.'

'But, my dear Flora, he is nothing.'

'And are my aunt and uncle nothing?' she asked, bristling.

'No, no, my love, I must always respect and value your relations. But this man Talacre—what do we know of him? He is an upstart, trying to impose upon my good nature.' He patted her hand. 'I beg you will not concern yourself with this, Flora. I shall deal with the fellow tomorrow.'

'I pray you will be polite to him, Quentin. He was a soldier. He was wounded at Waterloo.'

'Now, how do you know that?'

Under his questioning look Flora felt a blush rising and fought it down. She said airily, 'Oh, I heard some gossip in the town.'

They reached the side of the room just as the musicians struck up for another country dance. Quentin guided her to a chair and took up a position at her side.

He said slowly, 'Do you know, Flora, I believe you like Mr Talacre.'

She fixed her eyes on the figures leaping and skipping around the dance floor. She could not dissemble. The Viscount would see through that in an instant.

'I do,' she admitted. 'Our acquaintance is slight, but I think him an honest man.'

'Ah, but you are one who likes to think well of everyone, my love. You must be on your guard; you have lived a very sheltered life. There are many polite and charming men in this world who will befriend you for their own ends.' He turned to look down at her. 'As your future husband, it is my duty to protect you.'

Flora pressed her lips together to prevent the words that were on her tongue from spilling out. She wanted to tell him she did not need protecting, that she was more than capable of recognising and depressing pretension. But how could she rail at him for wanting to look after her?

As if reading her mind, Lord Whilton gave a gentle laugh. 'Ah, you would like to tell me to mind my own business, would you not? But you *are* my business, Flora. That diamond on your finger confirms it.'

She sighed. 'I know it and I am grateful for your concern, truly. But sometimes I feel…stifled! All my life I have been hedged about—cabined, cribbed, confined, as Macbeth would say—and it irks me, Quentin! I feel there is so much more I could be doing.'

'And so you shall, my love, once we are married. As my Viscountess you will have a great deal to do, including looking after Whilton.'

'And what of your other houses?'

'Yes, those, too, but we are agreed that Whilton Hall will be your home.' He flicked her cheek with a careless finger. 'Now, my dear, I shall take myself off to the card room until the end of the concert, when I will escort you back to Birchwood House. Until then, I shall not *stifle* you, but give you leave to dance with anyone you wish!'

Lord Whilton sauntered off and soon Flora was on the dance floor again, but somehow the lustre had gone from the evening. She learned from Aunt Farnleigh that Mr Talacre had taken his leave while she was waltzing with the Viscount and for once Flora found herself wishing that she might go, too. However, that was not possible and she chided herself for her selfishness. Lord Whilton was making a rare appearance at the assembly and it would be churlish of her to drag him away early from the card room.

The sun was shining when Matt made his second visit to Whilton Hall. He followed the circuitous drive that led to the redbrick carriage house and stable block, where he stopped to look across at the moated manor house, its creamy stone walls and the painted timber and rendering all reflected in the still waters of the moat. Access to the Hall was via a stone bridge and an imposing medieval gatehouse, where this morning, the faded oak doors in the arched entrance were closed against intruders.

Matt left his horse with a groom and crossed the bridge. As he approached the gatehouse a small wicket in one of the doors opened and a footman invited him to step through. Across the courtyard at the entrance door, an elderly butler was waiting to escort him into Lord Whilton's presence.

He was shown into an oak-panelled drawing room

with large, glazed bays on two sides that filled the room with light, somewhat reduced by the colourful stained-glass panels of heraldic symbols at the top of each window. A huge stone chimney piece dominated the room and the painted plaster walls displayed a warlike selection of swords, shields and pikes, the spaces between filled with dark portraits. As for the furniture, everything was constructed of heavily carved dark wood.

Matt thought this must once have been the manor's hall, a relic of an earlier age, and it did not surprise him to find the Viscount sitting in a high-backed oak armchair, like some medieval lord holding court. It was all a little theatrical—he half expected Whilton to put out his hand and insist that Matt kneel and kiss his ring.

The Viscount pushed himself slowly out of his chair and scooped up some sheets of paper from a table beside him.

'Good day, to you, Mr...' He glanced at the papers. 'Mr Talacre.'

If Whilton's intention was to intimidate his visitor, he had failed this time, thought Matt, amused. He inclined his head.

'I see you found my letters.'

'Yes.' Whilton gestured to a chair. 'Do sit down, Mr Talacre. You appear to believe I have a statue of yours here at Whilton Hall.'

'It is not merely my belief, my lord. I have documents and letters to corroborate my claim.' He slipped one hand into his coat and drew out a large packet, which he placed on the sideboard before sitting down. 'Copies of everything are here, verified and signed by a London attorney.'

The Viscount steepled his fingers. 'I purchased that particular statue in good faith. It is perfect in its setting.'

'It is even more perfect in the setting it was commissioned to fill,' replied Matt. 'You bought a stolen item, my lord. It must be returned.'

'You do not appear to understand, Mr Talacre. I am a collector of beautiful objects. But you know that, you have seen my fiancée.'

The Viscount was watching him closely and Matt was careful not to react. It surprised him that his host could talk of Flora Warenne in the same breath as an inanimate stone figure, but that was not his concern. He waited for Lord Whilton to continue.

'I appreciate fine stonework; it speaks of longevity, power. Permanence.' The Viscount waved a hand towards the magnificent chimney piece that dominated the room. 'You see how the overmantel here is ornately carved. The shields denote the Gask family arms through the years, altered and enhanced by successive alliances.'

'And the large wooden shield at the centre?'

'That is my own family arms, the red lion rampant of the Gasks.'

Matt inclined his head. 'And what, exactly, has this to do with my Rysbrack statue?'

'I dispute your claim, Mr Talacre. And besides, the Rysbrack is now in situ here and it is very fine. I like it. Perhaps we could come to an agreement.'

'Such as?'

'I will give you the difference between what I paid and the market price.'

It was Matt's turn to smile. 'Thank you, but no. That sculpture should be at Bellemonte, next to Aphrodite, his goddess.'

'Aphrodite?' The Viscount's brows rose.

'Rysbrack called them after the Greek gods, you see, not the Roman. Whichever names you use, both statues belong to Bellemonte Pleasure Gardens.'

'There, I believe, we must disagree.'

The Viscount fixed his cold blue eyes on Matt, whose gaze never wavered, and he replied in the same level tone that his host had used.

'No, my lord. *You* must agree to return my property.'

A momentary flash of anger crossed Lord Whilton's face and Matt wondered if he was about to be ejected from the house. But no. The Viscount laughed softly.

'Oh, I think not, Mr Talacre. You see, I am not minded to do so.'

'Then my lawyers will be in touch. Good day to you, Lord Whilton.'

'One moment.'

Matt was already moving towards the door but he turned back.

'Let us not be hasty,' purred Lord Whilton. 'It is possible I may be persuaded to change my mind. You interest me, Mr Matthew Talacre. I should like to know you better and learn more of these gardens you talk of. Dine with me here, tonight.'

The invitation surprised Matt.

'Your Lordship is all kindness. Sadly, I have another engagement.' He paused. 'The Antiquarians' lecture, at the Whilton Arms.'

A flicker of dissatisfaction flickered across the Viscount's face but he recovered quickly and waved one white hand in a languid manner.

'No matter. Wednesday, then.' The Viscount's lip curled. 'If you are free, that is?'

'Very well. I have no engagements on Wednesday.'

With a bow Matthew withdrew. It was not the result he had been hoping for, but at least the man had not refused outright to sell him back the statue. He could spare a few more days in Whilton, if there was a possibility of settling this matter without recourse to the law.

Chapter Seven

A faint drizzle was falling when Flora and her aunt and uncle arrived by carriage at Whilton Hall. The driver was instructed to negotiate the narrow bridge and gatehouse arch to the inner courtyard, where footmen were waiting at the entrance door, umbrellas at the ready to shield the guests from the rain.

In the drawing room the candles had already been lit to drive off the gloom of the lowering skies outside. They found Sir Roger Condicote and his lady were present and talking with the Viscount, who rose to greet his new guests.

He lifted Flora's hand to his lips before leaning forward to bestow a chaste kiss on her cheek.

'Welcome, my dear.' Keeping hold of her hand, he turned to address her aunt and uncle. 'I am very pleased you could all attend at such short notice.'

'Not at all, not at all, my lord,' declared Mr Farnleigh, smiling at the Condicotes.

'Indeed,' added Sir Roger, 'we are only too delighted to come.'

'Yes, yes,' gushed Mrs Farnleigh, moving into the room. 'As you know, in general we live very quietly, but to be invited to dinner, only days after the assembly, well, we consider ourselves blessed with a surfeit of pleasure this week!'

The Viscount gave a thin smile. 'It is only a small party; we await but one more guest.' He turned towards the small colourless woman dressed in widow's weeds and sitting in the corner. 'You already know my cousin, of course. Almeria is here once again, to act as my hostess for this visit.'

'Your servant, Mrs Gask.' Mr Farnleigh gave the widow a low bow before turning back to the Viscount. 'We are delighted to see you returned to Whilton Hall, sir. I hope you intend to make a long stay this time?'

'Alas, I can spare no more than a few days,' replied the Viscount, finally releasing Flora's hand. 'Which made it necessary for this sudden invitation. I could not leave the county without dining with my fiancée.'

'Pho!' cried Mr Farnleigh, smiling broadly, 'As to that, sir, you know you are welcome to take pot luck with us any evening. We don't stand on ceremony with you, my lord!'

'Just so.' The Viscount inclined his head and with a final, small smile for Flora, he wandered off to sit and converse with Lady Condicote.

'Well, well, Flora,' murmured her uncle, as she sat down beside him, 'We must put this invitation down to you, then, my dear. A cosy dinner for a few friends, arranged at such short notice—it shows His Lordship esteems you highly.'

'It shows a disregard for anyone else's convenience,' she retorted, albeit quietly. 'We were obliged to cry off from dinner with the Albrights tonight.'

'But you have spent the whole day with Jenny. And Mr and Mrs Albright were not at all offended that we could not dine with them.'

'No, they were most understanding,' Flora admitted. 'But it is not often Mrs Albright is well enough to host a dinner these days. I am sure she was looking forward to the company.'

Mr Farnleigh chuckled and patted her hand. 'Don't you worry, Flora, once your wedding is out of the way your aunt and I will have plenty of evenings to dine with the Albrights while you are off enjoying your new life as a viscountess!'

Flora said no more. She could not admit that she would have preferred to dine with her friends, rather than with her fiancé.

It had not always been that way. When Quentin had asked her to marry him, she had thought it the answer to her dreams. He was handsome, rich and extremely charming. She might not love him, but she enjoyed his company and thought that love would follow, once they were married.

That still might happen, but during this past year of their protracted engagement she had seen very little of her fiancé. He was busy in town, or visiting friends, and even when he was at Whilton Hall sometimes a whole week would pass without them meeting. Sometimes she wondered if he really wanted to marry her at all.

These disturbing thoughts were interrupted when the drawing room door opened. Her uncle looked up.

'Ah, this must be our last guest.'

The Viscount was already on his feet and going forward, saying, 'Welcome, Mr Talacre.'

Matt paused in the doorway, taking in the scene in one glance. The panelled room glowed softly with candlelight and illuminated the little group in the centre. He was surprised to see the Farnleighs there with their niece and he wondered if the elderly woman sitting beside Flora, and dressed head to toe in black, was a relative of theirs, until Whilton introduced her as his cousin, Mrs Gask. Come to add an air of respectability to the bachelor's household, he suspected.

Matt's eyes were drawn back to Flora. Her glorious red hair was caught up in a knot at the back of her head, with a few delicate curls allowed to frame her face. Pearl drops hung from her ears and a single strand of pearls circled her neck, accentuating the creamy skin on display above the low-necked gown.

The Viscount was coming towards him and he was obliged to drag his eyes away from Flora. He made some reply to Lord Whilton, accepted a glass of wine and went to sit down beside Mr Farnleigh. They conversed, but all the time his gaze kept straying back to Flora.

She was seated on the ancient, winged settee, newly re-upholstered in pale blue velvet that complemented the tawny silk of her gown, and when she turned to look at him her hazel eyes were large and luminescent beneath brows that might have been sculpted by the hand of a master. And her expression was one of shock and horror to see him there.

This makes no sense.

Why on earth would the Viscount invite him to a dinner where Flora was present? The fellow had been less than pleased at the assembly, when Matt had walked up with Flora on his arm. If he suspected he had a rival for his fiancée's affections, why would he bring them together like this?

Whilton was playing some deep game, but Matt wanted none of it. He behaved with perfect propriety, but made no attempt to speak to Flora while they waited for dinner to be announced. Then it could not be avoided. The Viscount escorted Lady Condicote while Sir Roger accompanied Mrs Farnleigh and Flora's uncle offered his arm to Mrs Gask. Matt had no choice but to follow on with Flora.

'What are you doing here?' she whispered as they made a slow procession to the dining room.

'I might ask you the same,' he murmured. 'I was expecting to talk business with His Lordship. I suspect he thinks I was flirting with you at the assembly.'

'You certainly tried to give him that impression,' she muttered. 'Your final comment about being *well entertained* was designed to taunt him!'

'It was irresistible.' His lips twitched at the memory.

She gasped. 'How dare you use me in your quarrel!'

'It was nothing to do with any quarrel, merely a natural ballroom rivalry.'

The Viscount had annoyed him with his superior air and Matt had known that his words, and the audacious glance he had thrown at Flora, would anger him. However, the lady was clearly not amused and Matt wished now he had not allowed his irritation to get the better of him.

He said in a low voice, 'It was badly done of me; I beg your pardon.'

There was no time to find out if he had placated her because they were already entering the dining room.

Matt saw at once that their host had set out to impress. The table was covered with an overabundance of silver and glass that glittered and winked in the candlelight. Having held the chair for Flora to sit down, he walked around to take his place between her aunt and Mrs Gask, who was seated at the foot of the table.

He was determined not to give the Viscount cause to think there was anything untoward going on between Flora and himself. As the dinner progressed, he divided his attention between Mrs Farnleigh and his hostess while around them conversation ranged from the new theatre opening in south London to the latest verses published by Lord Byron.

Finally, Matt heard his name on the Viscount's lips.

'I understand Mr Talacre here is the manager of some sort of…pleasure gardens in Gloucestershire,' he announced. 'Is that not so, sir?'

'I am part-owner of Bellemonte, yes.'

The Viscount waved one white hand. 'I stand corrected.'

'Mr Talacre has told us a little about this,' put in Mr Farnleigh. 'It appears the gardens were in a very poor state when he came across them and he has quite turned their fortunes around.'

'I must say it sounds all quite fascinating.' said Lady Condicote, admiring.

'Indeed?' The Viscount smiled, but Matt could see no amusement in those cold blue eyes. 'It appears I am the only one who knows nothing about this venture of yours, sir. Perhaps you would like to explain a little more about these gardens. Are they perhaps like Vauxhall, open to everyone?'

'As long as they can pay the entrance fee,' Matt replied. 'I employ wardens—constables—to maintain good standards of behaviour.'

Sir Roger chuckled. 'To keep the fine young bucks in check, I imagine!'

'Yes, when necessary. We provide entertainment, too, throughout the season. Concerts and balls. Even fireworks, upon occasion.'

'But who attends these entertainments?' demanded the Viscount. 'You are near Bristol, are you not? There can be no comparison with London Society. It must be full of cits and traders.'

Matt allowed himself a smile. 'Some very wealthy traders live in the city, my lord. We do not preclude anyone. There are also those who visit Clifton and Hotwells for the waters. They are often in need of entertainment and happy to make the two-mile journey to visit Bellemonte.'

'Hardly the *ton*, then.'

'Perhaps not, in the main.' Matt sipped his wine. 'But lucrative.'

'And your patron is the Earl of Dallamire, I believe,' added Sir Roger. 'Does he often attend?'

'Occasionally, when his duties allow.'

Flora watched and listened as Matt expanded on his theme. It was clear that he was very proud of Bellemonte. His enthusiasm was infectious and around her the other guests began to ask questions, keen to learn more. Only the Viscount was silent, his expression one of faint disapproval, while any comments he made were couched in friendly terms, but they were invariably critical. She guessed Quentin had introduced the subject merely to belittle Matt's achievements, although in her opinion, he had not succeeded.

'An admirable project, Mr Talacre.' Sir Roger raised his glass in Matt's direction. 'You have given employment to a number of ex-soldiers, too, I believe?'

'Yes. They are among my best workers. But there is still much work to be done,' Matt concluded. 'I want to return the gardens to their former glory. For example, opening up paths that have not been used for many years. And tracking down the missing statuary.'

Flora held her breath. This was clearly aimed at the Viscount and she looked towards him. Quentin, however, remained impassive and waved to a servant to refill his wine glass before making a reply.

'A daunting task, sir,' he said at last. 'I hope you will not be disappointed.'

'Oh, I don't think I will be, my lord. I have only one elusive piece yet to recover.'

If Flora had not been watching her fiancé so closely, she would have missed the quick glance he sent down the table to his cousin, who immediately rose from her seat.

'Ladies, it is time for us to retire to the drawing room,' she said in her nervous way.

Never had Flora been less eager to leave the dinner table. There was an undercurrent of malice in the Viscount's treatment of Matt Talacre. She did not think it would turn into outright antagonism with her uncle and Sir Roger present, but she knew it did not augur well for any future dealings between the two men.

Matt knew he had rattled his host with talk of Bellemonte and the missing statue, but once the ladies had withdrawn, talk moved on to politics and rumours that Lord Liverpool was about to dissolve Parliament. It would be the first election since Napoleon's defeat and the end of the war.

Matthew sipped at his wine and listened far more than he contributed to the discussion. His views differed widely from those of the Viscount, who clearly saw his rank and standing in Society as his right. No matter how successful Bellemonte might be, and how much money Matt might earn through his hard work, Whilton would only ever regard him as a grubbing tradesman and not a man to be taken seriously. Well, as to that, time would tell. Matt was sure that his case for recovering the statue would hold, but he wanted to avoid an outright confrontation. Dragging the matter through the courts would not suit either of them.

The servants were continually at the table, refilling the glasses, but Matt drank slowly. He needed to keep his wits about him. It was difficult to remain silent as the Viscount expounded his views on the poor and the slave trade, but if he was to stand any chance of negotiating with this man, he did not wish to quarrel openly with him. However, it was a relief when at last Whilton suggested they should join the ladies.

Flora was amusing herself on the pianoforte when the gentlemen walked into the drawing room. The Viscount came over and begged her not to stop, his words echoed by Sir Roger, who professed he always loved to hear her play.

'As good as anything one can hear in London,' he went on. 'Ain't that so, Lord Whilton?'

'I beg my lord will not feel obliged to answer that,' said Flora, laughing. 'I would not have him perjure himself.'

'I can say with perfect honesty that your playing gives me great delight,' replied the Viscount, smiling slightly.

'Oh, well done, sir, a most tactful answer!' she said. The other gentlemen were conversing with the ladies and she took the opportunity to ask the question that had been burning in her mind all evening. 'Why did you invite Mr Talacre to join us this evening?'

Her blunt question surprised him, but he was quick to recover.

'He has made himself agreeable to everyone in the

town, I would not like to be thought backward in my hospitality towards the gentleman.'

Flora glanced across to where Matt was talking with his hostess and Lady Condicote.

'Your meeting with Mr Talacre yesterday went well, then?'

'The man has some misguided notions. I was obliged to put him right.'

Flora hoped he would think her frown was due to the difficulty of the piece she was playing. She wished now that she had admitted she knew the reason why Matt had come to Whilton, then they might have spoken more freely. As it was, she needed to tread carefully.

'I hope you did not quarrel with him.'

He gave a gentle laugh. 'Not at all. The fellow had some ridiculous notion that the statue of Mars I purchased for my Italian garden belongs to his pleasure gardens. I have made it plain it is not the case.'

'And...he is content with that?'

'It is the only answer he will get from me.'

The piece came to an end. Flora let the last notes die away before looking up at the Viscount.

'Does he have any proof, Quentin?'

'Of course not,' he replied, not meeting her gaze. 'It is nothing to concern you, my love.'

She sat, watching him, and after a few moments he turned back to her, smiling.

'Now, Flora, your aunt tells me you have learned a new piece of music for me?'

'Yes. Beethoven.'

'Then I pray you will play it now and delight us all.'

Chapter Eight

By the time the party broke up Flora was exhausted. The Viscount displayed a barely concealed hostility towards Matt Talacre, although no one else seemed aware of it. Quentin lost no opportunity to disparage his guest with subtle hints, to which Matt responded with an unshakeable good humour that only irritated his host even more.

Carriages were called and the business of leave-taking began.

'You have had an uncomfortable evening, sir,' murmured Flora, holding out her hand to Matt.

'It was not all unpleasant.' He smiled down at her and she read understanding in his dark eyes, before he bowed over her hand.

'Until we meet again, Miss Warenne.'

The words, uttered in his deep, smooth voice, caused a little frisson of pleasure to run through Flora. A glance across the room showed her that the Viscount was glaring at them and she could not prevent a blush rising to her cheeks.

She mumbled something inarticulate and quickly withdrew her fingers, trying hard to look unconcerned. Was Quentin jealous? Perhaps he had cause, she thought, her eyes following Matt as he moved off to take his leave of her aunt. The man had a most disturbing effect upon her.

'Oh, by the bye, Mr Farnleigh.' The Viscount's raised voice caught her attention. 'I should like to call upon you in the morning, if I may?'

He walked across and took Flora's hands. She kept her eyes lowered, wondering why his touch did not rouse the same excitement, the same delicious ache deep in her body, that Matt's had done.

'I think we should set a date for the wedding,' said the Viscount. 'Do you not think so, my dear?'

Flora's head jerked up. Everyone had fallen silent, waiting for her answer. Quentin was smiling down at her and she adopted a teasing tone to cover her sudden awkwardness.

'And not before time, Quentin. We have delayed everything for a full year now.'

'I know it, my love, and beg your pardon.' He lifted her fingers to his lips. 'I mean to rectify that as soon as possible.'

Brittle as glass, Flora desperately wanted to snatch her hand away, but she dared not. Everyone was watching and the stillness around them was oppressive, menacing. Finally, her uncle's voice finally broke the silence.

'Aye, my lord, by all means call tomorrow. I am at home all day.'

The atmosphere changed. Everyone was chattering, Uncle Farnleigh was beaming and shaking the Viscount's hand, declaring he was very ready to discuss the arrangements. Only Flora was silent and troubled.

Why did she not feel unalloyed happiness at Quentin's announcement? The betrothal had elevated her from being a mere spinster within Whilton society, but perhaps that was the problem. Her position as the Viscount's fiancée, prolonged an extra year by the demise of the Viscount's godfather, had become too comfortable. Perhaps she was apprehensive of change.

Yes, that was it, she decided. Quentin had been absent from Whilton a great deal this past year and they needed to spend more time together. She would ask Aunt Farnleigh to take her to London to buy her wedding clothes. Since the Viscount had such a deal of business there it would provide an opportunity for her to become reacquainted with her fiancé—he might be busy during the day, but in the evenings they could attend balls and parties together, or visit the theatre.

'Well, my love, our coach is at the door, are you ready to leave?'

Aunt Farnleigh's touch on her arm brought Flora

back to the present. The Condicotes had already departed and Mrs Gask announced she would see them off before she retired. Flora accompanied her aunt and uncle out of the room, but as she reached the door she glanced back, her eyes instinctively seeking Matt Talacre. He had moved to the window and was standing with his back to the room, staring out into the darkness.

Matt heard the whisper of skirts as Flora left the room with the Farnleighs, the click of the door shutting behind them and then the Viscount's voice.

'So, it is only you and I now, Mr Talacre.'

Matt turned. 'Yes. It is time that I, too, took my leave.'

'Will you not take another glass of brandy with me first?' The Viscount was all smiles, but they did not reach his eyes.

'Thank you, but no. I intend to make an early start in the morning.'

'But we have not yet had time to talk together.'

'I think we understand one another well enough,' replied Matt, tired of these games. 'I shall instruct my lawyers to contact you.'

'Now do not be too hasty,' purred the Viscount. 'Surely there is no need for lawyers to be involved just yet.'

'There is every need, my lord. If we cannot come

to an agreement, then I must take measures to recover Bellemonte's property.'

'A costly lawsuit.' Whilton grimaced. 'Allow me a little more time to think about the matter.'

'You have had time, my lord. I first wrote to you some months ago.'

'Your letters were received and read by my secretary. Now you have brought the matter to my attention and I would like to consider your arguments.'

'They are very clear, my lord. It should not take you long.'

The Viscount looked pained. 'My dear sir, you do not understand. I am in the middle of arranging my nuptials. Tomorrow I hold discussions with Mr Farnleigh and then I must go to London to arrange matters there. I am sure you will agree that my new bride deserves my full attention.'

Matt listened, outwardly impassive, but he thought that if he was engaged to Flora Warenne, he would not have left her languishing alone in Whilton for the past two years.

He could hardly say so, of course. It was none of his business. Restoring the Rysbrack to its rightful place was.

'I do not think the matter can wait until after your wedding, Lord Whilton. Two weeks should be ample time for your lawyers to study the evidence and agree that I have a legal right to that statue.'

'A month,' the Viscount suggested. 'The end of June.'

It was a delay, but Matt could live with that.

He said, 'Very well, my lord. I shall expect to hear from you by the last day of June.'

With that he took his leave and rode back to the inn in the moonlight.

'What—am I to have no further part in the discussions for my marriage?' cried Flora, incensed.

She was in the drawing room with Mr and Mrs Farnleigh and Lord Whilton, and her uncle had just invited the Viscount to join him in his study.

'Flora, my dear child, we are already agreed on a date for the ceremony,' said Mr Farnleigh, spreading his hands. 'You and your aunt may now go ahead and make all your plans for the wedding itself. Lord Whilton and I are merely agreeing the financial settlements. It will be tedious stuff, nothing to interest you.'

Flora wished to say it was of great interest to her, but her aunt, who was beside her on the sofa, put her hand on her arm.

'Yes, yes, sir,' she said brightly. 'Off you go with His Lordship. Flora and I have plenty to occupy us now, July will be upon us before we know it!' Once the door had closed and they were alone, she went on, 'Let the gentlemen have their way on this, Flora. Your uncle will make sure everything is done correctly and to your benefit, you need have no doubt of that.'

'I know that, Aunt, but I should still like to be privy to the discussions.' She laughed suddenly. 'It is not as if they will be discussing anything that I do not know already!'

'No, no, my dear. Goodness, of course not!' cried her aunt, looking flustered. 'What a strange thing to say! Now, I really must go and speak to Cook, in case the Viscount can be persuaded to change his mind and stay for dinner.'

She hurried away, leaving Flora shaking her head and smiling. Clearly, Aunt Farnleigh did not want anything to upset the Viscount at this late stage in the engagement. Flora could understand that. She had been more surprised than anyone when Lord Whilton had proposed and the Farnleighs had been overjoyed when she finally accepted. It was such an excellent match for their niece.

She knew that one of the reasons they were so keen that she should be chaperoned at all times was to avoid any risk of impropriety before the knot could be tied. She remembered challenging them about it, shortly after the betrothal, and asking what harm could come to her in Whilton, where she had lived for the past sixteen years.

'A lady can never be too careful of her reputation,' Aunt Farnleigh had told her. 'It only takes a little thing to stir up all sorts of malicious gossip.'

Flora had thought it an odd thing to say, but she had

not let it upset her then and she dismissed it again now as prenuptial anxiety, wryly amused to think that her aunt should be so much more nervous about the coming wedding than the bride.

Flora was alone in the drawing room, engaged in arranging a vase of spring flowers, when the Viscount returned nearly an hour later.

'Well, my lord, it is all settled to your satisfaction?'

He surprised her by pulling her into his arms. 'And to yours, too, I hope,' he said, kissing her lightly on the lips. 'You have two months to buy your wedding clothes, is that enough for you?'

'More than enough, sir. After all, it is not as if we are being married in an abbey.'

'I hope you are not disappointed.'

'What, that we are to be married here, where I will know practically everyone? I am very well pleased with the arrangement.'

'So, too, am I.'

He released her and walked over to the mirror, where he studied his reflection before carefully pushing a stray lock of hair back into place. It was a conceit, but a very small one, thought Flora, and she turned away so that he should not see her smile.

'Aunt would like you to take dinner with us,' she told him, critically regarding her flower arrangement. 'She asked me to persuade you.'

'Alas, Flora, I cannot. I have much to do.' She heard him approach and felt his hands on her shoulders. 'I wish I could remain in Whilton longer, but there is business in London that requires my attention.'

'*More* business?' She sighed as she tweaked an errant dahlia back into place 'I thought Whilton Hall was to be our principal home, but you seem to spend most of your time in the capital.'

'I must be there when Parliament is sitting.' She felt his lips rest briefly on her bare shoulder. 'When we are married I shall spend a great deal more time here, I promise you, but this business will not wait.'

'Would that business concern Mr Talacre?' she asked, knowing full well the question was unwelcome.

'That need not concern you, Flora.'

'But it *does* concern me, Quentin.'

'Talacre is nothing, my dear.'

'I do not agree. Having met him—'

Smiling, he put a finger on her lips to silence her.

'Forgive me, Flora, but you have spent your life here in Whilton. You really must give me credit for possessing a little more worldly knowledge than you. I have met men like Talacre before. He is a fraudster, a charlatan. Why, who is to say that these gardens he talks of even exist? Or, if they do, they are probably nothing more than a patch of boggy land. No, no, my dear, you should put the fellow out of your mind. Will you do that for me?'

When she did not reply he said again, 'Flora?'

She turned back to face him. 'Why did you invite Mr Talacre to dinner, if you think so little of him?'

'To punish his audacity. The man deserved to be put in his place.'

'You were most impolite to him, Quentin. You were picking at him all evening.'

He looked amused. 'Is that what you thought I was doing?'

'I know it was,' she said firmly. 'Little barbs, designed to disparage.'

'No one else thought so, but then, they do not take such a great interest in Mr Talacre as you do.'

She looked him in the eye and said, coolly, 'It is merely that I abhor bad manners, Quentin. You demean yourself and your name.'

Her words hit home, as she had known they would. The Viscount was very proud of his lineage and he flushed angrily. Flora waited, wondering if he might lash out at her. She had never been afraid to speak her mind and until now the Viscount had always said how much he admired her for that, but she had never before criticised his behaviour.

He said coldly, 'You are being ridiculous, Flora. I was merely exchanging friendly raillery with our guest.'

'You were mocking him at every turn. It was subtly

done, but Mr Talacre knew it, only he was too much of a gentleman to show affront.'

'He is no gentleman!' the Viscount sneered. 'The fellow has no birth, no breeding, and he came to me with lies and false evidence, hoping to take from me what is rightfully mine! That I will not allow.'

She shook her head. 'Then why did you invite him to dine, when you are clearly at odds?'

The brief angry outburst was over and he merely curled his lip before replying.

'Because it amused me. I want to show Talacre I am not to be trifled with.'

'Is that wise, my lord?'

'The man is a nonentity,' he said dismissively. 'If he challenges me, I shall squash him. Like an insect.'

'Quentin!'

Flora could not quite hide her repugnance at this callous response and he quickly replaced his sneer with a look of concern.

'Have I shocked you, my dear?' He reached out and cupped her cheek. 'Really, Flora, you should not be surprised. Can you not understand that my dislike of the man is borne of jealousy?'

She stepped away, saying coldly, 'I have given you no reason to be jealous, Quentin. If you mistook my friendliness towards Mr Talacre as anything more, then I am sorry for it. I have never been in the habit of flirting with other men, whether or not you are present.'

'Ah, I know it, my love, I know it,' he said, catching her hand and pressing a fervent kiss upon it. He continued to hold her fingers between his own as he gave her a rueful smile. 'You must make allowances for a man who is impatient to make you his wife.'

Flora was tempted to say she had seen little sign of that impatience in the past two years, but held her tongue.

Receiving no response, the Viscount moved closer, pressing her hand against his heart and saying ruefully, 'Dear Flora, I am a brute to doubt you and I cannot leave for London until you tell me you forgive me for being a jealous fool!'

His words and manner disarmed her.

She smiled, 'There is nothing to forgive, Quentin.'

'Angel!' He kissed her cheek. 'I wish I did not have to leave you again so soon.'

'Perhaps I will come to London,' Flora suggested. 'Aunt Farnleigh and I can go there to buy my bride clothes and we might meet. What could be better?'

'Oh, my love, if only that were possible, but alas I shall be extremely busy.'

She laughed. 'So shall we, Quentin! I am sure we can find some time—'

'But how can I concentrate on my business, knowing you are in town and going into Society without me? I should be in a constant state of anxiety that one of my rivals will steal your heart!'

'Surely not!'

'I think you will find your aunt agrees with me. Once we are married I shall take you to London myself and you may shop at all the most fashionable haunts to your heart's content. But consider, my dear: we agreed, did we not, that this wedding is to be a very quiet affair. I am sure you will be able to find everything you need without making the long and exhausting journey to the capital.'

'But, Quentin—'

'No, no,' he interrupted her. 'I give you carte blanche to invite any modiste you wish to come to Birchwood House and dress you—you may send the reckoning to me!—but I should far prefer you to remain here in Whilton while I am in town. That way I shall rest easy, knowing you are safe.'

'Safe?' She frowned at the word, but he shook his head and continued.

'And I shall be returning to Whilton in a few weeks, for the Condicotes' ball.'

'Really?' She blinked at him. 'Why have you not mentioned this before?'

He beamed and flicked her cheek with a finger. 'It was to be a surprise. But you must see how our returning in three weeks' time for the Midsummer

Ball would greatly curtail your shopping expedition to London.'

'It would, but I should not mind missing the ball, just this once. After all, we can attend routs and dances in the capital.'

'Ah, my darling, I see what it is, you crave a larger society! You told me you had lived very secluded here and it is beginning to prey upon you, is it not? But that will change when you are my Viscountess. *Then* I shall make sure you go to all the best entertainments that London has to offer.'

He was smiling at her, but there was something in his voice and his face that told her everything was arranged and further argument was pointless.

'If I am to stay here, perhaps I might go to Whilton Hall and make preparations? It has been a bachelor establishment for so long I am sure some changes will be necessary.'

'You may look at it, by all means, but Whilton Hall is an ancient house filled with my family history. I would not have it changed, except to install you as its mistress.' He laughed and squeezed her hand. 'You will be the jewel, in a perfect setting.'

'Thank you, Quentin, but—'

He silenced her with an impatient hand.

'Dear Flora, when we are married there will be time and to spare to discuss all these little matters. Go and speak with Mrs Goole, if you wish. I am sure she will be only too pleased to give you a tour of the house and explain how everything is done.' He smiled at her. 'So, Flora, are we agreed? You will stay here and prepare for your wedding and I shall conclude my business as quickly as possible and hurry back to you.'

She could see he was eager now to get away. He gave her another swift kiss on the cheek and was gone.

After a few moments to gather her thoughts, Flora went off to the garden. There was still some time before dinner and she hoped a stroll in the fresh air would help to clear her head.

She was disturbed by the Viscount's rough dismissal of Matt Talacre and if it did spring from jealousy then she was sorry for it and must share some part of the blame. Quentin's decision to attend the Midsummer Ball was a surprise, and very flattering, but Flora could not help feeling a little disappointed not to be going to town. It was not so much the thought of visiting the fashionable modistes, for she knew her aunt's local seamstress was more than capable of making up gowns similar to those featured in the most recent editions of *The Lady's Magazine* or *Ackermann's Repository*.

No, it was a need to meet with Quentin in town, to quash the growing suspicion that Quentin did not wish her to join him in London. To allay her fear that, once they were married, he would leave her languishing in Whilton while he enjoyed himself in the capital or visiting his other country estates.

Flora sighed. Perhaps she was being too critical, she thought, as the scent and beauty of the flowering borders began to have their effect. Perhaps he really did care for her and wanted to wait until they were safely married before taking her out and about.

'Very well then, so be it,' she said aloud, reaching out to pluck a peony from the bush growing against a sheltering wall. 'But all that will change in July!'

'What happens in July?'

Flora jumped at the sound of Matt Talacre's voice and turned so quickly that she dropped her flower.

'What are you doing here?'

'I came to see you.' Matt scooped up the peony and held it out to her, smiling in way that did nothing to settle her agitated nerves. 'I was riding by when I spotted you walking in the garden. I climbed over the wall.'

'You appear to make a habit of trespassing in other people's gardens.' She took the flower from him, taking care not to touch his hand. 'If word should get back to the Viscount—'

'I doubt it will, but in any case, we are only standing here, talking, and in full sight of the house. There is no harm in it.'

'He will not believe that.'

And nor did she, when her heart was hammering so hard against her ribs she thought he must hear it.

His smiled disappeared. 'You are seriously concerned about talking to me. You need not be, Flora. You know I have no wish to steal you away from your fiancé. I came to say goodbye.'

'You are leaving?'

'I am going to London to discuss matters with my lawyers. I would normally consult Conham, too, but his Countess is close to her time. It is their first child and he will not wish to be distracted.'

'Naturally,' said Flora. 'He will want to know if he has an heir.'

'I do not think he minds if they have a son or a daughter, as long as the child is healthy. He is more concerned for Rosina. He loves her very much, you see.'

Flora found herself wondering if Quentin would show such consideration, when the time came. Or would he have business elsewhere that needed his attention?

'Lord Whilton is also gone to London.' She twirled the peony between her fingers, staring down at it.

'I doubt our paths will cross. We move in very different circles, you know.'

'Yes.' But thoughts of the Viscount had reminded Flora of something else that was troubling her. She burst out, 'I am sorry he was so rude to you last night.'

'You do not need to apologise for Lord Whilton, Flora.'

'Yes, I do.' She took a deep breath. 'It was because of me.'

He shook his head at that. 'No, he is angry because he knows the statue in his garden belongs to Bellemonte. Although I am sure he is a *little* jealous of me, too.'

Flora turned and walked on, determined not to respond to the wicked glint of laughter in his sable-brown eyes.

'The Viscount will not give up his property without a fight,' she warned, when he fell into step beside her.

'You consider yourself his property, then?'

'Of course not!' She blushed, angry at herself for being caught out by his teasing. 'I was referring to the statue.'

'Now that is most definitely *not* his property.'

'But can you really prove it?'

'I can, if I need to do so. I have given the Viscount until the end of June to decide. Sell the Rysbrack to me for what he paid for it, or we go to court and let the lawyers settle the matter.'

He reached across and took her hand, obliging her to stop.

'I should go now. Unless you are going to invite me to come in?' Even as she opened her mouth to refuse, he laughed. 'No, you are very wise not to do so. Goodbye, Miss Flora Warenne.' He kissed her fingers. 'I wish you joy with your Viscount.'

Flora watched him stride away, telling herself the man was a rogue, she was glad they would not meet again. But if that was the case, why was she fighting down a strong impulse to run after him?

Squaring her shoulders she turned resolutely away and hurried back to the house.

Matt left the path and made his way back to the beech tree that marked the spot where he had entered the garden. He scrambled up through its branches until he was level with the top of the wall before looking back. Flora had reached the terrace and he paused to watch her run up the steps and through the open door before he jumped down into the lane.

Magpie was waiting patiently where he had left her and he quickly untied the reins.

'It's a good thing we won't be seeing the lady again, old girl,' he murmured, rubbing the mare's bony nose. 'She's far too fascinating and that can only mean trouble.'

Chapter Nine

Flora busied herself with arrangements for the wedding, but by the end of a week all the immediate work was complete. She had helped her aunt to write the invitations and ordered several new gowns, which now had to wait for the seamstress to obtain the fabrics from the London warehouse.

Flora had also called at Whilton Hall, but her attempts to plan any changes were thwarted by the housekeeper, who insisted that everything had already been done in accordance with the Viscount's wishes. Flora curbed her annoyance at Mrs Goole's insolent tone, but she resolved to speak to Quentin about the woman as soon as he returned.

With little else to do, Flora found other thoughts were creeping back into her mind. The Viscount had assured her the statue of Ares in his garden was rightfully his and Matt Talacre was a fraudster. She should believe that. Quentin was, after all, her fiancé and she had known him far longer than Mr Talacre. But that was the problem: from what she knew of Quentin, she did not doubt that he might have suspected that the Rysbrack was illegally obtained, but it would not stop him keeping it.

For a week Flora tried to ignore the niggling doubts. It was not her concern. Then, when she and her aunt and uncle were dining with the Albrights, a chance remark sparked an idea.

'I am in such a quandary,' announced Mrs Albright, just before they went in to dinner. 'My poor sister has written to me. She is in a very bad way. Her heart, you know,' she informed her visitors. 'She is not expected to last much longer.'

'Oh, my dear ma'am, how dreadful,' said Mr Farnleigh. 'Is Mrs Boscombe living very far from here?'

'Sadly, yes. Near Bristol.' Mrs Albright sighed. 'Elvira has rooms at Hotwell House and has written asking if we might visit. She is Jenny's godmother, you see, and would very much like to see her one last time.'

'And I should dearly like to see Aunt Elvira,' put in Jenny. 'Do you remember her, Flora? She was so kind to us when we were younger.'

'Yes, I remember. She visited Whilton frequently when we were children. She was very kind to me, always ready to include me in her treats and outings.'

'But alas, we cannot go!' exclaimed Mrs Albright,

pressing a hand to her chest. 'My doctor has told me that I must rest. Such a long coach journey is out of the question and Mr Albright has sworn he will not go away and leave me while my health is so precarious.'

'I am quite happy to go on my own, Mama,' said Jenny. 'I can take Maria with me.'

'Do you think I would have a minute's peace if I allowed a slip of a girl like yourself to travel with only a maid for company?' cried her mother. 'It is unthinkable.'

'Mama! I am five-and-twenty,' Jenny protested, casting an amused glance across at Flora. 'Besides, I would be travelling in our own carriage—we would be perfectly safe.'

'But it would take you *days* to get to Bristol! No, no, it is out of the question.'

Flora had been thinking rapidly and she now addressed Mrs Albright.

'Perhaps I could go with Jenny. How would that be, ma'am, would it set your mind at rest?"

'Well, yes, of course, if there were the two of you... But your wedding preparations, my dear, you must have a great deal to arrange.'

But Flora had already thought of that.

'It is going to be a quiet wedding, because of the Viscount's recent bereavement.'

She was no longer sure that was the whole truth, but it stopped her friends and neighbours speculating upon why Quentin had insisted they should be married in Whilton's small parish church. She went on.

'The wedding is not until July, plenty of time for all the arrangements.'

'No, no, my dear, you cannot possibly go so far without us,' cried Aunt Farnleigh, looking alarmed. 'It is not to be considered.'

'But we would not be gone very long,' said Flora. 'If Uncle Farnleigh will allow us to use his travelling chariot, we could go post and do the journey to Bristol in a day. I remember you telling me that it has a removable coachman's seat, did you not, sir?'

She looked an enquiry at her uncle, who nodded. 'Well, yes, that is a possibility, I suppose…'

'I could take Betty with me, too, as well as Jenny's maid, because it carries four passengers,' added Flora, forestalling her aunt's next objection. 'We could also take our own footman, on the back.'

'And I would happily pay the cost of them travelling post,' put in Mr Albright, relieved to see a solution to the dilemma of how to transport Jenny to her godmother.

'There you are then,' cried Flora. 'We would be gone only a few days. All I need now is for my aunt to give her permission.' She smiled across the table at Mrs Farnleigh. 'Do say I may go, Aunt. It would mean the world to Mrs Boscombe to see Jenny once again and I should like to do all I can to help.'

It took some time for Jenny and Flora to persuade Mr and Mrs Farnleigh to agree, but at last Flora's arguments won the day and she was able to sit back while the dinner table conversation moved on.

There were a few details to her plan that she did not intend to divulge until she and Jenny were on the road, but for now she was very well satisfied with the outcome of the evening. She hoped that by the time she and Jenny returned to Whilton, she would have learned everything she needed to know about Mr Matthew Talacre and Bellemonte Pleasure Gardens.

Having agreed upon the trip to Bristol, events moved quickly. While Flora and Jenny decided what clothes to take, Mr Albright made arrangements for the postillions and horses at the various posting houses. He also sent a man to bespeak accommodation for the two ladies at the Hotwell House or some respectable lodging close by. Mr Farnleigh, meanwhile, gave orders for his travelling chariot to be dragged out of the coach house and prepared for the eighty-mile journey with hired post boys.

Within days everything was ready and it was on a fine June morning that Flora waved goodbye to her aunt and uncle and set off to collect Jenny Albright. Her maid, Betty, was beside her in the carriage and

Edwin, one of the Farnleighs' footmen, was sitting up at the back to provide extra protection.

It was not until they stopped for the second change of horses that Flora informed Jenny of her plans. She invited her friend to step out of the carriage and take a short stroll along the lane to stretch their legs. Then, once they were out of earshot of their maids, she announced they would be making a short stop later.

'I shall advise the postboys to divert to Bellemonte,' she told her astonished friend. 'It is in Gloucester and only a few miles north of Bristol.'

'Bellemonte!' exclaimed Jenny, round-eyed. 'Did not Mr Talacre mention such a place?'

'Yes,' said Flora, her eyes dancing. 'He owns the pleasure gardens there. And a hotel, where I hope to bespeak a room. I would like come back and stay there for two nights, once I have seen you safely to Hotwells.' She saw that Jenny was looking horrified and went on quickly, 'There is nothing improper in it, Jenny. Mr Talacre said he was going to London on business, so he will not even be there! I merely wish to see the gardens for myself and I know my aunt and uncle would never agree to a visit.'

'I am surprised Betty has agreed to it,' retorted Jenny.

'Well, she hasn't yet,' Flora admitted. 'But she is such a dear, loyal soul that I know she will not fail me.

I shall give her something to ease her conscience, of course,' she added thoughtfully, 'And perhaps it would be wise if I paid your maid something, too.'

'No, no, I shall take care of Maria,' said Jenny. 'She may be a little shocked at your behaviour, but she would no more give you away than she would me. But why must you stay overnight? Can you not visit there for a day while I am with Aunt Elvira?'

Flora hesitated, wondering how far to take Jenny into her confidence.

'The Viscount has some business dealings with Mr Talacre, which have reached an impasse, and I want to help,' she said at last. 'I thought if I stayed at Bellemonte I could see the place for myself. And if I could talk with the people who work there, I would be able to glean a little information about the man's true character.'

Jenny put a hand on her friend's arm. 'Flora, is that wise?'

Wise? Flora thought sadly that so far in her life she had been allowed to do nothing that was *un*wise. She was tired of it.

She said, 'Perhaps not, but what harm can it do?'

Her friend looked so concerned that Flora's resolution faltered, but only for a moment.

'Let us wait until we get to Bellemonte before making a final decision,' she said, smiling. 'Who knows, the hotel may well be full, in which case I shall be obliged to make a day trip to the gardens from Hotwell House.

'Now, I can see that the postillions are waiting to set off. We had best return before we make them late for the next change!'

It took several hours to reach the village of Bellemonte, but it was still daylight and the summer sky was a clear blue, painting everything in the best light. Flora had to admit she was pleasantly surprised when they turned off the main highway on to a well-maintained road and drove past the Dallamire Arms with its fresh paintwork and a cheerful sign swinging above the door.

From there the carriage entered a large cobbled square and slowed as the horses walked around, passing glossy black railings with a pair of large gates at the centre and, above the gates, a metal arch with *Grand Pleasure Gardens* picked out in gold.

'Well, I must say that looks very enticing,' remarked Jenny, impressed.

'Enticing.' Flora savoured the word. 'Yes, it does, doesn't it?'

She leaned forward to get a better look out of the window. Beyond the railings she could see shrubs and colourful flowerbeds lining a wide path which eventually curved away into the trees and out of sight. There was already a fair number of people moving through the gates, some branching off on to a second path and she caught sight of a large building through the trees before their carriage swung around and came to a halt outside a large and imposing house built of creamy sandstone.

'And this must be the hotel.'

As she waited for the footman to climb down and open the door, Flora surveyed the building, the tall sash windows, each one topped with a neat stone triangle that echoed the grander pediment over the central door. It looked more like a private house than an hotel, except for an impressive doorkeeper who had stepped out as soon as the carriage drew up and was already making his way down the path towards them. Flora looked at Jenny.

'Would you like to come with me, while I make my enquiries?'

'Well, that was surprisingly easy,' said Flora, when their mission was accomplished and they were on their way again. 'How fortunate that they have sufficient rooms available—they appear to be extremely busy. And you will have a room to yourself, Betty.'

Her maid, sitting opposite, did not look particularly pleased with the news. She turned to share a disapproving glance with Jenny's maid before addressing her mistress.

'It ain't right, Miss Flora, I'll tell you that now. I

should be sleeping on a truckle bed in your room with you.' She gave a disparaging sniff. 'After all, 'tis nothing more than a public inn, when all is said and done. Who knows what might happen in the night?'

'It is a very respectable hotel, Betty,' Flora corrected her, but gently. She knew her maid's grumpiness stemmed from anxiety for the safety of her mistress and she was careful not to tease her. 'Miss Albright and I were both very impressed with the hotel and its servants, were we not, Jenny?'

'I would prefer you not to be staying there, if I am honest,' replied Jenny, 'But since you have made up your mind to it, I cannot see that any harm will come of it. Not when you have the estimable, *sensible* Betty to look after you.'

Flora's heart swelled with gratitude for her friend. Jenny had said exactly the right thing to put Betty in a better mood. The maid's plump cheeks grew even rosier and she preened herself a little.

She said gruffly, 'Well, that's as may be, miss, but I do know how to go on in such an establishment, even if I do say so myself. And I'll make sure Miss Warenne comes to no harm.'

Having smoothed the maid's ruffled feathers, the two young ladies sat back and watched as the fields gradually gave way to houses. Before long they were bowling through the city of Bristol towards the village of Hotwells.

'We shall soon reach our destination, I think,' said Jenny, 'As soon as we are shown to our rooms I shall send a note to my aunt, telling her I have arrived. Aunt Elvira moved here because the waters taste so much better than Bath, but I believe she is so ill she rarely leaves her room now. I hope she will be well enough to see me this evening, but I think it far more likely she will prefer me to call in the morning.'

'I would very much like to come with you to see her, if I may,' said Flora. 'Either this evening or tomorrow, before I set off for Bellemonte. And when I return, we will have a day to explore the delights of Hotwells and Clifton!'

Jenny gave a rueful smile. 'I am not sure what delights we shall find here. From everything I have learned, Hotwell House is full of those who are chronically ill and have no appetite for the entertainments on offer in Clifton village. However, it suits me very well to stay here, since all I want to do is be with my godmother.'

By this time the carriage had descended a narrow and winding road to the banks of the River Avon. When it came to a stop, the ladies stepped out and looked up at Hotwell House, towering above them.

Built a century earlier, it was a tall, stuccoed building, rather austere in aspect and constructed on a rocky ledge protruding slightly over the river. Tree-covered cliffs rose steeply behind it and cut into the rock was a series of steps that led up to the village of Clifton, which boasted a pump room, theatres and assembly rooms.

Flora could not imagine many of the Hotwell's residents making the steep climb up the steps to the village and she said as much to Jenny.

'No indeed, poor things,' replied her friend. 'I cannot help but think they would be better living in Clifton, where there is more to divert them.'

'Yes, I think that, too,' murmured Flora, looking up at the severe building towering above them. She thought the place looked tired and drab compared to Bellemonte, with its colourful gardens, the grand pleasure baths and the warm, welcoming frontage of the honey-coloured hotel, and everything built around the pretty square.

Having paid off the postillions and stabled Mr Farnleigh's coach, Flora was obliged to make arrangements for another hired carriage the next day to take her to Gloucestershire. She did not object. She had a generous monthly allowance and was happy to pay for her trip. She would far rather that than have a reckoning sent to Mr Albright—or even worse, her uncle—and have to explain why she had visited Bellemonte.

Jenny and her maid would not disclose that she had spent two nights at Bellemonte unless directly challenged. As for Betty and Edwin, who had accompanied them, they were devoted to Flora and she knew she could rely upon their discretion. The Farnleighs were so much older than their niece that they had come to rely upon their servants to look after her.

From the first moment Flora came to live with the Farnleighs the servants had been her allies. When Aunt Farnleigh thought Flora was having a gentle riding lesson in the south field, she and her groom were galloping over the hills, and when the Albrights took her to the assembly and she returned later than she should, not one of them mentioned it.

This outing was a little more daring, but Flora still hoped that it might go undetected.

Bellemonte was basking in the hot afternoon sun when Flora arrived. In the quiet square she could hear shouts and laughter coming from the far side of the high wall which bounded the grand pleasure bath. At that moment, before she made her way into the shadowed interior of the hotel, she felt slightly envious of the young gentlemen cavorting in the cool waters.

Flora was shown to her room by a female servant while a footman carried her portmanteau, leaving Betty with nothing to do but follow on with her own small bag.

'Well, at least I have a room adjoining yours, Miss Flora,' she said, once they were alone. 'That's a mercy.'

'It is, but I do not want you to keep to your room, Betty,' said Flora.

She was unpacking her clothes and shaking out the gowns before passing them to her maid to hang on the pegs in her dressing room.

'Of course I won't be doing that, Miss Flora. I shall be accompanying you everywhere. You can hardly go out and about alone!'

'No, but when I am not *"out and about"*, as you put it, I should like you to engage the servants in conversation. I want to know what they think of Mr Talacre.'

'Lord, miss, you want me to listen to tittle-tattle?' asked Betty, scandalised.

Flora shook her head. 'Not exactly, but you can tell a great deal about a man from the way he treats those in his employ. I need to find out if he is an honest man.'

'You are mighty interested in this gentleman, if I may say so, miss. Are you sure you ain't sweet on him?'

'Don't be absurd,' said Flora briskly, although she could not bring herself to look Betty in the eye. 'Mr Talacre has business with the Viscount, and I am trying to discover the sort of man Lord Whilton is dealing with.'

'Well, I think His Lordship should be doing that for himself and not dragging you into such matters,' retorted Betty.

'He didn't drag me into anything,' Flora protested.

She shook out the last of her dresses and held it up. 'I shall wear this one, I think. A promenade gown is perfect for taking a stroll through the gardens before dinner. What do you think?'

'I think this whole escapade is sheer madness,' declared Betty, narrowing her eyes at her mistress. 'To wander around the pleasure gardens, even with a maid in attendance, is not seemly.'

'Oh, what nonsense!' Flora laughed at that. 'I saw several ladies doing just that when we arrived and none of their maids looked half as terrifying as you!'

Betty had known Flora too long to take offence at this, but she scowled blackly and shook her head at her mistress.

'Aye, and you aren't too old for me to box your ears if I have any more of your cheek, Miss Flora!'

Chapter Ten

A sunny June afternoon was the perfect time to visit the pleasure gardens and Flora was impressed with what she saw. She felt perfectly at ease, strolling along the shady paths with Betty, and there was nothing to disgust her in the people she saw along the way. They appeared to be mostly wealthy tradespeople or minor gentry strolling through the grounds, although there were a few decidedly fashionable young bucks cutting a dash. One or two of the gentlemen cast a second glance at Flora, but Betty's fearsome scowl prevented anyone approaching them.

Flora spotted several wardens, all in dark green breeches and waistcoats and with the Bellemonte emblem embroidered upon their matching coats. She recalled Matthew telling her they were employed to keep the peace and remove any rowdy or drunken revellers.

She also took note of the number of statues throughout the gardens, many of them in the centre of small clearings on each side of the path. They were all very fine, but none looked at all similar to the one Quentin had installed at Whilton Hall. Not that she was any judge of these things, of course, but the pleasure gardens were very large and there were so many side paths and little tracks that it would take some time to explore everything.

As she stepped into yet another secluded recess, this time with a stone bench beneath a wooden arch covered with roses, her maid emitted a loud sigh.

'Are you not enjoying yourself, Betty?'

'It's all very pretty, ma'am.'

This was said so woodenly that Flora almost laughed.

'But you have seen enough for today, is that it?'

'Aye, well, I'm not as young as I was,' said Betty, 'and we had a full day's travel yesterday. It fair takes it out of a body.'

'Very well,' said Flora, taking pity on her maid. 'We will go back now.'

When they reached Flora's bedchamber, a glance at the little carriage clock she had placed on the mantelshelf told her it was still early.

'Goodness, we were out for little more than an hour!'

'It seemed a lot more than that,' muttered Betty, following her into the room. 'And in the heat of the day, too!'

She sounded aggrieved, which Flora realised was

due to tiredness. She sent her maid off to lie down, saying she was quite capable of removing her own pelisse.

'There is a good two hours until dinner,' she added, when Betty hesitated. 'I dare say we shall both feel better for the rest.'

However, when she was alone, Flora did not lie down upon her bed. She pottered about the room, then tried reading her book, but she could not settle. Perhaps the hotel could provide her with a newspaper, or a lady's magazine, something to pass the time. From the adjoining room came the faint sound of snoring and she decided not to wake Betty. She would go down herself and enquire.

She had reached the landing and was halfway down the final flight of stairs when she saw Matt Talacre in the hall, talking with the manager. She froze and was about to retreat, when he looked up and saw her.

There was no escape. His eyes held hers and although her brain told her to turn and flee, her body would not obey. She watched as his initial surprise gave way to a warm smile.

'Miss Warenne.'

He walked across to the bottom of the stairs and there was nothing she could do but carry on. The way his eyes crinkled when he smiled had set loose a net full of butterflies inside and she gripped the handrail tightly as she made her way down the last few steps, afraid her legs might give way.

'This is a delightful surprise,' he said, reaching out to take her hand when she was at last standing on the tiled floor of the hall. 'Welcome to the Bellemonte Hotel.'

'Thank you.'

Flora's cheeks were flaming and she was aware that the manager and at least two other servants were in the hall, watching them. Matt was still smiling and gripping her fingers. Then he suddenly seemed to realise their situation and released her.

'You are here with Mr and Mrs Farnleigh?'

'No. But I have my maid,' she said quickly. 'She is upstairs.'

'Of course.' He looked around. 'Will you take some refreshment with me? Tea, perhaps. We have a very comfortable morning room here, overlooking the square.'

'Tea would be very…refreshing,' said Flora, although she would have liked to ask him for wine, or brandy, to steady the tumult inside her.

After a word to a hovering footman, Matt escorted her into the room and to a small table by one of the windows. She was relieved to see they were not alone—there were two other couples on the far side of the room.

'Now,' he said, sitting down opposite. 'Tell me what

brings you to Bellemonte and without your aunt and uncle.'

Why, oh, why did I come here?

Flora breathed deeply, struggling to regain her composure and maintain some sort of dignity.

'Miss Albright is visiting her godmother in Hotwells.'

'And is she staying here, too?'

'No. She is putting up at the Hotwell House. I stayed there with her last night, but I thought, since we were so close…'

Flora stopped, thankful that the arrival of a maid with the tea tray obliged them to pause their conversation. She then elected to pour tea for them both, giving herself a few extra moments to compose her reply.

She would have liked to appear nonchalant, to admit to nothing but idle curiosity bringing her to Bellemonte, but that was impossible. Far better to tell the truth.

'I wanted to find out if all you had told me was true.' His brows went up and her cheeks grew even warmer. She said, 'Lord Whilton said you were trying to trick him. I did not know who to believe.'

'Since you are going to marry the Viscount, surely you should believe him.'

'His Lordship might have misunderstood the situation.' She knew she was clutching at straws and expected him to say so. When he remained silent, she burst out, 'I thought you would still be in London, or I should never have come!'

'No, I can believe that. But what did you hope to achieve?'

'I hardly know. I just thought, if I could see Bellemonte for myself, inspect the statue of Aphrodite and compare it to the one at Whilton…'

'And have you seen it?'

'No. Not yet. I took a short walk there when I arrived, but the gardens are much larger than I envisaged…'

He drew out his pocket watch. 'I am free for a couple of hours. I could take you to Aphrodite now, if you wish? When you have finished here, of course.'

Flora sipped her tea. It was out of the question. She must subdue this new, wayward spirit that had been kindled within her these past weeks. Coming alone to Bellemonte was quite reckless enough. Besides, she was here on Quentin's behalf and to accept Matt Talacre's escort would be tantamount to consorting with the enemy.

She did not even need to consider her answer—she must refuse.

'Unless you think your Viscount would not like it.'

He was smiling, a faint challenge in his dark eyes. Flora put down her cup.

'I will fetch my pelisse.'

Flora hurried up to her bedchamber, telling herself

there would be no impropriety in touring the gardens with Matt Talacre as long as Betty was there as a chaperon. However, when she entered the maid's room she found her faithful servant sleeping soundly. Flora quietly closed the door again and, quickly donning her pelisse, she ran back down the stairs.

Matt was waiting for her in the hall.

'No maid?'

'She is asleep and I did not have the heart to wake her.' Flora avoided his eyes. 'She was exhausted by our earlier walk in the gardens, even though we did not make a full circuit.'

'Has Miss Albright's godmother visited the gardens?' he asked her. 'As you have seen for yourself, it is within easy reach of Hotwells.'

'I do not think so. Certainly not recently. She is too ill to go out now. I went with Jenny to visit her this morning and she is very frail.'

'I am sorry to hear that,' he replied, sincerely.

'Yes, it is very sad. She wrote to ask if Jenny could come and see her, only with Mrs Albright herself in poor health, her parents could not come. That is why I offered to accompany her.'

'And Bellemonte just happened to be on your way.'

'Yes. It seemed too good an opportunity to miss.'

'Even knowing I would not be present?' he teased her.

'*Especially* since you would not be present!'

Flora tried to sound severe, but it was difficult when she was so at ease. It was as if she had known Matt Talacre for years, rather than a few weeks. She discovered that he was an excellent guide, too, very knowledgeable about the shrubs and trees as well as his plans to make the gardens more profitable.

'I beg your pardon,' he said, after a while. 'I have been talking non-stop at you since we set off.'

'Not at all, I am finding it all very interesting. It is a pleasure to walk here with someone who knows so much.' She chuckled. 'My poor maid found the whole thing so tedious, when we came here earlier.'

'A good thing to let her sleep then, this time.'

'Yes.' She smiled back at him. 'A very good thing.'

Matt did not take Flora directly to the statue, but diverted along several of the smaller paths, taking his time, pointing out to her the more exotic plants and explaining his ideas for opening up new paths. It was a pleasure to walk with her, she showed a genuine interest in the gardens and posed intelligent questions. But no matter how much he liked Flora Warenne, however enjoyable he found her company, she was betrothed to Lord Whilton. Nothing could come of their friendship, so why was he taking so much trouble with the lady?

Because she can help me persuade the Viscount to return the statue. That's all.

Matt told himself that repeatedly as he conducted Flora through the gardens, refusing to acknowledge it could be anything more. He would never allow himself to fall in love. He had felt its sting himself, once, and seen the pain it caused his mother.

No, he was very happy to flirt with a pretty woman, but that was all.

At length they reached a clearing edged with a circular stone balustrade and, at the far side, the statue of a Greek goddess.

'Pray allow me to present Aphrodite,' he said. 'This area was totally overgrown when I first came to Bellemonte. It was not until I had cleared all the encroaching plants that I discovered the plinth for Ares is here.' He pointed to the low flat stone protruding some inches above the grass. 'If you look closely you can see marks on it, identical to those on the statue in the garden at Whilton Hall. They are also similar to the markings you will find over there, on Aphrodite.'

Matt watched as Flora inspected the empty plinth, then she walked over to the statue of Aphrodite. He was struck by how cold and lifeless the stone goddess appeared when compared to the vibrant creature studying her. Flora Warenne exuded warmth, with her hazel eyes and lovely smile, and that glorious flame-red hair. When she was near it was a struggle not to reach out and touch the creamy softness of her cheek. He imagined how it would feel to pull her close and kiss those coral lips. They would taste of ripe strawberries, he imagined. Or peaches, warmed by the sun.

She came back towards him and Matt quickly shifted his gaze, afraid his thoughts would be all too clear in his eyes.

'I wish now I had looked closer at the statue at Whilton,' she told him. 'I did not see any marks on the back of it.'

'Perhaps that is for the best. I would not want to put you at odds with your fiancé.'

The briefest hesitation, then she raised her chin and looked at him. 'You will never do that, Mr Talacre. I will not allow it to happen.'

Her voice was cheerful enough, but he had seen a shadow flicker across her face. A momentary sadness that did not sit well on a soon-to-be bride. He brushed aside a sudden tug of concern. Flora Warenne was no business of his.

He waved one hand towards the statue.

'Aphrodite looks a little lonely, doesn't she, standing all alone here? Lord Whilton has a few more weeks to decide if he wants to settle this privately. If not, I will take the matter through the courts, which I do not think he would like.'

'No, Quentin would abhor the gossip arising from that.' She bit her lip. 'But he is a viscount. He has influence, power.'

She was anxious for him and Matt was surprised how much that mattered. He shrugged.

'The Earl of Dallamire also has some influence,' he said. 'He has written to tell me I have his full support.'

'I am glad of that.'

She looked up, smiling, and a jolt of desire hit Matt like a body blow. By heaven, how he wanted to take her in his arms, to kiss those soft lips! He summoned up the devil-may-care grin he always used to disguise his feelings, only this time it did not work. Their eyes met and held a fraction too long. He felt something shift between them. Something dangerous as a rockfall, or an earthquake, only neither of them dare admit it.

Abruptly Flora turned away from him. 'Thank you for showing me the statue. I think we should be going back now.'

No. He did not want to lose her just yet. He said, 'But there is so much more yet to see.'

'There is no more time, I have ordered an early dinner to be sent up.'

'Then it must wait for another day... Tomorrow?'

She hesitated. It lasted only a moment, but to Matt if felt like a lifetime. Then she nodded.

'Tomorrow.'

'Very well, madam.' He stifled a sigh of relief. 'Allow me to escort you back to the hotel.'

Flora placed her fingers on his proffered arm, alarm bells clamouring in her head. She had come to think of Matt as a friend, but that last look they had shared frightened her. She was in very great danger of feeling more for the man than was seemly for a woman who was promised to another.

She should not meet with him tomorrow, but she knew with a frightening, exhilarating certainty that she would not cry off. She resolutely silenced the alarm bells. Matt Talacre was a gentleman. She trusted him and they would be walking in a public place. What harm could come of it?

Back in her bedchamber, there was still no sign of Betty. Flora slipped off her pelisse before knocking loudly on the door and calling to her maid. She received a croaky reply and opened the door to find the poor woman with a handkerchief pressed to her mouth and looking decidedly hollow-eyed.

'Ooh, Miss Flora, I don't know what's the matter with me, I ache all over. And I feel so dreadful!'

'Oh, my goodness!' Ignoring Betty's command not to come too close, Flora crossed the room and laid a hand on the maid's forehead. 'You have a fever. Perhaps it is all the travelling we have done. No, no, do not try to get up. You must remain in bed and I shall order dinner to be brought up for both of us.'

'But I must get up. *Someone* must attend you.'

'I am sure they will have a maid who can do that,' Flora told her. 'For now, you need to rest. You are in no state to look after anyone.'

Betty was inclined to be tearful, but Flora was adamant. She settled her maid back against the pillows, straightened the covers and went off to find someone to help.

Chapter Eleven

Flora woke to bright sunshine and a feeling of happy anticipation. The hotel maid assigned to wait upon her brought in her breakfast and helped her to dress and then, after checking on Betty to make sure she was no worse, Flora left her room and went downstairs. Yesterday's doubts had been put to rest. She liked Matt, she felt happy and comfortable in his company—surely there could be no danger in that.

None at all, she decided as she skipped down the stairs. She would enjoy this little break from her dull, predictable life and return to Whilton refreshed. Then she would be ready to take up her role as Quentin's wife.

Or so she told herself.

Matt saw her on the stairs just as the long-case clock was chiming eleven. He smiled and touched his hat as she came up to him.

'Good morning, Miss Warenne. I understand your

maid is unwell. Nothing serious, I hope?' He added, when she looked surprised, 'I make it my business to know what goes on in my hotel.'

'Yes, of course. I think Betty is exhausted from all the hours we spent in the carriage on Monday and she has contracted a slight chill. However, she does seem a little better this morning, thank you.'

'I hope my people have been looking after you.'

'Why, yes. Your manager, Mr Cripps, has been most helpful and supplied me with a maid to take Betty's place.' She read a question in his eyes and lifted her chin a little as she went on, 'She will attend me later, but I think, at six-and-twenty, I do not need a chaperon for a mere stroll with you in a public garden.'

Matt nodded. Her trust in him was gratifying, but misplaced. It was going to be difficult to resist the temptation to flirt with Flora when she was looking particularly lovely. She was wearing a dark green spencer over a cream-coloured muslin gown, embroidered at the hem with acanthus leaves, and perched atop her flaming hair was a jockey cap in the same colour as her spencer. She unfurled her lace parasol and smiled at him.

'Shall we go, Mr Talacre?'

Silently, Matt offered her his arm. Difficult? It was going to be well-nigh impossible!

For Flora, the hours flew by. The sun was shining even brighter than yesterday, dappling the tree-lined paths and intensifying the colours of the flowers and foliage in the gardens. Once they had made a full circuit Matt escorted her up to the viewpoint, from where they could look out over Bristol with its gleaming spires. Then he invited her to turn back and admire the view of the pleasure gardens.

'From here you can see how we are renewing parts of the gardens, replanting flower beds, restoring walls and adding more saplings.'

'It is quite wonderful,' she told him, 'and impressive. To have made so much progress in just a few years.'

'It is hardly a gentlemanly occupation.' He grimaced and stripped off a glove. 'You can see here the results of my labours.'

Flora tightened her grip on the parasol to prevent herself from reaching out and touching the scars and calluses on his hand.

'No, it is much, much better,' she said fiercely. 'You should be very proud of what you are doing here. Not only are you rebuilding the gardens and making them a success, you have given employment to so many former military men.'

She was looking up at him, fire sparking in her eyes. Matt felt as if an iron band was tightening around his chest.

'Do you really think that, Miss Warenne?'

'I do. It is a very fine achievement. I only wish I—'

Flora broke off, her lashes falling quickly over her eyes, shielding her thoughts.

'You only wish...?' he prompted her.

'N-nothing,' she muttered. 'I only wish everyone was so concerned for their fellow men.'

They made their way back down the hill and gradually Flora began to relax again. Listening to him talk of his work in the gardens, she had suddenly been frustrated with her own small existence.

I only wish I could help you with your plans, was what she had wanted to say, but that would imply criticism of her fiancé.

And I am being disloyal enough, she thought, as they approached the Pavilion. I am enjoying the company of a man Quentin might well consider an adversary.

She pushed that thought aside. She wasn't here to take sides, but to find out the truth about Matt Talacre's claim to the statue and to do what she could to mediate between the two men. She had hoped Betty might be able to find out something of the man's character, but now she would have to rely upon her own judgement.

That was why she had accepted Matt's escort, she told herself. The fact that she very much wanted to spend more time with him was purely coincidental.

That thought set her inconvenient conscience ringing with something that sounded very much like hollow laughter.

When they reached the Pavilion, Matt explained they would not be taking tea in the original tea rooms.

'They are large enough for the quieter winter months,' he said, as he escorted her through the building. 'But the number of summer visitors has increased so much that I had tables moved here, into the ballroom.'

He ushered her into the large, bright salon and Flora stopped for a moment to look around. It was much bigger than the assembly rooms at the Red Lion. Long windows ran the full length of one wall, most of which were open today, giving a view of a colourful flower garden. At night the chandeliers would be ablaze with candlelight, making the gilded plasterwork around the ceiling glitter.

Several musicians occupied the small dais, entertaining everyone with a selection of traditional folk songs and country airs, but Flora imagined an orchestra playing there, music filling the air while the dancers twirled and skipped in a joyous, colourful spectacle.

'It is a magnificent room,' she remarked as he led her between white-clothed tables where small groups were enjoying refreshments served by soft-footed servants. 'What happens if you wish to have a ball?'

They had reached an empty table by one of the open windows and he held her chair for her to sit down before responding.

'You mean *when* we have one,' he corrected her. 'We will be holding our weekly ball tonight, in fact. The tea rooms will close early today and everything will be cleared away in readiness for the dancing.'

'That must take a great deal of effort.'

'We have practised it many times. Everyone knows exactly what to do.'

'Like an army drill?'

He grinned. 'Exactly that.'

'I am impressed,' she replied, twinkling back at him.

'Thank you. Now let me see if we can impress you with our tea and cake!'

The tea was accompanied by an assortment of small delicacies: sponge fingers and puffs flavoured with lemon or almonds as well as biscuits and slices of fruit cake. Flora discovered that she was quite hungry and nibbled a macaroon while her escort entertained her with amusing anecdotes about the characters who attended the concerts and balls held in this building.

His passion for Bellemonte shone through, as did the affection in which he held his patrons, from those who could only afford the luxury of an occasional visit to the rich merchants and gentry who had purchased season tickets and attended every ball and concert.

When at last they made their way back into the square, she thanked him for his time.

'I cannot remember when I have enjoyed a day so much.'

'Thank *you*, Miss Warenne. Bellemonte means a great deal to me and I am glad to have your approval. After I was wounded at Waterloo, I found it difficult to adjust to life in England. I had been a soldier for too long, you see. I was accustomed to being busy. Conham employed me as his aide-de-camp and when he became Lord Dallamire and sold out, he kept me on, but it was never enough. There was no challenge in it.'

She smiled at his enthusiasm.

'And you find Bellemonte challenging?'

He grinned and waved his arm. 'Just look about you. The gardens are constantly changing with the seasons and the weather. I work with the gardeners to keep them looking their best throughout the year and with the wardens and the watchmen who keep out footpads, pickpockets and ladies with a more, er, unsavoury reputation. And then there is the hotel. It is proving so successful that I can now consider expanding on to the spare land behind it.'

'And what of the pleasure baths?' said Flora, glancing at the tall wall on the far side of the square. 'Are they successful?'

'Yes, they are. The swimming pool is popular with young gentleman.'

Flora sighed. 'I have often thought that I should like

to be able to swim. Perhaps you should build a private pool for the ladies, too.'

'Perhaps I shall, if you promise to come and use it.'

'I cannot swim.'

'No difficulty there,' he murmured. 'I could teach you.'

She quickly looked away from his smiling eyes. The idea brought images to her mind that made her blush, but it saddened her, too, knowing this would be her only visit to Bellemonte.

When they left the Pavilion, Flora took Matt's arm as they walked to the hotel, revelling in the solid strength she could feel beneath the fine woollen sleeve. Being this close she could see that no padding was required to widen the shoulders of his coat and the flat plane of his stomach suggested he was no stranger to hard, physical exercise.

Unlike Quentin.

No. She would not compare the two men. Quentin had many good qualities. Only she could not bring them to mind just now.

Flora released Matt's arm as they entered the hotel's elegant lobby.

'I am obliged to you, Mr Talacre, for giving up so much of your time.'

'It was a pleasure, ma'am. I should like to ask you to dine with me, but I suspect you would say no.'

'I should indeed. That would be most improper.'

'And you will not come to the ball tonight?'

'Completely out of the question.' She ruined the effect of this firm response by adding, 'Besides, I have not brought a ballgown.'

'It is a masquerade. I could find you a mask and a domino and your gown would not be seen. In fact, no one need ever know you were at the ball.'

She shook her head. 'Please, do not tempt me. You know I cannot.'

'But you would like to.'

Flora hesitated. She could not lie. The thought of dancing with Matt Talacre in that lovely ballroom was almost irresistible.

'Very much.' She swallowed a sigh and squared her shoulders. 'Thank you for a most enjoyable day, Mr Talacre.'

He took her outstretched hand and bowed over it.

'I shall come to your room at ten o'clock, in case you change your mind. If not, ignore my knock. I promise you I will not persist.'

And with that he turned and walked away, leaving Flora to make her way upstairs to her bedchamber. She would not go, of course, even though she was flattered by Matt Talacre's attentions. She had thoroughly enjoyed his company and her spirits were quite buoyed up by her outing, so much so that she was still smiling broadly when she found Betty waiting for her, a little pale but determined now to resume her duties.

Even the maid's irate greeting could not dent her good humour.

'And where in the world have you been, miss?'

Flora laughed. 'Goodness, Betty, you sound just like my old governess.'

'Your aunt sent me along to look after you,' Betty scolded her with all the authority of an old and trusted retainer. 'Goodness knows what she would say if she knew you was going here there and everywhere alone!'

Not by the flutter of an eye did Flora correct her maid's assumption.

'I have been no further than the gardens,' she replied, handing over her parasol before removing her cap and spencer. 'Since you are in no condition to talk to the servants for me, I must make my own judgement about Bellemonte and its owner.'

'Aye, well, it ain't your place to be making judgements,' Betty told her. 'It is no business of yours and you should leave all that to Lord Whilton.'

Flora held her tongue. She knew that one word would silence her servant, but she would not utter it. She was sincerely fond of Betty, who had looked after her since she was a child. She knew that the older woman had her best interests at heart, so she meekly accepted these strictures and set about coaxing her maid out of her ill humour.

She was in part successful, and Betty was further

reassured when Flora confirmed she would be dining alone in her room again.

'I am that glad to hear it, miss. If I am honest, just getting up and dressed has quite tired me out. I shall be glad to get back into my bed again. And an early night will do us both good.'

'I am sure it will,' Flora agreed, although the idea of retiring while it was still light was more than a little depressing, particularly when she thought of the dancing that would be taking place almost within sight of her window.

'And there'll be no need for you to change out of your day dress, Miss.'

'Oh, but I think I should,' said Flora, surprising herself as much as her maid.

'But why, miss, if you are dining alone again? You didn't do so yesterday.'

Flora had quite decided she would not go to the Pavilion Ball tonight, but somehow she was not quite ready to give up the idea. Her maid gave a long-suffering sigh and went over to the linen press.

'Very well, then, Miss Flora, there's the sarsenet, or perhaps the green cotton.'

'No, the Venetian gauze, I think.'

Betty looked at her, aghast. 'Surely you would not waste your new evening gown on a solitary dinner in your bedchamber!'

But Flora would not be moved, and with a tut of

disapproval the maid fetched out the gown and helped her mistress to dress.

'There.' Betty stood back with a grudging nod of approval. 'It does look very well on you, miss.'

Flora turned back and forth before the mirror to observe how the tawny gown with its gauze overdress caught the light as she moved. She turned to give her maid a kiss on the cheek.

'Thank you, my dearest Betty.' She put a hand to the row of pearl buttons down the centre of the bodice. 'And the advantage of this gown is that I can undress myself. It means you need not worry another moment about me. No, no, I will brook no arguments on this. In fact, I *order* you to go to bed and rest, as soon as you have finished your dinner!'

Throughout her solitary meal Flora battled with her conscience. Her sensible self was adamant that her resolve was as strong as ever. She would not go out. But another, more rebellious spirit was eager to kick over the traces of her dull, conventional life. Just a little more.

Why else did you choose this gown, she asked herself, if not to prove that you can make a choice and resist temptation, when the time comes? If Mr Talacre should call you will see him, face to face, and refuse.

Yes, exactly that, she decided, signalling to the hotel servants to clear away the remains of her dinner. In a few weeks she would marry Viscount Whilton. She would go with him to London and take her place in Society, where there would be far greater lures and enticements than she faced here, tonight. She needed to be prepared, to know she could face temptation and not weaken.

However, when the servants withdrew and Flora was alone, with only the faint sound of Betty's snores for company, the truth crept back in and would not be ignored. She *wanted* to go to the ball tonight and dance the night away.

More specifically, she wanted to dance with Matt Talacre. One last time.

Chapter Twelve

Would he come?

The hands of the little carriage clock were moving ever closer to the hour. Ten o'clock. Flora paced the floor, her silk skirts whispering in the silence.

If he did not call for her, then the decision was made, she would not go to the Pavilion Ball. She would go to bed and return to Whilton tomorrow without seeing Matt Talacre again. That was what she *should* do, but she did not think she would be strong enough to refuse, if he came to her door.

She was caught up in a giddy excitement she had never known before. It was as if, by leaving Whilton, she had slipped the leash, at least for a few days. She had an opportunity to dance in a glittering ballroom with a man she had come to look upon as a friend. It would all be quite harmless, but she knew that was not how others would see it, and if Quentin found out, it was very likely that he would call off the marriage.

She was playing with fire, but she could not stop now, even if it consumed her.

Matt reached the door of Flora's room and paused. He should not be doing this. He did not flirt with married women and Flora Warenne was as good as married. He tried to ease his conscience by telling himself that was the point of befriending her. She was betrothed to Lord Whilton and Matt hoped she would use her influence with the Viscount over the matter of the Rysbrack statue.

He knocked softly on the door. Perhaps she had thought better of it and would not answer. But then the door opened and his relief was so great he could not stop the smile that surged up from somewhere inside him.

'Good evening, Miss Warenne.'

She looked a little pale as she regarded his cloaked figure, then her eyes fell to the folds of black silk draped over his arm.

'You have a domino for me.'

'As you see. Will you allow me?'

She nodded and stepped out into the corridor, quietly pulling the door closed behind her. He draped the cloak about her, resisting the temptation to allow his hands to linger on her shoulders, then he held up two strips of black silk by their ribbons.

'I have masks, too, you see.'

Moments later he was escorting her down the stairs. The hall was bustling with others dressed for the masquerade, some in cloaks, others in costume to disguise their identity. No one spared a second glance for one more masked couple, shrouded head to foot in their enveloping dominos.

It was a warm summer night and it did not take them long to walk the short distance to the Pavilion, where the dancing had already commenced and the music flowed out through the open windows. As they approached the door, Flora hesitated.

Matt glanced down at her. 'Nervous?'

'A little.'

'You need not be. I will look after you.' He placed his hand over her fingers and felt them tremble. 'I give you my word I will keep you safe.'

She said quietly, 'I shall rely upon you do to so, sir.'

The ballroom at night was every bit as magnificent as Flora had imagined it and the orchestra was excellent. Her nerves settled once she was on the dance floor. After all, this was the reason she had come. Matt Talacre was a good dancer and an attentive partner, and she was soon lost in the joy of the music, caught up in the lively, colourful world of the dance.

Matt remained at her side for the next two dances, and the next. They only left the floor to partake of a simple supper, where they laughed and chattered together as if they had known each other for ever.

Afterwards Flora went back with him to the ballroom for two more sets before finally allowing him to guide her through one of the long windows and out into the balmy night air.

'Are you glad you came?' he asked.

'Oh, yes, I do not know when I have enjoyed myself more! What I mean is,' she went on, 'this ballroom and the orchestra are both far superior to what we have in Whilton.'

'Ah, so your pleasure has nothing to do with your dancing partner.'

'As to that, I could not possibly say,' she replied primly.

Through the slits in his mask his eyes blazed, as if they were on fire. Something inside her flipped over and she scolded herself for being fanciful. Reflected light from the ballroom, she told herself, refusing to read anything more into his heated look. She quickly turned away and began to stroll along the terrace.

'You cannot say,' he repeated, falling into step beside her. 'Not even a hint?'

'Pray do not try to flirt with me.'

'Hah, would I dare?'

'I think you would dare a great deal,' she replied, suddenly serious.

'Not tonight. Tonight, I gave you my word I would keep you safe.' He hesitated, 'However much I want to take you in my arms and ravish you.'

She felt faint at the very thought of it. 'Please, don't say such things, Mr Talacre.'

'Will you not call me Matt?'

'You know we can only ever be friends.'

'I am Matt to my friends. And my lovers.'

She uttered a little cry of frustration. 'Can you never be serious?'

'I was never *more* serious.'

There was no laughter in his voice now and Flora's heart began to race, knowing that what she said next, what she did, could change everything.

The air around them almost crackled, charged with energy. Her pulse was jumping, she felt so alive, so aware of the man beside her. His powerful presence, the sound of his voice, the touch of his hand. Most of all the fresh scent of him, reminiscent of pine forests mixed with something exclusively male that made her want to reach out and grab him.

Flora took a step back in alarm, but it was not Matt Talacre who frightened her. It was her own wayward body.

'We...we should return to the ballroom,' she stammered.

'Do you really want to dance again?'

'No.'

Her happiness was draining away, replaced by an aching sadness for what could never be.

'No, neither do I.' He held out his arm. 'Will you walk with me? Nothing more, I swear. We will just talk.'

After the briefest hesitation she rested her fingers on his sleeve and they left the terrace. He guided her towards the pleasure gardens, where the lamps were still alight, although almost no one was walking there now.

They strolled along the dimly lit path and he said, 'I have enjoyed dancing with you tonight.'

'So, too, have I,' she murmured.

'More than I should, since you are betrothed to another man.'

'Yes.'

'And that will not change.'

'No.' Flora released his arm, but continued to walk beside him, hands clasped in front of her. 'I should not have come tonight. It was very wrong of me.'

Something was obstructing her throat and she was obliged to swallow, hard, before she could bring herself to continue. To repeat the argument that had been revolving in her head all evening.

'I love my fiancé, Mr Talacre. We have been engaged for two years. Everything is settled. I cannot cry off now.'

'No, of course not. After all, we only met a few weeks ago.'

'And have seen each other, what, a half a dozen times?'

'Yes. We hardly know each other.'

'Quite.' She kept her eyes fixed on the path ahead of them.

'In fact,' he said, 'we are little more than strangers.'

They halted. His voice was deep and dark as the shadows around them. Flora turned to face him.

'Strangers,' she agreed, as his mouth came down upon hers in a kiss that rocked her to the core.

She clung to Matt, returning his kiss with a passion she had not known she possessed. It would have shocked her, if she had been capable of thought. He teased her lips apart, exploring her mouth with his tongue, and she felt something unfurling deep inside, a curl of desire spreading into every part of her body. His hands roamed over the thin silk of her gown and she felt her breasts tightening in response. A sigh escaped her as Matt trailed kisses along her jaw and down over her neck. She pushed her body against his, not knowing what it was she wanted, except that it was more than this.

There is no more. You are betrothed to another man.

The thought was like sudden shower of cold water. She struggled in his hold and immediately he let her go.

'Oh, I am sorry,' she gasped. 'I am so sorry. I cannot do this...it is wrong!'

***

Flora's distress was all too clear in her voice. Matt dragged in a harsh breath, and another, fists clenched at his sides as he fought down the desire that threatened to overwhelm him. The hood had slipped back and her fiery curls trembled as she sobbed.

He said raggedly, 'No. No, don't cry, Flora, this is not your fault.'

'Oh, but it is,' she cried, looking up. 'Don't you *see*, I should never have come to Bellemonte!'

Instinctively he opened his arms and she fell against him, tearing off her mask and burying her face in his shoulder as the tears flowed, unrestrained. He held her, resting his cheek against her hair until at last she grew calmer.

'I beg your pardon,' she said, her voice muffled against his coat, 'I should not have allowed this.'

'Nay, sweetheart. Don't blame yourself. We were swept away by the music and dancing and the night air.'

'And I know you are not the marrying sort,' she muttered, 'You told me so, yourself.'

'Yes, I did, didn't I?'

Matt looked up at the black canopy of the trees overhead. It was true, marriage was not for him. Neither was stealing another man's bride.

He reached up one hand and gently pushed an errant curl behind her ear.

'I should have known better than to escort a beautiful woman to a ball. It was inevitable I would want to kiss her.'

His attempt at easing the mood fell flat. Another shuddering sob racked Flora's delicate frame and his arms tightened. This was not what he had planned. He had wanted to show Flora the gardens, to strengthen their friendship in the hope that she would help him recover his property. Instead he had proved himself to be the very worst sort of rogue. He had known from the first that Flora was an innocent and yet he had flirted outrageously with her.

Confound it, he had damned well nearly seduced her!

Reluctantly he let her go. She had found a handkerchief from somewhere and was wiping her eyes.

'I think I should go back to the hotel now.'

'Of course.'

He scooped up her mask from the floor and handed it to her, standing silent. She fixed it in place just as a party of revellers came into view and surged unsteadily along the path. Matt helped her pull up her hood.

'I had better escort you.'

He thought she might object, but she merely nodded and they set off, side by side, not touching. In silence.

'What will you do now?' asked Matt, as they approached the entrance gates. He could see the square, flickering with lamps, before them.

'I shall go back to Whilton and forget all about this.' She added, after a slight pause, 'Not completely, I am not sure I shall ever do that.'

'I only hope I have not ruined you,' he murmured.

'Not at all,' said Flora robustly. 'It was only one kiss.'

But what a kiss! Matt had never experienced such heat, such desire with any woman before. He had been lost as soon as their lips met.

Forbidden fruit always tastes sweeter. You'll get over it. As will Flora.

He straightened his shoulders. He must make this as easy as possible for her.

He said, 'Aye, 'twas a very pleasant interlude, Miss Warenne, and hopefully no one will ever know of it. You will go back and marry your Viscount; I will continue to manage Bellemonte. Our paths will not cross again.'

'And the statue of Ares?'

'It will be returned to Bellemonte, but I shall leave any future negotiations to the lawyers.'

She nodded. 'I sincerely hope you are successful.'

They had reached the gates and Matt stopped.

'It is but a few steps from here to the hotel. You had best go alone. I will watch you, all the way. To make sure you are safe.'

'Thank you.' She hesitated, then said in a rush, 'It was foolish of me to come here. Naive. And yet, I do not regret it. Any of it.'

She was gazing at him, her eyes shining with tears, and a faint, brave smile trembling on her lips. It took every ounce of Matt's willpower not to drag her back into his arms.

'Goodbye, Flora. Be happy with your Viscount.'

Without a word she hurried off, the black domino floating about her, giving the impression that she was some ethereal creature, gliding across the square. Matt watched her until she disappeared into the lighted portal of the hotel, then with a sigh he turned and strode back into the gardens.

Chapter Thirteen

'Well, my dear, I have had a letter today from Lord Whilton,' said Mr Farnleigh, beaming at Flora across the dinner table. 'He will be with us again this week. Is that not capital news?'

Flora looked up quickly. 'But the midsummer ball is not until next Wednesday!'

'He has completed his business and will be back at Whilton Hall by Friday.' He beamed at her. 'That will put the roses back in your cheeks, eh, my dear?'

'Just what I was thinking,' said Aunt Farnleigh. 'You have been looking decidedly peaky since you returned from Hotwell House. It was very good of you to go with Jenny Albright, my love, but really, for you to put up in the Hotwell House, filled with the sick and dying, cannot have been good for you.'

'We were in no danger at all, Aunt,' replied Flora, smiling. 'Those taking the waters are in the main elderly and infirm, but not infectious. And Jenny was so glad to see her godmother. Mrs Boscombe was considerably cheered by her visit.'

Flora had felt very guilty for leaving her friend to visit her ailing godmother alone, as she had been at pains to tell Jenny when the carriage came to collect her from Bellemonte, early on the Friday morning.

Jenny had been equally quick to assure her there was nothing she could have done.

'I spent every hour I could with Aunt Elvira and was fit for nothing but to fall into bed each night. You would have been obliged to amuse yourself for the whole time. I am sure you were much better off at Bellemonte.'

As to that, thought Flora, moving her food around her plate, her visit to Bellemonte had solved nothing. She realised now that it had been a foolish, fruitless outing, born of her desire to escape Whilton, just for a while.

She had gone to the gardens at Whilton Hall and seen the marks on the statue for herself and she was convinced it was indeed from Bellemonte. But what good did it do? She could not explain that to Quentin without telling him of her visit to Gloucestershire and she dared not do that, because she had embroiled others in her deceit. Not only was Jenny complicit in the secret, but her maid, Maria, as well as Betty and Edwin.

Flora had known all three servants for years. They

had accompanied Jenny and Flora on many of their childhood picnics and outings, mended their torn gowns, bathed grazed knees and mopped up their tears. They had often covered up the childish misdeeds of their young charges, but Flora knew that this secret was quite another matter and she had charged them all that, if asked directly, they must not lie to their employers. The decision to go to Bellemonte had been hers and hers alone. She would take full responsibility, if word should get out, and do her best to defend them.

Flora could not believe that her aunt and uncle, or Mr and Mrs Albright, would turn off such old retainers who had had no choice but to obey orders, but still guilt weighed down her spirits. She had heard nothing so far to suggest anyone in Whilton knew of her visit to Bellemonte and she could only hope that nothing occurred to change that.

Mr Farnleigh cleared his throat. 'I believe, my dear Flora, that the Viscount's decision to cut short his time in town is a sign of his affection for you.'

'I should believe that more readily if he had informed *me* of the decision, sir!' she said, finally giving up on her meal.

Aunt Farnleigh tutted. 'Hush now, Flora. It is only proper that he should write to your guardian.'

'It is positively medieval!'

'Ah, now we know the cause of Flora's malaise,' her uncle chuckled. 'She is moping for her sweetheart.'

She blushed at that, but thought it best not to protest. Lord Whilton was not the man who featured in her dreams each night, or who occupied her thoughts for most of her waking hours. Since returning from Bellemonte she had not been able to get Matt Talacre out of her head. She could not forget their final meeting, or the kiss they had shared. She could not forget the feel of his lips on hers, his arms about her. At night she was a prey to dreams where she was lying with him, their naked limbs tangling, and she would wake, trembling in the darkness, her body aching with desire so overpowering she wanted to weep.

Preparations for the wedding had been carrying on while Flora was away and there was plenty to keep her busy: fittings for her new gowns, invitations to be written, menus for celebratory dinners to be discussed. The dreams of Matt Talacre were purely wedding nerves, she decided. His kiss had awakened something, brought her body alive to the pleasures that awaited in the marriage bed. She had heard whispered conversations and gossip between married women of her acquaintance, but had never known what it meant, until she had gone to Bellemonte. Now she knew why parents were so careful with their daughters.

Her aunt and uncle had kept her well chaperoned.

Even those two early occasions when she thought she had lost her heart, she had never been allowed to be alone with her admirer. She had engaged in only the mildest of flirtations with any gentleman, until she had met Matt Talacre. It was no wonder that one kiss from him should liquefy her bones and send the hot blood coursing through her body. How much better would it be when Quentin at last took her in his arms and kissed her that way?

She was still mulling over these thoughts on Friday, when Lord Whilton arrived at Birchwood House. She watched him from the upper landing window as he rode up the drive on his long-tailed bay. How could she have forgotten what a handsome man he was? Straight-backed in the saddle, his slender frame looked very elegant in a blue riding jacket. With his fair hair and blue eyes, he reminded her of a prince from a fairy tale. She was so relieved that at last he was here. He would put all her doubts to rest.

Flora went back to her room to remove her apron and tidy her hair before going downstairs. Learning that Lord Whilton was with her aunt and uncle in the morning room, she almost ran across the hall and opened the door in time to hear her uncle speaking.

'We should tell her—'

He broke off when he saw Flora and she said, smiling, 'Tell me what, Uncle?'

'No, no, not you, my dear,' he said hastily.

'The new scullery maid,' added Aunt Farnleigh. 'A trifling matter.'

Flora gave an uncertain laugh. 'Surely that is of little interest to His Lordship?'

'Indeed, it is nothing of consequence!' The Viscount crossed the room towards her. 'My dear Flora, I hope you have missed me?'

She gave him her fingers and she waited for the tremor of excitement as he kissed her hand. It never came.

'Welcome back, my lord.'

'So formal.' He shook his head at her and murmured, 'I like to hear my name on your lips, my dear.'

'Yes of course. Quentin. We did not expect you back so soon.'

'I could not stay away,' he said, sitting down with her on the sofa. 'I was eager to return to my future bride. I want to dance the night away with her at the Condicotes' Midsummer Ball. And, of course, I must make Whilton Hall ready to receive its new mistress.'

Flora was surprised. 'When I called, I was informed everything had been arranged and there was nothing for me to do. In fact,' she added, recalling the housekeeper's frosty reception, 'Mrs Goole appeared to resent my being there.'

'I think you misunderstood the woman, my love.

And you will recall my saying that you need not trouble yourself over these little things. Goole is perfectly capable of running Whilton.'

Flora paused to consider her words before replying. 'I wonder—is she perhaps afraid I shall try to usurp her position?'

She saw him frown, his eyes suddenly wary, but it was gone in an instant and then he was laughing.

'Usurp her? No, no, my dear. Goole knows that her position is secure. I do not expect you to involve yourself with the housekeeping. I should not wonder if she is a little in awe of my future Viscountess.'

Flora wanted to say she had found the woman's manner almost hostile, but Quentin had already turned towards her uncle and engaged him in conversation. Well, no matter. She would deal with Mrs Goole herself, once she was mistress at Whilton.

The Viscount stayed for a full hour before declaring he must go.

'Until Wednesday, Flora,' he said, kissing her hand. 'I cannot tell you how much I am looking forward to dancing with you at the ball on Wednesday.'

'Truly? You intend to stand up with me for more than one dance, this time?' She could not help sounding a little sceptical.

He laughed. 'I would partner you for every dance, if that were possible, but how can I deprive our friends and neighbours of that pleasure? And you dance so beautifully that I take great pleasure in watching you.' He flicked her cheek with a careless finger. 'I shall be there with you, my dear, never doubt it!'

He took his leave, but Aunt Farnleigh barely waited for the door to close behind their visitor than she turned to reprimand her niece.

'I could not help but overhear you, Flora. You really should show a little more deference to the Viscount.'

'Why? If we are to be married, we must be able to speak freely to one another.'

'But it is not wise to antagonise him. He has done you a great honour in offering for you.'

Flora hesitated. 'I would rather he showed me greater affection, Aunt.'

'That is not the way of these great men, my love. Be assured, after you are wed you will find him a most thoughtful husband, intent upon making you happy. Why, in the two years since your engagement, we have never seen anything to concern us.'

'But how often have we seen him in those two years?' she argued. 'The number of times he has come to Whilton cannot add up to more than a few months.' She bit her lip. 'I wonder sometimes if I am doing the right thing in marrying him.'

That brought a cry of protest from her aunt. 'Oh, my love, pray do not be saying such a thing! Whatever are you thinking?'

'Better that I should voice my doubts now, than when it is too late,' replied Flora, playing with the ring on her finger.

'My dear Flora, calm yourself.' Her uncle smiled at her in a kindly fashion. 'This is nothing more than wedding nerves! The Viscount will make you an excellent husband. He is kind, considerate, and you like each other well enough. Stronger feelings will follow, once you are living together, and you will have plenty to occupy your time, which is what you want, is it not, my love? You know he has several houses besides Whilton Hall, for you to look after.'

'And there will be your visits to London,' added her aunt, 'Summers spent in Brighton, perhaps. Oh, heavens! You will be the envy of every other young lady in the county!'

Seeing the Farnleighs' happy faces, Flora realised they would not understand why she was anxious about this marriage. She barely understood it herself, except that today, after talking with the Viscount, she had been aware of a mild feeling of disappointment. He was attentive, his tone caressing, but her insides did not flip over when he smiled at her, nor did her pulse jump at his every touch.

Oh, do be sensible, Flora, she scolded herself. You are fretting over silly, girlish fancies. Just like whatever was the problem with the scullery maid. It is nothing of consequence.

* * *

Sir Roger and Lady Condicote's midsummer ball at Condicote Manor had become the highlight of the summer for their friends and neighbours. This year was of especial interest, because Lord Whilton had returned from London expressly to attend the ball and dance with his fiancée, Miss Flora Warenne, just one month before their marriage in the little parish church at Whilton.

Flora knew all eyes would be on her tonight. She had dressed for the occasion in a new gown of iridescent blue silk that shimmered as she moved, changing from deepest midnight and azure to the palest ice blue. It was low at the neck and high at the waist with tiny puff sleeves and was the first of many gowns the local seamstress was making for her, in readiness for her wedding.

Looking at herself in the mirror before they left Birchwood, Flora wondered aloud if, perhaps, the shot silk was a little too extravagant for a country dance, but her aunt was quick to reassure her.

'By no means, my love. Lady Condicote has decreed you and Lord Whilton must open the ball.'

Flora shuddered. 'I wish she had not. I am unused to being the centre of attention.'

'I know, my love, but on this occasion, it can do no harm. It is only a country ball, you know. It is not as if it is London where people might remember—'

Mrs Farnleigh broke off so suddenly that Flora looked at her in concern.

'Remember what, ma'am?'

'Oh—your...your parents, of course.'

Her aunt was looking so flustered that Flora was puzzled.

'But that would be a good thing, wouldn't it?' she said. 'In fact, I should like to meet someone who knew my mother, it would be interesting to talk to them.'

'Well, well, and perhaps you shall, one day,' said her aunt, taking her arm. 'But enough of this silly talk. Let us go downstairs, my love. The carriage will be at the door and you know how your uncle hates to keep the horses waiting.'

Lady Condicote and her husband were waiting to greet their guests as they arrived. A few words were exchanged, compliments received and returned, and then the Birchwood party was free to move on towards the ballroom.

Lord Whilton was waiting for Flora at the door and, as he came towards her, she felt her spirits lift a little to see the admiration in his eyes.

He took her hand and kissed it. 'My dear, you look beautiful tonight.' He leaned closer. 'Only wait until we are married. I shall give you the family sapphires to wear and you will look truly magnificent!'

'Oh?' She touched the string of pearls around her

neck. 'Are my mother's jewels not grand enough, then? I understand they were a present to her, from Papa, on the occasion of their marriage.'

'They are perfectly acceptable for a country dance,' he assured her, 'but as my wife you must wear only the finest jewels.'

He stayed beside her, talking with her aunt and uncle until it was time for the first dance, when he escorted her to the middle of the floor.

As first lady, she had the privilege of calling the dance and had chosen one she knew the Viscount liked and danced well. She hoped this would encourage him to stay at her side, at least until supper, but after a second dance she could tell he was not enjoying himself. His smile was strained, she heard him sigh more than once, and although he was perfectly polite as he led her from the floor, she knew he was relieved when Sir Roger came up to claim her hand for the quadrille.

As she stood with Sir Roger, waiting for the music to begin, Flora looked for the Viscount and was pleased to see him partnering Lady Condicote on the far side of the room. At least he was not snubbing his hosts. However, at the beginning of the next country dance, she spotted him heading off in the direction of the card room. She sighed, knowing she would not see her fiancé again until the end of the night.

Flora kept her head high and her smile in place as she performed the familiar steps, but she elected to sit out the next and gently dismissed her partner. She made her way to the supper room, where a selection of wines and punches had been set out on a long table for guests to help themselves.

As she ladled punch into a cup she heard the sounds of another familiar tune striking up in the ballroom, but for once it did not excite her. She felt overdressed and wished she had kept this gown for a grander occasion. She had worn the shot silk to impress Quentin, but even that was not enough to keep him at her side.

Flora sipped the punch and reminded herself that she should not be disappointed. She had always known the Viscount preferred cards to dancing. In the past she had not allowed it to worry her, but tonight he had promised much. He had said he would dance the night away with her and she was angry and disappointed that he had let her down.

'Good evening, Miss Warenne.'

She froze. The sound of that deep, familiar voice at her shoulder set her heart beating so hard she was obliged to put her other hand around her punch cup before she could turn.

'Mr Talacre.' She tried to steady her galloping nerves, aware of the people around them. 'What, what a pleasant surprise. I did not know...'

'Lady Condicote sent me an invitation and I thought I should come. I have made so many friends here, you see.'

She wanted to reach out and touch him, to make sure he was real, but instead she threw him a warning glance.

'Please do not mention my visit to Bellemonte,' she said quietly. 'No one knows of it. They must never know.'

'As you wish.' He gazed at her for a moment. 'I could not stay away.'

Flora's heart was thudding and it was difficult to breathe. She should not feel like this. It was as if he had stepped out of her dreams. She shook her head.

'I… I do not know what to say.'

'Then do not say anything.' He removed the cup from her fingers. 'Will you dance with me?'

'I am sorry, I cannot.'

'But you love to dance, as do I.' He smiled. 'I take great pleasure in dancing.'

'I thought most men preferred cards.'

He shook his head. 'Not this man. Well, madam?'

No. She could not. Could she?

Why not? Quentin has not kept his promise. Why should you not dance with someone else?

Matt held out his arm, his eyes warm with understanding.

'One dance,' he said.

Slowly her hand slid on to his sleeve. 'One dance.'

Flora accompanied him back to the ballroom, where the orchestra began to play a familiar tune. She forced herself to be calm, knowing that it would be easy to make a mistake, even in a dance she knew well. She did not want to draw attention to herself or her partner. They must do nothing to cause talk or speculation.

One dance. Two. It was impossible not to enjoy oneself with a partner as proficient as Matt Talacre. She agreed to dance the Scotch reel with him and he matched her for skill and enthusiasm. She forgot everything but the sheer exhilaration of the moment.

The music ended and they stood on the dance floor, happy and breathless.

'Thank you,' exclaimed Flora, 'that was wonderful!'

She was laughing up at him, looking radiant in her blue gown, her cheeks flushed, eyes bright. Matt told himself to bow and walk away. Flora was marrying Whilton in a few weeks' time, everyone here knew that. If he danced with her again, tongues would wag.

He glanced towards the orchestra.

'The next is the last dance before supper. A waltz. Will you dance it with me?'

The reel had left Flora dizzy and elated. She could barely keep still, eager to dance again. The waltz was well accepted now. Even her aunt and uncle had learned it and had been known to join in.

She gave Matt her hand and a beaming smile. 'Of course I will!'

They joined the dancers forming a circle about the

dance floor, ready for the first section, *la marche*. It was slow and sedate, the couples promenading around the floor in stately fashion. Then came the *pirouette*. Matt's arm went around Flora's waist, holding her close. She raised her hand to clasp his in an arch above their heads and slowly they began to move around each other.

Flora had often danced the waltz, most recently with the Viscount at the assembly, but this time was different. Her heart was singing, she felt more alive, more aware of every breath, every beat as she moved around her partner. Then she glanced up to find Matt's eyes fixed on her, his gaze dark and intense, and she could not look away. Her steps never faltered. They were as one, circling, hearts beating, oblivious to everything and everyone. Time stopped. It was just the two of them, and the music.

The tempo changed. Their gazes still locked, they performed the final dizzying steps. Matt pulled her around until they were dancing breast to breast and her heart was hammering as they whirled about in one last, frantic circuit of the dance floor.

The music ended and everyone came to a stand, laughing and chattering, applauding the orchestra and each other.

Everyone except Flora and Matt. She felt his arms drop away from her, but she could not move. Couples went off towards the supper room, but still she gazed at him, her eyes questioning. Matt was staring at her as if he, too, was unable to comprehend what had just happened.

'Well, well,' drawled a cold, sneering voice. 'Mr Talacre. I do believe you have plans to steal my lady as well as my statue.'

Chapter Fourteen

Lord Whilton's icy tones cut through the fog in Flora's head. She saw Matt's brows snap together and she was suddenly alert to the very present danger. She summoned all her inner strength to face the Viscount, head up and smiling.

'That is nonsense, Quentin. We have merely been dancing.'

'But it was a waltz, my dear.'

Matt heard the menace behind the words. His hand itched to move, to reach for the sword he no longer carried, but that might be construed as an admission of guilt.

'A waltz, yes,' said Flora. 'And if you had been present, I would have danced it with you.' She stepped closer and took Whilton's arm. 'Now, shall we go into supper? I take it that is why you came to find me.'

'Yes, it was.' His cold gaze swept over Matt. 'We will speak later, Mr Talacre. That is, unless you are leaving now?'

* * *

Despite the storm raging inside him, Matt conjured a smile of disdain.

'Leave, before the ball has ended? I see no reason to do that. Until later, my lord.' He gave a little bow and strolled away.

Confound it, I should not have come tonight! he thought, walking off the dance floor. Lady Condicote's invitation had presented him with an opportunity he could not resist: the chance to see Flora again. Since their meeting at Bellemonte he had not been able to get her out of his mind. He had thought—hoped—it was a mere flirtation, but tonight, dancing with her, holding her in his arms for the waltz, had proved him wrong.

Flora had felt something, too, he would stake his life on that. He had seen it in her eyes, but whether it was infatuation, or something more, he did not know. Lord, what a coil!

'What did you mean by dancing with that man?' demanded the Viscount, as he escorted Flora out of the ballroom.

'It would have caused comment if I had not.'

'I forbid you to dance with him again.'

'Then I suggest you quit the card room and dance with me for the rest of the evening,' she retorted. 'That was the reason for your coming, was it not? To dance the night away with me.'

'It was, yes.'

The admission gave her some satisfaction and she squeezed his arm.

'Thank you, Quentin,' she said, more warmly. 'I shall look forward to it.'

They went into the supper room, where the Farnleighs were seated at one of the first tables they passed. Mr Farnleigh immediately jumped up.

'It is quite a crush in here, my lord. I doubt you will find another table free now. Won't you join us?'

'Thank you, Aunt, we would be delighted!' Flora replied before her companion could refuse and Lord Whilton acquiesced, but with only just enough grace to avoid comment. She had expected as much and, if he was quiet during the meal, she chattered quite enough for both of them.

She was desperate to avoid a tête-à-tête with Quentin until she had examined her own feelings. She had convinced herself that the kiss she had shared with Matt at Bellemonte meant nothing. It had been caused by the situation: the dancing, a balmy night and the attentions of a charming man.

Seeing Matt again tonight, laughing with him, dancing in his arms, had turned her ordered world upside down. She did not love Matt. How could she, on such a brief acquaintance? But the bigger question was, could she marry the Viscount?

She was not sure now that she wanted to do so,

but the wedding was only weeks away. All the arrangements had been made, money spent, invitations sent out. To withdraw now would have serious consequences, for everyone. Even now she could hear her uncle's response, if she told him of her doubts.

You would be a fool to throw away an excellent match and for what? A charming rogue you know nothing about. He has probably broken more hearts than you could count.

She could believe the last quite easily, but it made no difference to her wayward heart. She knew now she did not love Lord Whilton, so could she—should she—marry him?

Before supper was finished the effort of constantly chattering while her brain tried to wrestle with her problems had taken their toll. Flora fell silent, and when Mrs Farnleigh remarked that she was looking a little pale, she admitted that she had the headache.

'Oh, my poor girl, that is not like you, I hope you are not sickening for something.'

'No, no, it is merely the heat,' muttered Flora.

'Perhaps, my dear, you should go home,' suggested the Viscount.

Flora was momentarily surprised at his concern, until she realised it was a convenient means of getting her out of the way. He would not have to spend the rest of the evening dancing with her and could instead indulge his passion for cards.

The new fiery spirit in Flora wanted to declare that she was very well and would happily dance with him until dawn, only the dull throbbing pain in her skull told her that would not be sensible. So, instead, she gave him a wan smile.

'Yes, my lord, I think that might be best.'

'Then I am sure Mr and Mrs Farnleigh would oblige…?'

'Oh, yes, of course,' exclaimed her uncle, looking anxiously at his niece. 'We will take her home directly.'

The Viscount rose. 'Very well. No need to delay, sir, I shall make your apologies, for all of you. I am sure our hostess will understand.' He turned to Flora, all affectionate concern. 'You must go home and rest, my dear.'

He kissed her hand and Mrs Farnleigh, watching this display of affection with approval, said quickly, 'Pray do not be anxious, Lord Whilton. We shall take good care of her.'

With a final nod and a smile, the Viscount walked out of the supper room, leaving Flora and her aunt and uncle to make their way home.

No sooner had Matt returned to the ballroom than Lady Condicote appeared at his side. She presented him with a dance partner for the next set and he could not refuse. He politely stood up with a very shy young lady who barely opened her mouth during the whole time they were dancing. Perhaps he should have been more attentive, but all he could think of was Flora in his arms, laughing up at him, making his heart soar.

He had just escorted his young partner back to her party when he felt a touch on his arm. Matt looked around to find Lord Whilton at his side.

'A few moments of your time, Talacre, if you please.'

With a shrug he followed the Viscount out to the terrace.

'I cannot think you brought me out here to enjoy the night air, my lord,' he said.

The Viscount strolled over to a low balustrade that separated the terrace from the gardens below and stared out into the darkness.

He said coldly, 'If you thought to enlist Miss Warenne's aid to recover the statue, then you are mistaken.'

'Am I?' Matt was surprised. The statue was the last thing on his mind.

'You are. The decision will be mine and mine alone.'

'I beg to differ. The decision will lie with the courts,' Matt repeated what the lawyers had told him. 'Good title to the statue remains with Bellemonte and does not pass to you, even if you were the unwitting purchaser of a stolen item.'

The Viscount said nothing. He continued to stare out over the gardens, washed in shades of blue-grey moonlight. Matt waited and at length Whilton turned back and laughed softly.

'This is no subject for a ball, is it? We should discuss this another day. We agreed I would give you an answer by the end of the month, but perhaps you would like to hear it a little sooner.'

'If you have made a decision, you can tell me now.'

'Ah, such plain speaking, it will not do,' murmured the Viscount. 'Join me for dinner tomorrow.'

Matt made no attempt to hide his impatience. 'Is that really necessary? I should have thought you were wishing me at Jericho.'

'Ah, but I like to observe the proprieties, Mr Talacre.'

In the moonlight, Matt saw the Viscount smile. He had no desire to dine with Lord Whilton, but if it meant he could bring an end to the matter a little quicker, then what had he to lose?

'Very well, if that is what you wish.'

'I do wish it. We dine early,' said the Viscount. 'Country hours.' He gave a little bow. 'Until tomorrow, Mr Talacre.'

With that he sauntered off, leaving Matt to wonder just what the devil that had been about.

The look Whilton had given him in the ballroom suggested he would like to run him through and Matt did not trust this sudden display of urbanity. The man was up to no good: he would be wise to be on his guard tomorrow night.

For propriety's sake, Matt stood up for a couple more dances, but when he learned that Flora and the Farnleighs had already left he decided that he, too, had stayed long enough. He called for his horse and was soon on his way back to the Red Lion.

The evening had given him much to think about. The Viscount's invitation to dine had surprised him, but although recovering the statue was important, he could not stop his thoughts straying to Flora. Talking with her, dancing with her this evening had proved to him how much he wanted her, not only in his bed, but by his side.

A wife, a friend. For ever.

It was strange, unsettling. Matt had never felt like this before about any woman. Not even the French widow who had cheated him. He rubbed a hand over his eyes. If this was love, then he was in love with Flora Warenne. But did she love *him*? She was not in love with Lord Whilton, he was certain of that, but she was engaged to the man. Their wedding was only weeks away.

'Perhaps she is merely amusing herself.'

Even as he voiced the thought, Matt knew it was not true. He looked up at the moon sailing in the cloudless sky. He needed to see Flora. Until he had talked to her, he would take nothing for granted.

***

When Betty came in with Flora's hot chocolate the following morning, she also brought with her a note.

'It's from Lord Whilton, Miss Flora. Delivered by hand just as I was coming up the stairs!'

Brimming with curiosity, the maid put the hot chocolate on the table beside the bed and held out the folded paper. Flora took it and placed it on the covers before her. Was Quentin still angry with her? Perhaps he had decided to cry off from their engagement.

The flicker of hope she felt at that thought was telling. She had spent a restless night, going over and over the same argument. It was not just that she did not love the Viscount, she did not even like him very much. The little things that had annoyed her over the past two years had coalesced to become an insurmountable problem. He was vain, arrogant and selfish. It was clear to her now that she had known this for a long time, but had chosen to ignore it.

Until last night, when she had danced with Matt Talacre and observed the Viscount's reaction. If he had been consumed with a lover's jealousy she might perhaps have forgiven him, but that was not the case. He saw her only as one more possession, much as he regarded the statue of Mars installed in his garden.

As for Matt, perhaps he was like those early suitors, the ones who had courted her assiduously, then drawn back before declaring themselves. But for now that was unimportant—she could not even consider the matter while she was betrothed to Lord Whilton.

She glanced again at the letter. Perhaps Quentin, too, had realised they had made a mistake.

'Thank you, Betty, you may go.'

Flora waited only until the door had closed behind her inquisitive maid before snatching up the letter.

It turned out to be an invitation to dine at Whilton Hall that evening. Without the Farnleighs. Flora put her hand to her mouth. What on earth should she understand that to mean? Did he think their wedding day was close enough now that he could take her to his bed?

The very idea of it made her shudder. She must put an end to this, and quickly.

Having made her decision, Flora was impatient to get the meeting over as soon as possible. She finished her breakfast and set out for Whilton Hall, hurrying through the woods and gardens until she reached the moated house. She followed the footman across the hall and walked past him into the drawing room even as he was announcing her.

Lord Whilton was standing in the window embrasure, deep in conversation with his housekeeper. They both turned quickly as she entered, but it was Mrs Goole's expression that caught Flora's attention. The woman's eyes positively blazed with anger.

'That will be all, Goole,' said the Viscount.

Thus dismissed, the housekeeper lowered her eyes and hurried out of the room. Quentin walked over to Flora and she allowed him to take her hands, but as he raised first one and then the other to his lips, her mind was racing with conjecture over the little scene she had just witnessed.

'My dear Flora, this is most unexpected. Did you receive my note?'

'I did.' He was still holding her hands and she gently pulled them free. 'I did not want to wait until this evening to see you.'

'Should I be flattered?'

He was smiling, but she saw the wary look in his eyes. She took a deep breath and plunged into the speech she had been preparing as she walked here.

'I am very sorry, Quentin, I cannot marry you. I do not love you and I am sure you do not love me.'

'Love is not important.'

'It is to me. I did not think so, at first, but now… Now I do not believe we can be happy without it.'

She began to pull the diamond ring off her finger and he stopped her, putting his hand over hers.

She said quickly, 'Please, Quentin. I want us to end this charade now.'

'There are things to be considered, my dear, before you contemplate terminating our engagement.'

'I have thought about it very carefully, I assure you.'

'I do not think you have considered everything, my dear. This is about your parents.'

She frowned. 'My parents?'

'More specifically, your mother.'

'I don't understand.' Flora shook her head. 'My parents died sixteen years ago.'

'Yes, on their way to France. Do you know why they were going there?'

'The Treaty of Amiens had been signed. We were at peace. Everyone was going there that summer.'

'But not all for the same reason. Your mother and father were not going as visitors, my love. They were quitting England, for ever.'

'No, no,' she laughed at him. 'That is ridiculous. They left me with my aunt and uncle in order to enjoy a little travel abroad.' Her laughter faded. 'What is it? Quentin, why are you looking at me in that way?'

'Ah, my poor Flora, I am sorry to be the one to tell you this,'

'Tell me what?'

'Your father was taking your mother abroad to save her life. You see, she had been spying for the French.'

Chapter Fifteen

'No!' Flora felt sick. 'No, that is not true, Quentin. My mother would not do such a thing. She could not be a spy...my father was a government official!'

'That is the point, my dear. Your mother was very well placed to mix with members of the government. They held regular dinners for His Majesty's ministers, where she heard secrets and plans that she passed on to her French masters.'

She threw up her hands. 'No, stop! I do not believe you. I would know, I would have been told, if this, this *abomination* was true!'

The Viscount's smile was sympathetic, but it sent a chill running through her.

He said softly, 'Alas, it is all too true, my dear. Your father hoped to reach France before the treason was discovered. He would have succeeded, too, if their carriage had not overturned. Once they were dead, your uncle persuaded the ministers involved not to make the matter public, which would have been highly humiliating for the government. He also managed to silence any rumours and protect the good name of Warenne.'

She put up her chin. 'If everything was hushed up, how do you know of it?'

'Your uncle told me, when I asked for permission to pay my addresses.'

'My *uncle*?' Flora stared at him, trying to make sense of everything he had said. 'But why? Why would he do that?'

'He felt it his duty to tell me the truth.'

'His duty to tell *you*, but not me?' Flora's confusion turned to anger. 'How dare he keep something like this from me!'

'My dear, he was trying to protect you.'

'Protect me, by keeping me in ignorance?' She laughed again, but this time it was a bitter sound. 'And knowing this, you still considered me a suitable bride? I thought breeding and respectability were paramount with you.'

'Breeding, certainly. Your father's lineage is impeccable. The Warenne name goes back centuries. William de Warenne fought with the Conqueror and was made Earl of Surrey by his son, William Rufus. I have traced your history. Your father was a direct male descendent of the first Earl.'

She shook her head. 'No, that makes no sense. My father was a gentleman, but he had no fortune, no pretentions to greatness!'

'But he should have done. His family's descent is well documented.'

'You have studied it all?'

'But of course. I wanted a wife with a bloodline to match my own.'

She looked at him in amazement. 'You are marrying me for my *bloodline*?'

'A little more than that, my dear. Your father had a right to arms and I have ascertained that right now applies to you. Your heraldic arms will be impaled with mine. I have already ordered several shields with the new design. Once we are married, they will be displayed prominently in every room. Our combined ancestry must command respect.'

That word, impaled, made her shiver. Flora stared at the man in front of her. She had always known that he was proud and arrogant, but she could not believe that he had chosen her purely for her bloodline, like some prize animal.

'Quentin, does anyone care for that sort of thing now?'

His brows went up and he said coldly, 'Of course they do. I would have preferred a bride with an unblemished line on the distaff, but it is the male line that is important. Your mother will be forgotten. She is an irrelevance.' Flora winced at that. He went on. 'Do not worry, Flora, no one else knows of your mother's treachery. And they never will, as long as you marry me.'

'Oh, this is absurd,' she exclaimed. 'I will not stay here another moment!'

She tugged the ring from her finger and held it out to him.

He said, 'Think, before you do anything foolish, Flora. If you cry off, I shall make certain that your history is known. And not only in Whilton. It will be reported in the London papers and throughout the country. All your friends will know your parents were traitors, that they were fleeing to France to escape justice.'

He gave an eloquent shrug. 'Perhaps that does not worry you, to have everyone know you are the daughter of a traitor—two, when you think that your father was going to help her to escape. But think of how it will rebound upon your aunt and uncle. They suppressed all the evidence against your mother. Of course it is still in the government papers, for anyone who wishes to look.'

'Like yourself?'

'Exactly. The Farnleighs took you in and gave you a home. Did you never wonder why they came to Whilton? They needed to start afresh, you see. Somewhere no one had heard of your parents. Rumours were already beginning to circulate in London, but after the tragic accident your uncle, together with your father's friends, silenced the whispers. Moving to a quiet town was an ideal solution.'

She said defiantly, 'After all this time no one would be interested in such an old story.'

'Oh, but they would, my dear, if certain papers came to light. You see, after your uncle told me about your past, I made a few enquiries of my own. I have obtained a number of letters your mother wrote to her contact in Paris. They were sent via a go-between on the English coast.' He waved to a large leather wallet resting on the sideboard. 'Your behaviour recently made me think you might want to cry off so I brought the letters with me from London. I thought you might like to see them. Go on, my dear. Take a look.'

She walked across and picked up the wallet. Inside were a number of folded papers. She pulled one out and read it, then a second.

'Where did you get these?' she asked, sitting down on a chair next to the sideboard.

'I sent an envoy to France to see what could be discovered. By a mixture of, er, persuasion and bribery he came back with these.' He laughed. 'They cost me a great deal of money, but I believe it was worth it.'

Flora's blood turned to ice. If all this was true and it became known about her mother and Papa's attempts to save her, she knew she would not be the only one tainted. Her aunt and uncle would be damaged by association. The Farnleighs' comfortable, respectable existence would be destroyed.

And Matt. He had an implacable hatred of French spies. And with good reason, she thought, remembering what he had told her. He would want nothing more to do with her.

'I do not believe any of this, my lord!'

'Not even those letters, in your mother's handwriting?'

'They might be forgeries.' She put the papers back in the wallet and placed the ring next to it on the sideboard. Then she rose, her legs not quite steady. 'I shall go back to Birchwood House and ask my aunt and uncle.'

His smile only drove the ice further into her bones.

'Yes, do that, Flora. And then you will put on your finest gown and come back to Whilton Hall. We shall dine together and say no more about this painful subject.'

'No. Even if everything you have said is true, I shall never come back here.'

'Oh, I think you will, my dear,' he murmured. 'You will do as I say. Or your shameful history will be public knowledge by the morning.'

Without a word she turned and walked towards the door.

'Come alone tonight,' he told her, as she grasped the handle. 'My cousin is here; she will play chaperon for you.'

***

Flora hurried back to Birchwood House, by turns running and walking. Her thoughts were in turmoil. It could not be true; Quentin was playing some cruel joke upon her. But why would he do that, if it could be easily disproved?

She was quite out of breath by the time she reached the house, but on learning that her aunt and uncle were in the drawing room, she ran across the hall to join them.

'Ah, Flora, there you are my love, what a time you have been!' declared Aunt Farnleigh, as she went in. 'You have just missed our visitor. Mr Talacre was here and—'

'Mr Talacre?'

Her uncle nodded. 'Why, yes. He called to pay his respects, after the ball last night. He asked after you particularly and stayed talking for a good half-hour. Perhaps it is for the best that you were not here. Dancing the waltz with him might not have been the kindest thing to do, Flora. The poor fellow may well have been beguiled, although we had made it quite plain to him that you were engaged.'

She waved an impatient hand, afraid to think of Matt until she had asked the question that was burning her mind.

'Was Mama a French spy?'

She watched them both, expecting a puzzled frown

or a shocked disclaimer. They looked at one another and her aunt burst into tears.

Flora forced her shaking limbs to move to the nearest sofa and sat down.

'So it is true.'

Mr Farnleigh went over to his wife and put one arm about her shoulders.

'What have you heard?' he demanded.

Flora repeated everything the Viscount had told her. When she had finished, he sighed.

'Charles—your father—fell in love with Mary in Ireland. He had no idea that her family supported the revolution in France. And Mary herself never said anything about it. He brought her back to England as his bride and we thought them well matched. She was always such a sweet, quiet girl.

'It was only later that we learned of it. Charles came to me for help, when he discovered she was passing secrets to the French.'

'But why, how?' said Flora. 'I don't understand. Papa worked for the government; he would not betray his friends or his country.'

'Not knowingly,' said her uncle. 'Apparently, Mary was very fond of one of her Irish cousins and it was he who persuaded her to spy for the French. He moved to Deal, in Kent, in ninety-six and Mary wrote to him there regularly. Charles thought nothing of it—after all she was a long way from her home and all her family, it was only natural that she would correspond with a cousin.

'Your father had an active role in government at the time, forever holding dinners for his political friends and allies with Mary as his hostess. She was passing on everything she heard at the dinner table.'

'And there was plenty for her to tell,' put in Aunt Farnleigh, bitterly. 'Charles and his colleagues never considered that they would need to guard their tongues in front of his wife!'

'Her cousin was only a go-between,' added Mr Farnleigh. 'Her letters were being smuggled across the Channel to his French masters. Then Charles began to suspect someone in his household was passing on secrets and when he mentioned it to Mary, she confessed the whole. It was quite deliberate, she had been revealing names, dates, places—details that could be very useful to the French. Charles realised it could only be a matter of time before the truth came out.'

Aunt Farnleigh nodded. 'That was when he came to us. The Treaty of Amiens had just been signed and he wanted to take your mother to France, where she had been promised sanctuary. He asked if we could give you a home.'

'You *knew* they would not be coming back?' asked Flora.

She remembered it so vividly. She had been ten years old, excited to be spending a few weeks with her aunt and uncle while Mama and Papa enjoyed an excursion to France. They had all been so happy, talking of what they would do when they were back together again. It had all been a pretence.

'Oh, my love, it was such a difficult time,' said Aunt Farnleigh, wiping her eyes. 'My brother loved Mary so much, he could not bear to leave her.'

Suddenly Flora felt very much like a child again.

'Why did they not take me, too?' she asked, in a small voice.

Her uncle was looking uncomfortable, frowning and biting his lip as he struggled to find the words to explain.

'There were already rumours in Whitehall, Flora. It had to appear as if he and Mary were off on a short jaunt. Leaving their beloved daughter behind was the perfect bluff.'

Flora's world was collapsing around her. She gripped her hands together. She wanted to weep, or scream.

'How could they?' she whispered. 'How could they abandon me?' She shook her head. 'Papa was always very busy, but Mama was with me constantly. How could she? How could she desert her own child?'

'Oh, my dear, it was a very dangerous situation, you must believe that,' said her uncle, begging her to understand. 'Mary knew she had destroyed your father's career, that they must give up the life they had known. As for Charles, he was distraught. Mary's treachery might be discovered at any moment and he wanted to do the best for you both. She would have been executed if she had been caught, so he knew he must get her out of the country, but he could not bring himself to subject you to the hardships and difficulties he knew they would face in France.'

That would have been nothing to me, compared to losing my parents.

'Instead, he used me,' she muttered. 'I was a pawn, sacrificed for their safety.'

Uncle Farnleigh shook his head. 'Leaving you behind broke their hearts, believe me.'

'Yes, yes,' cried her aunt. 'Your mama never forgot to take her pearls, Flora. She left them for you. With instructions that we were to give them to you on your eighteenth birthday, the age she was when she married your father.'

'But you were never going to tell me that, were you?'

'How could we?'

Aunt Farnleigh began to weep and Flora closed her eyes, wondering how she would ever live with the pain of it.

'We were all four of us guilty of deceiving you, Flora,' said her uncle. 'I am so very sorry.'

'Everything you told me then was false,' she said. 'A ruse to convince me and the world that they were coming back.'

'Yes.' Aunt Farnleigh dabbed her eyes. 'But then we

heard about the accident and, well, we were so thankful that you were safe with us.'

The tears burning Flora's eyes could no longer be held back and she gave a sob as they spilled over. With a cry Aunt Farnleigh flew across the room to sit beside her.

'Oh, no, no, my love, do not weep.' She put her arms about Flora. 'We loved you every bit as much as your parents. They knew we would bring you up as our own.'

It was a blessed relief to allow the tears to fall, but Flora only indulged for a few moments. There were still so many questions and time was short.

'Why did you not tell me?' she asked, trying to keep her voice calm.

'After the accident it was all hushed up and we did not think it necessary,' explained Aunt Farnleigh. 'No one remembers it now and we knew it would only upset you.'

'But Lord Whilton knows of it,' said Flora. 'You told him.'

'Of course.' Uncle Farnleigh nodded. He walked over to take up his favourite stance, before the fireplace. 'Having asked permission to pay his addresses, it was only right to tell him.'

'But it was not right to tell me.'

'We wanted to protect you,' said her aunt. 'It would only have caused you distress to know the truth, whereas it would be quite wrong not to inform a prospective husband.'

Flora suppressed her anger. She knew it was the way of her world, to protect the weaker sex from unpleasant truths. A sudden thought occurred to her and she looked up.

'Were there other *prospective husbands*, then?' She did not miss the look exchanged between her aunt and uncle and she went on. 'I can think of at least two gentlemen who showed a decided partiality for me, but they suddenly changed their minds. Did you tell them the sordid details, too?'

'No, no, my love,' exclaimed her aunt, close to tears again. 'Never any details. Your uncle was always most discreet. He only *hinted* at some past scandal. Lord Whilton was told the same, but he made his own enquiries and insisted upon being told the whole. And you must see, it makes it particularly gratifying that he was still prepared to offer for you, even after he learned your true circumstances.'

Flora fought back a sharp retort to that. What good would it do now?

'That is why you have been protective of me,' she muttered. 'Why we have lived quietly in Whilton all these years. It was always important that I should not attract attention or cause a scandal. You were afraid someone might remember the rumours and began to ask questions.'

'My love, you know that every woman needs to be careful of her reputation,' said her aunt. 'We love you like a daughter. We should have been just as watchful, whatever your history.'

Flora nodded. A lot of things made sense now: the excessive care the Farnleighs took of her, why she had never gone to London for her come out. She rose and shook out her skirts.

'I am going to walk in the garden. I need a little fresh air.'

'Would you like me to come with you?'

'Thank you, Aunt, but no. I shall be better on my own. I promise I shall not leave the gardens.'

After all, where could I go now?

'Yes, yes, of course my dear,' said her uncle. 'This has been a great shock to you, I can see that. However, I think it is for the best that you know everything before you marry. I wanted to tell you myself, but His Lordship was against it.'

She nodded, recalling how she had walked in upon their conversation and her aunt had passed it off as a discussion about a servant. If it hadn't all been so tragic she might have laughed. How absurd to think Quentin would ever show concern for a lowly scullery maid!

'Lord Whilton has warned me he will make all this public if I cry off.'

'Good heavens!' Mrs Farnleigh clapped her hands

over her mouth and turned her frightened eyes upon her husband.

'Surely you would not change your mind at this late stage!' he said to Flora.

'Uncle, he is trying to coerce me into marrying him!'

'No, no, I am sure you misunderstand. The man loves you. He is desperate to have you for his wife, that is all.'

She gave a bitter laugh. 'He is desperate to put my family crest into his coat of arms!'

'Well...well, what of that? A man wants to be proud of his wife.'

'Grandfather Warenne believed it was all a fabrication, did he not, Aunt?' Flora looked towards Mrs Farnleigh. 'That is what Papa always said. There is no coat of arms in any of the early family portraits.'

'When the crest was attributed to your family is not important,' her uncle replied. 'You are entitled to use it.'

'But that's the point,' said Flora. 'Quentin believes in all this antiquated nonsense. He wants a brood mare. He is marrying me in order to have an heir.'

'Of course he wants an heir,' retorted Aunt Farnleigh. She flushed a little. 'We talked of all this, Flora, how it is a wife's duty...'

'Yes, but then I was not being coerced into marriage!'

Her uncle scoffed. 'I am sure the Viscount was not serious. It is far more likely that he was shaken by your sudden talk of crying off. No, no, trust me, Flora, the Viscount is a sound man. He has been more than generous over the marriage settlement and he will make you a good husband. And for most of the year you would be settled at Whilton Hall, very close to us and to all your friends.'

He patted her clumsily on the shoulder.

'Take a turn around the garden, my dear. Consider all the advantages of being a viscountess. A married woman has far more freedom, you know, and in time, you will have a family to occupy you. And there is the Viscount's fortune. I can assure you, my dear, having drawn up the marriage settlements I know you are going to be a very wealthy woman! There is your place in Society to consider, too: a place you richly deserve! You would be a fool to throw it all away at this late hour.'

Flora's head was spinning, but she knew she needed to make a decision. And quickly, she thought, remembering the Viscount's final threat.

'Excuse me,' she said. 'I would like to walk in the garden now.'

As she left the room her aunt's voice followed her, shrill and trembling with anxiety.

'Please, Flora. Think very carefully about this! If the Viscount did denounce your mother, it would reflect badly on us all. We would be obliged to leave Whilton and this house—our home for the past sixteen years.'

Flora closed the door as the words gave way to sobs. Not stopping to fetch a wrap, she made her way to the garden door. As she reached the gun room door, Scamp barked and scratched on the panels. He had been her companion on so many solitary walks it came naturally to her to let him out and together they made their way to the gardens.

Outside, clouds were building for a thunderstorm and the air was still and heavy, adding to the oppression on Flora's spirits. At first she strode around the gardens, raging against those she had believed loved her. Every one of them had proved false. Her parents had abandoned her and the Farnleighs had been complicit in the lies told to a ten-year-old girl.

Gradually her pace slowed and the fierce anger inside abated. How could she blame her aunt and uncle when they had only ever wanted her happiness? She remembered how kind they had always been. The Italian greyhound puppy they had given her to help assuage the grief of losing her parents, the trouble they had taken with her education, interviewing countless governesses to find one who combined kindness with good teaching skills. Her uncle's patience when he taught her to drive his gig.

Even when Lord Whilton had approached them, asking permission to pay his addresses, they had not tried to exert their influence. He was allowed to call, to court her. True, she had refused him the first time, but when he had asked her again she had accepted. It had been her decision and hers alone. Would her answer have been any different, had she known the truth?

She remembered she had thought the Viscount very agreeable when they had first met. He was tall and good-looking, with his golden-blond hair and blue eyes. He had been charming, too, in those early months. A little lacking in humour, perhaps, and he was not as fond of dancing as Flora, but in every other way she had thought him most acceptable.

Was it the arrival of Matt Talacre that had changed all that? Matt's rugged features could not be called classically handsome and his lean body was too muscular, the broad chest hinting at strength rather than elegance, yet he had an animal grace when he moved. She remembered dancing with him. It had been more than a pleasure. She had been transported, as if they were the only couple on the dance floor.

Flora had reached the sheltered rose garden and sank down on a stone bench. If Quentin's godfather had not died last year, she would have been married by now. She would have known nothing of her past. She would never have met—

No! Flora quickly pushed that last thought away. Any feelings she had for Matt Talacre must be firmly crushed. He must be as dead to her now as her parents. Aunt and Uncle were a different matter, however. She did not doubt they loved her. Nor did she doubt that they now regretted not telling her the truth about Mama.

'But what else could they have done?' she said aloud. 'How do you tell a young girl that her parents have deserted her?'

Hearing the distress in her voice, Scamp jumped up beside her and nosed at her clasped hands. Absently she fondled his ears while she closed her eyes, thinking back.

She clearly remembered when they had told her she was an orphan. It was the only time she had seen tears in her uncle's eyes and Aunt Farnleigh had held her close while she cried, their tears mingling. Despair welled up in Flora. Her eyes stung.

She had lost her parents, but her aunt had lost a beloved brother. They had done their best. None of this was their fault, nor hers, but it was her actions now that would decide their future happiness. With a sob she pulled the spaniel on to her lap, buried her face in his soft coat and wept.

Chapter Sixteen

The sky was heavy and overcast when the Farnleighs' landau left Birchwood House for the short journey to Whilton Hall. Inside the carriage Flora sat alone, dressed in her white muslin evening gown with a muslin fichu embroidered with white work around her neck and fastened at the front. Her hair was piled up and dressed with white rosebuds. A glance in the mirror as she left her room had reflected her countenance, pale but resolute.

The threatened storm had not broken by the time she reached the Hall, and she ordered the driver to stop at the stables, preferring to walk. To delay her arrival just a little longer.

As she alighted, she saw the groundskeeper, Jepps, limping across the bridge. She was a little surprised when he avoided her eyes and did not respond to her greeting. Whenever they had met in the gardens he always greeted her civilly, and they had often exchanged a few words about the plants.

Perhaps he was uncomfortable outside his usual milieu—or perhaps he had told the Viscount of her first encounter with Matt Talacre in the gardens. She doubted that, because Quentin was not in the habit of speaking with his servants, other than to issue orders. Not that it mattered now, she thought as she made her way across the courtyard and prepared herself to meet the Viscount.

The door to the entrance hall was already open and she stepped inside, handing her cloak to the waiting footman. It was as she followed him across the hall that she noticed Mrs Goole standing to one side, watching her. The housekeeper turned and walked off almost immediately, but the look in her eyes stayed with Flora and added another unsettling thought to those already in her head.

The Viscount was waiting for her in the drawing room. Candles were already burning to dispel the gloom of the leaden sky outside, but the dark portraits and black, heavy furniture oppressed Flora. Even the gaudy heraldic crests on the elaborately carved overmantel seemed to taunt her now.

'Welcome, my dear.' Quentin came forward. He held out one hand, the diamond ring resting in his palm. 'May I?'

She watched impassively as he slipped the ring back on to her finger, then he kissed her hands, one after the other, before leading her to a chair. It had been placed beside the carved oak armchair that he favoured and was a similar style, only less ornate.

A seat for a consort beside her lord.

The Viscount poured two glasses of wine and carried them across the room.

'My cousin will join us shortly, but for now we will drink a toast,' he said, handing her a glass. His eyes rested for a moment on her ring finger, then he raised his own wineglass. 'To my beautiful bride.'

'You will excuse me if I do not join you in that toast, just yet.'

He laughed. 'Still cross with me, my love?'

She had no desire to smile as she asked, bluntly, 'Is Goole your mistress?'

His good humour vanished. 'That need not concern you.'

'I will not share this house with her.'

He shrugged. 'Very well, it can be arranged. There, will that do?'

She inclined her head. He had not denied it and she had achieved a victory, of sorts.

'Let us talk of more pleasant matters.' He sat down in his own chair and stretched out his long legs, entirely at his ease. 'It is four weeks to the day until our wedding. It will be a quiet affair, of course.' He glanced at her, as if to say that she now understood the reason. He went on, 'Rather than a grand ball beforehand, I thought we might enjoy a quiet family dinner here with my cousin and your aunt and uncle. What do you say?'

Flora murmured her assent. In her present mood she had never felt less like dancing. He reached over and caught her hand.

'Excellent. I am delighted we are in agreement. I think we shall deal very well together, Flora, my dear!' He pressed his lips against her fingers, then raised his head, listening to the sounds of footsteps approaching. 'And this must be our guest.'

'Guest?' Flora quickly snatched her hand away and sat up. 'I thought we were dining alone—'

'Mr Talacre, my lord!'

After the heavy grey rainclouds and even darker entrance hall, Matt blinked in the candlelight of the medieval drawing room.

He walked forward, preparing to make his bow, then he saw Flora and stopped. She was sitting in a chair next to the Viscount and her shocked face told Matt she had not expected to see him. At that moment came a flash, quickly followed by a crash of thunder that seemed to rock the very foundations of the house.

The Viscount rose, laughing.

'Well, well, that is quite an entrance, Talacre. And just in time,' he said, as the torrential rain beat against the windows. 'Pray sit down, sir. As you can see, my fiancée has honoured us with her presence. I hope you do not object?'

'Not at all, my lord.'

Matt gave a small bow and sat down on a settee opposite his host. He had no idea what was going on here, but he would play along. For now.

Flora had not been home when he had called at Birchwood House that morning. The Farnleighs had not said where she had gone, but part of him had wondered, hoped, that she had gone to Whilton Hall to break off her engagement. Obviously, that had not happened, but it was equally clear to Matt that she was unhappy.

The Viscount returned to his high-backed chair and kept up a flow of desultory small talk until his timid little cousin bustled in, breathlessly apologising for being late. A soft-footed servant followed her into the room and served Matt and Mrs Gask with glasses of wine. The Viscount indicated that his glass should also be refilled, but Matt noticed that Flora had barely touched hers.

When dinner was announced, Lord Whilton rose and held out his hand to Flora.

'Come, my love, let us lead the way to the dining room.' He had to raise his voice slightly over the sound of the rain, hammering against the glass. 'I am sure Mr Talacre will be happy to escort my cousin, is that not so, sir? My fiancée and I have had so little time together recently, I cannot get enough of her.'

Matt's jaw tightened. The Viscount kissed Flora before pulling her hand on to his arm. She looked pale and strained, as if she was not enjoying his attentions. Could it be the Viscount suspected she was not indifferent to his guest? Damn the man for taunting them both like this!

Matt gave his arm to Mrs Gask. He had no idea how much Whilton knew about his meetings with Flora, but he was determined not to betray himself. Or Flora. Matt felt the anger swell within him. Whilton was a scoundrel to make her so unhappy.

The dinner was a tense affair, with thunder rumbling around the house, and rain still pattering against the windows. Only the Viscount appeared to be at ease. Matt and the two ladies did their best to join in the conversation, but there was a palpable sense of relief when at last the meal was over. Whilton made a show of escorting the ladies to the door and kissing Flora before she left the room. When the two men were alone, Matt resumed his seat and waited for the Viscount to speak.

'What a pleasant evening this has been,' he drawled, indicating to the servant to refill their wineglasses. 'I hope you are enjoying it, Mr Talacre?'

'How could I not?' Matt replied. He waited until the

servants had withdrawn and they were alone before continuing. 'However, I did not come for a sociable evening, my lord. You promised me a decision.'

'Such haste!' The Viscount looked pained. 'My dear sir, surely we should discuss the matter first.'

'There is nothing to discuss. You have seen my letter and the evidence. It is quite clear cut. You have only to agree and I will reimburse you for what you paid and arrange for the statue to be removed.'

The Viscount listened with a faint, supercilious smile on his face.

'And yet,' he purred, turning his wineglass between his hands, 'and yet, Mr Talacre, I am minded to refuse.'

'You would prefer a long and costly legal case?'

The Viscount sneered. 'You see, I do not think you could bear the expense.'

'I believe I can.' For a long moment they eyed one another across the table. 'Is that your final word on the matter, Lord Whilton?'

'I believe it is.'

'Very well.' Matt rose. 'I shall take my leave.'

'Oh?' The Viscount sat up. 'What, sir, will you not stay and take brandy with me?'

'I will not.'

'But the ladies are waiting for us to join them.'

'Then pray give them my apologies. Goodbye, my lord. My lawyers will be in touch.'

Matt left the room, cursing himself for a fool. This

matter could have been settled weeks ago if he had not given Whilton the benefit of the doubt. He knew his hesitation was in part down to Flora Warenne. He paused in the hall, glancing towards the thin strip of light shining at the top and bottom of the drawing room door. He had thought...

No! He almost snatched his greatcoat from the servant waiting at the door and shrugged himself into it. Flora was going to marry Lord Whilton. Time to put her out of his head. Completely.

He picked up his hat and gloves and headed out into the courtyard. At least the rain had ceased and the sky was clearing: he should make the journey back to the Red Lion before it was completely dark.

In the drawing room, Mrs Gask was sitting quietly on a settee with her embroidery while Flora paced back and forth, unable to settle. Through the latticed windows small patches of moonlight lightened the sky. The storm had passed. She heard the thud of the outer door and quickly went out to the entrance hall, where she addressed a servant sitting by the small window.

'Has someone gone out?'

'Why, yes, ma'am. Mr Talacre.'

Flora paused only long enough to order her carriage before turning on her heel and hurrying back to the dining room. She entered without ceremony and saw the Viscount lounging back in his chair, a glass of brandy in his hand.

'Why did you invite him, Quentin?'

'Invite whom, my dear?'

'Mr Talacre.'

'It amused me.' He turned his head and gave her a malicious smile. 'I thought it would amuse you, too. The man has developed a tendre for you.'

Flora was too angry to blush. 'If that is the case, then it was unkind to taunt him.'

'The man is an upstart. He deserved to be cut down a little. I wanted to show him he could not have you. Or that wretched stone figure. It was the knowledge that I will not part with the statue that caused him to leave so abruptly, you know. I hope you aren't heartbroken; I know you have quite a liking for the man. In fact,' he said, rising from the table, 'I think you might be more than a little in love with him.'

He was smiling and she stared at him, repelled by the cruel streak that made him revel in the misfortunes of others.

'You know I do not love you, Quentin. I cannot understand why you should still want to marry me.'

He put a finger beneath her chin, obliging her to look up.

'Because, my dear, our children will be beautiful. More importantly, they will carry our blood in their veins. Your ancestors came over with the Conqueror and mine can be traced back to Gascony. We will be uniting two ancient, noble families.'

With a shudder Flora turned and walked over to the window. She stared out into the dusk while the Viscount continued.

'You also have many qualities that will make you an excellent consort, my dear. As well as your breeding, you have all the accomplishments required of a viscountess. And you are exceedingly desirable.' She had not heard him approach, but when he spoke again, his breath was on her neck. 'Why not let me take you to bed now, Flora?' he murmured, his hands on her shoulders. 'It is only a few weeks until the wedding, we do not need to wait...'

He gently moved aside the fichu and she felt his lips on her skin. Quickly she twisted away from him.

'Don't touch me!'

His lip curled. 'You forget, madam, I have the power to ruin you.'

'I forget nothing,' she retorted. 'I have promised to marry you and I shall come to your bed on our wedding night, not before.'

She held his gaze, angry and defiant. At length he shrugged.

'As you wish. I can wait a little longer for you.'

'Very well.' She maintained her haughty tone. 'Then I shall bid you goodnight. I have already ordered the landau; it should be waiting by the time I reach the stables.'

He frowned, but made no attempt to argue. 'Then allow me to escort you.'

She nodded. Not by the flutter of an eyelash would she show how relieved she was to be leaving. She collected her cloak and maintained a frosty silence as the Viscount walked with her, out through the gatehouse and across the bridge. Her carriage was waiting and he handed her in.

'You will go home directly, Flora,' he ordered, as she sat down and arranged her skirts.

'Where else would I go?'

She snarled out the words, but her anger only amused him. With a laugh he shut the door and stepped back as the carriage pulled away.

Chapter Seventeen

Flora leaned back against the squabs and closed her eyes. The niggling doubts about the Viscount had gone. He was arrogant and cruel. He had brought her and Matt together out of malice, enjoying their discomfiture. She remembered the look in Matt's eyes when he saw her sitting beside the Viscount. Shock, but dismay, too. The attraction between them had not been her imagination.

There was no hope that they could even be friends, but she wanted to see him, to tell him why she was marrying the Viscount. Tomorrow might be too late. Now Quentin had decided not to sell the statue Matt would want to see his lawyers as soon as possible. If she was going to talk to him it must be now. Tonight.

Flora opened her eyes and looked out. The heavy clouds had moved off and in the west the clear sky was a fiery orange from the setting sun. It was early enough. Her aunt and uncle would not expect her to return yet. As the carriage slowed to pass out through the gates of Whilton Hall she quickly issued new orders to the coachman. He was not to take the road to Birchwood, but carry on to Whilton. And he must hurry.

Having let down the window, Flora left it open. She wanted to breathe in the fresh air as they rattled at pace between the flower-filled hedgerows. It calmed her and helped to curb her impatience. It was a good three miles to the town, the road following a circuitous route through farmland. Ahead, she could see the small wood that marked the halfway point in her journey. Not long now.

The carriage rattled on and soon they were plunged into shadow as the road carved its way through the wood. It was more sheltered here, the trees were still dripping from the recent rains and the air coming through the window was redolent with damp earth and leaf mould. Something just off the road caught Flora's eye. Staring into the shadows she saw a black and white shape. A horse, standing among the trees.

'Stop, stop!'

The coachman pulled up at her sharp cry. Flora opened the door and jumped out, not waiting for the steps to be let down.

'That is Mr Talacre's horse.' She looked around, eyes searching the gloom. 'If Magpie is here, where is her rider?'

The coachman looked about him and pointed with his whip.

'Over there. No, you stay here, ma'am, let Amos go!'

Flora paid no heed. Before the footman had even climbed down, she was running towards the figure lying half hidden in the ferns at the edge of the trees. It was Matt, face down on the ground and lying so still that her heart stopped.

Steeling herself for the worst, she tore off her gloves and put two fingers on his neck, as she had seen her doctor do when checking for a pulse.

'Is...is he dead, miss?' asked Amos, running up.

She shook her head. There was no doubt; she could feel the steady beat against her fingers. The dripping trees has soaked his greatcoat, but there was an ominous, darker stain on the sleeve and she feared what else they might find if they moved him.

'He is unconscious,' she said, trying to speak calmly.

'Looks like he's taken a shot through the arm,' observed Amos, standing over her.

'Yes. It will be easier if we remove his coats before we turn him.'

She worked the heavy coat off his shoulders and eased the sleeve down his injured arm, then did the same with his evening coat, exposing a billowing shirtsleeve, soaked with blood. She saw a small hole in the material and, biting her lip to steady her nerves, she used her fingers to tear it wider, revealing the bullet wound beneath.

Flora dragged the fichu from her neck to make a pad against the wound.

'Amos, give me your neckcloth. We must bind up his arm.'

As soon as the makeshift bandage was secure, she asked Amos to help her turn the unconscious man. Together they carefully shifted Matt on to his back, his coat and greatcoat beneath him. Blinking away a tear, Flora gently removed the leafy debris that was stuck to his face. There was a bruise blooming on his temple where his head had fallen upon a protruding stone, but a careful examination of his clothes show no other signs of blood.

A shift in the wind direction sent a chill breeze along the road and Flora shivered.

'His clothes are wet; he will be growing chilled out here. We must get him into the carriage and take him to Whilton. But carefully, we do not know if he has any internal injuries.' She looked around. 'Ask John Coachman to come and help us.'

The footman hurried off and she looked doubtfully at Matt's large, solid frame. Even with three of them, how would they ever manage to carry him safely to the coach?

A movement in the shadows caught her eye and she looked up.

'Jepps! Whatever are you—no! Don't you dare run

away!' she charged him, in her sternest voice. 'Come here.'

The man approached slowly, his face haggard. Flora stared at the rifle he was carrying in one hand.

'You...*you* did this?' she demanded, horrified.

'I didn't want to,' he muttered, his voice breaking. 'His Lordship ordered me. I told him I couldn't, but he said he'd have me whipped and turned off if I didn't do as he said.'

Matt was stirring. Commanding Jepps not to go away, Flora looked down at him.

'Don't move,' she said. 'You have been shot.'

'Aye, the villain winged me. The devil of it is I came off Magpie.'

'The mare is still here,' she assured him. 'Keep still now, you have lost a lot of blood.'

'Nothing a good night's rest won't cure.' He tried to sit up and fell back, his face twisted in pain. 'Confound it! I fell on my bad leg,' he gasped. 'Can't get up.'

She placed one hand against his chest. 'Then do not try. We will carry you.'

Matt was not listening. His attention had switched to the groundskeeper.

'Jepps, isn't it?' The man nodded silently and Matt's eyes fell to the rifle. 'Was it you who shot me?'

'Lord Whilton ordered him to do it,' said Flora.

'The devil he did!' exclaimed the coachman, who had come up with Amos.

Matt kept his eyes on Jepps. 'Then why the deuce are you still here?' he demanded.

'Miss Warenne told me to stay.'

'Aye, and we'd've caught 'im soon enough if he'd run off,' muttered the footman, taking the rifle away from Jepps.

'We need him to help get you into the carriage,' she explained.

'As simple as that!'

Matt's laugh ended in a grunt of agony and Flora said, quickly, 'Hush now, we need to move you.'

Between the four of them they carried Matt to the coach without mishap, but lifting him inside required some manoeuvring. At last he was lying on the bench seat and Flora gently placed his injured arm across his chest. She thought he had lost consciousness again, but just as she was spreading his evening coat over him, he spoke.

'Where's Jepps?'

'Here, sir,' said a voice from the dusk.

'Step closer, man.'

Flora sat down opposite Matt in the carriage as Jepps appeared in the doorway.

'I am that sorry, Mr Talacre, sir,' he said, white-faced and almost shaking with terror. 'His Lordship brought the rifle this morning and told me I was to waylay you in the woods. But it's been almost ten years since I fired at anything but a gamebird! As soon as

I put my eye to the sights I knew I couldn't do it. 'Tis a very different thing to shoot one of your own rather than a Frenchie in battle. And in cold blood, too! But I was shaking so much and my finger caught the trigger—'

'Aye, well, I suppose I should be thankful you weren't actually aiming for me! Don't worry, I am not going to press charges.'

'You—you ain't going to have me arrested?'

'No. But I don't think you should go back to Whilton Hall.'

'No, sir, I was thinking that myself.' Jepps swallowed. 'Once His Lordship knows I failed he'll be mad as fire.'

'Aye, he will. I think it would be best for you to disappear.'

'Run away, you mean?' The man looked even more frightened.

'No, I don't, but I want Whilton to think that's what you have done. You will come with me tonight and in the morning I will send you off to Bellemonte with a note for Cripps, my manager. He will set you on in the gardens.'

Flora had been listening silently from the shadows, but now she gasped. 'Is that wise?'

'Whilton is unlikely to think I have employed the man who shot me.'

'No, but how are you going to explain his presence at the Red Lion?'

'I'm not going back to the Red Lion.'

She was just about to demand what he meant when Amos appeared behind Jepps.

'I've fetched the mare and secured her to the carriage, Miss Warenne. We're ready to set off now.'

'Tell me,' Matt asked the footman, before she could answer, 'is there somewhere on the Banbury Road I can put up for the night? Somewhere you and your master are not known?'

Amos scratched his head and declared that was a question for John Coachman.

'Then ask him, if you please,' said Matt. 'Take Jepps with you and find him a seat on the box. He is coming with me.'

'What is your plan?' said Flora, when the others had gone. 'Do you think the Viscount might come looking for you?'

'It's possible, if he thinks his plan has failed. More to the point I don't want you mixed up in this. If your carriage is seen in Whilton town at this time of night, there will be the devil to pay.'

Flora was about to say she did not care a jot, but at that moment Amos returned.

'There's a posting inn not too far from here, sir. The King's Head. John knows of it, but he's never had occasion to stop there. Jepps says he ain't known there either. He hasn't been further than Whilton since he arrived in Warwickshire.'

'Excellent,' said Matt. 'Tell John to drive there now, if you will.'

'But as steadily as he can!' added Flora.

'Don't fuss, woman,' Matt muttered as the carriage pulled away. 'I have had much worse than this.'

Flora strained her eyes against the darkness but it was impossible to see his face clearly. She heard him drag in a breath and slid to her knees on the floor beside him.

'Are you in pain?' she asked softly.

'My arm hurts like the devil, but that's to be expected.'

'And your leg, is that troubling you?' She looked at his knees, which were bent up to fit him on the bench seat.

'It's not so bad. I shall be better once I can stretch out in a bed.'

She looked out of the window as the coach slowed a little.

'We are turning off on to the road towards Banbury. It is the mail coach route, so the going should be a little smoother.'

'With you beside me, I feel nothing.'

She chuckled, encouraged by his teasing.

'You are clearly delirious, sir!'

'Not so confused as to think you were on your way

to Birchwood House when you came upon me,' he retorted. 'Where were you going?'

She flushed a little. 'To Whilton, to find you. I was so incensed at Quentin's behaviour that I wanted to apologise.'

'You have no need to apologise for the Viscount.'

'But I do. Quentin tricked us both this evening. He behaved despicably. And then, to order Jepps to shoot you—I can never forgive him for that.'

'Then why the devil are you marrying him?' he demanded.

'I must.'

'But you don't love him. You could not love such a man!'

'No.' There. She had admitted it, but could she tell him the rest of the sorry tale? She heard him sigh.

'If you must sit on the floor, rest against me. This side of my body is unhurt.'

Flora, too tired to argue, relaxed against him. He was such a kind man. Honourable, too. That was what made it so hard to tell him the truth about her family. He might not hate her, but it was inconceivable that he would be able to forgive her mother's traitorous actions.

'Tell me.' He reached out and put his good arm about her. 'Tell me why you must marry him.'

She hesitated a moment longer, then, sitting in the

darkness on the floor of the rocking carriage, she told him all she had learned that day.

'So, you see,' she ended, 'if I do not marry Quentin, he will make sure my mother's treachery is made public, and my father's, in carrying her out of the country. It would destroy the Farnleighs. They brought me to Whilton sixteen years ago and have made their home here. They would have to leave the town, their friends, the life they have made for themselves.'

'But they must bear some of the blame,' he said angrily. 'They concealed the truth from you. They kept you here, virtually a prisoner, in this little town.'

'The Farnleighs love me, they only wanted my happiness. They did what they thought was best.'

'Benevolent gaolers.' His arm tightened around her shoulders. 'You should have had so much more, Flora! A London Season, a chance to meet a man who was worthy of you.'

'No, no, that would never have happened. If I had known the truth, I should have had to divulge it to a suitor and who would want such a wife? Uncle Farnleigh admitted he had merely *hinted* at my past to at least two of my admirers and they withdrew at once, despite the fact that I am not a pauper.'

'Then they were fools not to see your true character!'

Flora sighed. If the matter could be kept a secret, if it was shared only with her immediate family, then perhaps there might be a chance of happiness. But she knew if she did not marry Quentin he would divulge her past to the wider world and there would always be whispers, slights. Society would not readily forgive her for the sins of her parents.

She said, 'If I refuse, Lord Whilton will destroy everyone I love. He has already tried to destroy you, merely to prevent you recovering your statue. By the bye, I know it is genuine. I saw the marks on Aphrodite when I was at Bellemonte and when I went back to Whilton Hall I compared them. They are an exact match.'

'Yes, I know. My lawyers shall fight that battle and win it.'

His voice was fading. She said, penitently, 'I beg your pardon, you should be resting.'

'No, I am glad you have told me.'

She leaned her head against him. 'I am so sorry this happened to you, Matt.'

'Hush now, I have been in worse fixes than this. But no more for now.'

No more, ever.

Flora closed her eyes against the tears that threatened. She had no future with Matt Talacre. If she jilted the Viscount, he would tell the world she was the daughter of a French spy. She knew Quentin's spiteful nature; he would also go out of his way to make sure Matt's patrons knew her history. It would ruin him and, even if he didn't hate her for it, Flora would hate herself for destroying everything he had worked so hard to build.

Chapter Eighteen

The carriage rumbled on. Flora remained on the floor, Matt's arm about her shoulders and the beat of his heart against her cheek. She must have dozed off, because she woke to find the landau had stopped. Outside was the noise and lights of a busy coaching inn and she quickly scrambled back on to the seat.

'The King's Head, I presume,' said Matt. 'Put up your hood and stay in the corner of the coach.'

The door opened and Jepps looked in. 'We are at the inn, miss. Best you stay in the carriage and we'll look after everything. We had a talk about it on the way here, me and Amos and your coachman. If Mr Talacre don't object, we'll say I'm his man and that we was attacked and our horses stolen. Your driver came past and took us up, but we'll not say where he's from and if you ain't seen, then no one will be the wiser.'

'Well done, man,' said Matt. He had struggled to sit up and was holding his injured arm against his body. 'That is pretty much what I was thinking.'

Jepps nodded. 'Now to get you out, sir. Can you walk, if Amos and I help you?'

'Aye. Step down and I'll get myself to the door.'

Flora watched Matt climb to his feet and steady himself with a hand against the wall.

'Thank you, for everything, Flora.'

'What will you do?' she asked, trying to put off the inevitable goodbye.

'As soon as I can ride, I will go back to Bellemonte. A few days at most. Go home now, Flora.' He bent and brushed his lips against her cheek. 'Don't worry, we shall come about.'

Silently she watched him struggle to the steps, where Amos and Jepps were waiting to help him down. Then all she could do was sit in the darkest corner of the carriage while they supported Matt across the busy yard.

It felt like hours before Amos returned. He opened the carriage door and examined the handle, as if looking for a fault.

'All sorted, ma'am,' he muttered, not looking in. 'The landlord holds footpads responsible for the attack and we told him we was going Banbury way, so no reason for him to think anyone from Whilton is involved. And if we get a move on, we can have you home again by midnight, which won't raise an eyebrow from the master and mistress now, will it?'

On these reassuring words, Amos slammed the door

and scrambled up on to his seat. They set off back out into the darkness and Flora settled herself more comfortably against the squabs, but sleep eluded her. Had the landlord believed the tale they had concocted? Would he send for a doctor to look after Matt? Then there was Jepps. He might take the chance to carry out the Viscount's orders to kill Matt. Somehow, she did not believe he would do that, but she could not be sure. She had never felt so helpless!

Flora resolutely shut out all the questions, but that left her with the memory of Matt's words and his parting kiss. A kiss that went all the way to her heart.

Thankfully, by the time Flora returned to Birchwood House, Mr and Mrs Farnleigh had retired and Betty was too drowsy to do more than help her mistress undress before returning to her own bed, so Flora was saved from any questions about her evening. At least for a while.

At breakfast, she responded to her aunt's enquiry by saying the Viscount had invited Mr Talacre to dinner, but that he had left early.

'Mr Talacre!' exclaimed her uncle. 'Now why should he do that?'

'I believe there was some business they needed to discuss.'

'Strange, I would have thought, since he had invited

you to come alone…' He trailed off, shrugging a little. 'But if the fellow did not tarry, then no harm done. I suppose you and Lord Whilton have now settled your, er, differences?'

'As to that, we shall see,' replied Flora with a smile that she was far from feeling.

Quentin would know by now that something had gone wrong with his plans and she had no idea what he would do next.

Matt stirred. His head ached, his mouth was dry and when he moved a searing pain shot through his left arm, making him wince. He opened his eyes to find a stranger bending over him.

No, not a stranger. Jepps. It was all coming back to him now.

'You are still here,' he muttered.

'Aye, sir. I gave you my word!'

The man sounded aggrieved, which would have made Matt smile, if he hadn't been so parched.

'I need water,' he said. 'And something to eat.'

'Water I have here.' Jepps helped him to sit up. 'If you can manage to hold the glass, sir, I'll go and tell the landlady to send up your breakfast.'

Matt frowned as he took in the man's homespun garments. 'Don't tell me you passed yourself off as my valet dressed like that!'

'Why, no, sir.' Jepps looked at him as if he was a

fool. 'You mentioned gardens, so I said I was your groundsman, come to look at some plants with you.'

He went off and Matt sipped at his water, thinking that the man had surprised him for the second time. He was intrigued by the fellow, but the entrance of a maid with his breakfast tray put to flight everything but the problem of how to eat it with only one good arm.

Despite his injury, Matt enjoyed his meal and left only empty plates to be removed with his coffee cup. When the servant came to take them away he asked her for pen and ink and spent the next hour propped up in his bed with a board across his knees, writing.

'Ah, Jepps, I need you to fold these for me,' he said, when the man came in some time later. He pointed to the first of the sheets. 'That one is for you to give to Cripps at Bellemonte—I have written the direction on the other side. I take it you can read?'

'Of course, sir. I ain't no heathen!'

Matt hid a smile as he handed him a small purse. 'This should be enough for your journey.'

Jepps took the purse, then picked up the letter and scanned it.

'This is mighty generous, Mr Talacre. How do you know you can trust me?'

'If you were intent on robbing me, you have had plenty of time to take the purse from my coat, and find the other one in my saddlebag. The fact the money is still there is encouraging.' Matt grinned. 'My leg aches like the devil, but I am not quite bedridden, I checked everything earlier this morning.'

Jepps began to stammer his thanks, but Matt waved a hand to silence him.

'How you fare at Bellemonte is up to you; if you show promise my man there will soon promote you. Now, this other note is for the landlord of the Red Lion in Whilton. I want you to find a reliable fellow to go and fetch my portmanteau.' He held out another handful of coins. 'That's enough to pay my shot and he can keep what's left. The letter doesn't say where I am and impress upon the messenger that he is not to mention it. Tell the man I will reward him for his trouble when he returns here with my belongings.'

'I'll get on to that right now, sir.'

'Very well. The landlord tells me the coach to Banbury isn't due for another two hours yet, so when you have done, there should be time for you to take a drink with me. I need diverting,' he explained, seeing the man's look of surprise. 'Until I have my portmanteau, I have nothing to read!'

It was not long before Jepps returned to Matt's room, carrying two tankards of ale and reporting that he'd sent one of the grooms to Whilton.

'He's a bright lad, sir, and the landlord said he's not one to blab.'

'That's good,' said Matt. 'Now pull up a chair and tell me about yourself.'

'Ain't nothing much to tell,' came the wary reply.

'Come, man, I don't believe that. An ex-solider, ain't you? And with a defective leg. We have that much in common.'

'I doubt it, Mr Talacre. You was an officer, I'll be bound!'

'I volunteered at the age of nineteen, but was fortunate to be promoted to the rank of captain before I took a bullet in the leg at Waterloo. Now, what about you?'

Matt gave Jepps the smile that he had always used to put soldiers at their ease and it wasn't long before they were exchanging tales of their experiences in the Peninsula.

'And was it the injury that forced you out of the army?' asked Matt.

'Aye, sir. A badly set fracture left me with one leg much shorter than the other. I couldn't walk that far, either, so I was no longer fit for duty. I made my way from Portsmouth to London, looking for work, but couldn't find anything. No one wants a cripple.'

Matt heard the bitterness in his voice and recognised it. He had felt much the same for many months after he had been wounded.

'How long have you worked for Lord Whilton?'

'It must be five years now. He came across me begging on the streets of London,' Jepps took another drink of his ale. 'Sent me to Whilton Hall.'

'That was very generous of him.'

Jepps shrugged. 'He said he wanted someone to look after his property, to patrol the grounds and keep them free of poachers and the like, but the wood is too small to attract more than children, catching the odd rabbit. And as for the gardens, they were in a sorry state. I'm no gardener, sir, but I do what I can, the others don't really care, although I think that will change when Miss Warenne becomes mistress.'

'She visits the gardens a lot, does she?' asked Matt, trying to sound casual.

'Oh, yes, she likes to walk there with that dog of hers. Very friendly she is, sir. A real lady, if you ask me.'

He frowned a little and Matt wondered if Jepps shared his opinion that Flora was too good for the likes of Lord Whilton. Not that he would ask.

He drained his own tankard.

'Well, let's hope you don't have to see the Viscount again, Jepps. You'll be working in my gardens in future.'

The man's smile was strained, but it was there. He said, 'And very glad of the work I shall be! Now, if you've finished your ale, I'll take these tankards back downstairs.' He gathered them up, saying, 'You know, sir, I was thinking that meeting Lord Whilton again was the worst thing that had ever happened to me. But now, well, perhaps it was meant to be.'

Matt frowned. 'What do you mean, meeting him *again*?'

'I recognised him, see, when I was a beggar in London. I saw this fine gentleman walk by and so I spoke to him. Thought he might remember me and spare me a few pence. Didn't know he was a viscount then, of course. When he offered to set me on at Whilton Hall I thought he was being charitable. But now I've thought more of it, I do believe he was buying my silence. Didn't want his new friends to know that he was such a bad officer.' He shook his head. 'Worst thing I ever did was to help *Captain* Gask.'

Matt sat up. 'Wait, you mean, he was a soldier?'

'That's right, sir. I met him in Portsmouth. I'd been there for some months, because of my leg, and that's when I met His Lordship. Only he wasn't a viscount then, of course. No idea how he ended up there, but he'd been attacked and lost everything save the clothes he stood in. It being winter, I gave him my cloak and we got chatting, friendly like.

'A month or so later I met a couple of troopers who'd been under his command and from what they told me I wished I hadn't.' He scowled. 'He ran out on his men during a skirmish on the way to Corunna. The officers preferred to believe he'd been killed in the fight, but a few troopers saw what happened and knew he'd deserted.'

'Interesting,' said Matt. 'I—'

He was interrupted by a knock at the door and the landlord came in to say that the doctor had arrived.

'Oh, very well, send him up.' Matt held out his good hand. 'Off you go, Jepps. Safe journey into Gloucestershire.'

He watched the man walk out with that awkward, halting gait, then lay back against the pillows and prepared himself for the doctor's examination.

Flora kept herself busy all morning, but she could not relax. She knew at some point the Viscount would call and she did not know when. It was something of a relief when he eventually appeared, late in the afternoon.

She was in the morning room, mending a flounce on one of her gowns when he was shown in. She put aside her sewing and rose to greet him, schooling her features into a look of polite welcome.

'My lord.' She held out her hand. 'I am sorry, my aunt and uncle have gone into Whilton, although I expect them back before very long.'

He came forward and kissed her fingers.

'No matter, it was you I wished to see, my dear.' He looked up at her, smiling, although there was a wary look in his blue eyes. 'You came directly home last night, I hope?'

She inclined her head.

'As I told you last night that I would.' He was still holding her hand and she made no move to pull free. 'However, I did order the coach to stop for a while on the road.' A tiny sigh escaped her. 'I was too angry to come back immediately, I needed to compose myself. I did not wish my aunt and uncle to know we had argued.'

'Ah, Flora, you do not know how I regret our little... contretemps. I could not sleep last night, thinking of it.'

'I, too, spent a restless night,' she replied, with perfect truth. 'I can only beg your pardon for my little outburst. Whatever your quarrel with Mr Talacre, it is no concern of mine.'

'No, no, you were right to chide me, my dear. I fear I allowed my jealousy to override my judgement.'

'Jealousy!' Her eyes widened. 'My dear sir, why on earth would you be jealous of Mr Talacre?'

'Because you appear to regard him very highly.'

With another smile she freed her hand and moved away to sit down in an armchair, indicating with a gesture that he should do the same.

'I admit he is very charming,' she said, arranging her skirts more becomingly. 'But, Quentin, he is hardly a gentleman. He makes his money from...pleasure gardens.' She let the words hang there, knowing he despised anything that hinted at trade.

He sat down, his face losing some of that wary look.

'I am glad you have not grown too fond of the man, Flora,' he said, becoming serious again. 'Because I have some bad news. Unless you have already heard?'

She shook her head, eyes wide and questioning. When had she learned to be so devious and deceitful? Heavens, her acting would rival the great Mrs Siddons!

He went on, 'Mr Talacre appears to have left town.'

'What!'

'Yes. Without paying his shot, too, which is inexcusable.'

'And you are sure he did not return to the hotel last night? Perhaps something has happened to him.'

'I fear I am to blame.' Flora's eyes flew to his face at that, but her racing pulse steadied when he continued. 'I refused to sell him that statue and now he is gone scurrying back to Gloucestershire, like a kicked dog.'

Voices could be heard in the hall. Flora looked around just as the door opened and Mrs Farnleigh hurried in.

'Lord Whilton, this is a pleasant surprise!'

'It is indeed,' exclaimed her husband, following her close behind. 'If we had known you intended to call, we should not have gone out.'

Flora listened as pleasantries were exchanged and refreshments ordered. She kept her eyes on the Viscount. She wanted to know what steps he had taken to find Matt. She was wondering how she could introduce the subject again when her uncle saved her the trouble.

'Goodness me, what a to-do in Whilton this morning, my lord, have you heard?'

'Mr Talacre has absconded without paying his bill?' said the Viscount, his countenance grave, 'Yes, I had heard.'

'No, no, worse,' cried Mrs Farnleigh, sitting down and fanning herself vigorously. 'The poor man was set upon!'

'Indeed, ma'am?' murmured Quentin, sitting very still. 'Pray tell me more.'

Aunt Farnleigh was only too happy to oblige.

'Well, we were visiting the Albrights this morning and on the way back we stopped off in the High Street. I needed a new pack of sewing needles, you see, and that is where I heard it. From Mrs Newsome, the haberdasher! Her son is an ostler at the Red Lion and he had it from one of the chambermaids. She said that someone had called on Mr Talacre's behalf to pay his bill and collect his bag.'

'Oh? And do we know where the gentleman is now?' asked the Viscount.

'No! That's the thing,' replied Mr Farnleigh. 'The messenger said Talacre was attacked by footpads last night and was too afraid to disclose his whereabouts.'

Mrs Farnleigh clasped her hands together. 'He must

have been on his way back to Whilton after dining with you, my lord. I have never heard of anything like this in the area before. Thank heavens they did not come upon Flora!'

'The road to Birchwood does not go anywhere near the town, Aunt,' she replied. 'I was never in any danger. I had John Coachman and Amos with me, too. Any rogue would think twice before stopping the carriage.'

'But this is all very worrying,' declared the Viscount, frowning. 'You see, one of my own men has absconded. I thought nothing of it at first, but now you have told me about Mr Talacre, I wonder.' He looked across at Flora. 'You know Jepps, my dear, the lame groundsman. My people have been searching for him, checking in all the barns and outhouses.'

'Oh, heavens, do you think he has been set upon, too?' cried Mrs Farnleigh, even more alarmed.

'Possibly, or he may even be the culprit,' murmured the Viscount. 'But do not upset yourself, madam. That shambling walk of his cannot be disguised. If he is still in the area, my people will find him.'

'In the meantime, I shall have an extra man on the carriage whenever we go out,' Uncle Farnleigh decided. 'And if you ladies step out of doors, then Amos must go with you.'

Lord Whilton nodded. 'A very good idea, sir. I believe this means you must give up your solitary walks to Whilton Hall, Flora. I would not for the world have anything happen to you, with only a month until our wedding.' He held his hand out to her. 'I must take my leave. My love, will you accompany me to my curricle?'

With her aunt and uncle looking on, she could not refuse. She rose and went out of the room on the Viscount's arm.

'This business with Talacre is very odd,' he remarked as they walked along the drive to the stables. 'Why should the fellow wish to hide away?'

'Perhaps he is fearful of another attempt on his life.'

'And you are sure you saw nothing on your way home last night?' he asked her.

'I am quite sure,' she replied. 'There was no one on the road when I returned to Birchwood House.'

'And Talacre has not been in touch, to tell you where he is?'

She managed a very creditable laugh. 'Good heavens, Quentin, why should he do that? As your fiancée, I am the last person he would contact.'

'But we both know the man finds you very...desirable.'

'And *I* know Mr Talacre is a gentleman, whatever you may think of him!' she said, sharply. 'He is far too honourable to encroach on another man's territory. You are allowing your suspicions to run away with you again, my lord.'

'Yes, I beg your pardon. I thought for a while it was not only the statue of Mars the man coveted.'

'Yes, you said as much at the Midsummer Ball,' she retorted. 'I have not yet forgiven you for that remark!'

He laughed gently. 'Pray, do not glower at me in that way, my love, you should be flattered by my concern.'

'I assure you, Quentin, you have no need to be concerned about Mr Talacre.'

'I am sure you are right,' he agreed. 'I have no doubt that if the fellow *was* attacked, it has given him an aversion to Whilton and he has now scuttled back to Gloucestershire.'

'And do you think he will continue the dispute over the statue?' she asked him, as casually as she could.

He waved a hand. 'He may try, of course, who knows? It is a small matter.' He paused for a moment, then said smoothly, 'Once we are married, I may be minded to sell him Mars, as a mark of my munificence. What say you?'

A chill shivered down Flora's spine. Was that a threat, or was he merely saving face, knowing Matt had a legal claim to the statue? Her reply was suitably cautious.

'You must do what you think best, Quentin.'

'I shall. As soon as I have you safe.'

His words and the smug tone he used convinced Flora it was a warning.

'I have to leave for London tomorrow,' he said, when

they had almost reached the stables. 'I regret I cannot stay here myself, but I shall send over one of my own men to protect you until I can install you at Whilton Hall as my wife. They are all out searching for Jepps today, but one will come to Birchwood House at first light.'

'Really, Quentin, there is no need for that!'

'There is every need, my sweet. Your safety is paramount with me and I will take no chances.'

She heard the implacable note in his voice and knew there was no point in arguing. She would be a virtual prisoner until the wedding. And after that…

She shuddered, not wanting to think of the future.

Flora's betrothal to Lord Whilton had given her a great deal more freedom over the past two years. Not because the Viscount was there to escort her—in truth, he had been absent for a most of the time—but her aunt and uncle, considering her to be a sensible young woman, had allowed her to do very much as she pleased. As long as she was accompanied by a servant, they rarely enquired closely into her movements.

That would change once Quentin's man was installed at Birchwood, her every move would be reported back to him. It shattered the faint hope she had of seeing Matt once more before he went back to Gloucestershire.

The Viscount's curricle was waiting in the stable yard and he stopped and took her hands. 'You will explain it all to your uncle and aunt for me, if you please. I am sure they will appreciate my concern. And when I return to Whilton,' he said, carrying her hand to his lips, 'I shall claim you, as my bride!'

Flora pinned on a smile as she watched him drive away, his tiger clinging on to the back. Her anger and unease were growing. She had no illusions about her forthcoming marriage. Quentin did not care for her, she was just another possession, to be guarded and kept safe at Whilton. And why should he think it necessary to provide her with an escort, unless it was to keep her away from Matt Talacre.

The memory of their parting reared up. There had been no words of love, but it had been warm, affectionate. So different from this chilly farewell. She was overwhelmed with a sudden, fierce longing, a need to see Matt just once more. She knew there could be no hope of lasting happiness with him, but the surge of desire was a physical ache, too strong to ignore.

Turning, she noticed the coachman standing in the doorway of the coach house and went over to him.

'I trust there have been no repercussions from last night, John?' she asked quietly.

'No, miss. No one suspects that we did more than drive you home from Whilton Hall.' He paused. 'His Lordship's tiger was asking a lot of questions, though. Asked if we'd heard something on the road, a gunshot or the like. But don't you worry, Miss Warenne.

Amos and me knows better than to be taken in by his sort and we wouldn't have said anything, even if you hadn't greased our palms so generously last night.' He smiled down at her and tapped his nose. 'We'll stick to our story and no one will be any the wiser.'

'Thank you, John, that is a comfort.' She hesitated. 'I wonder if you would now do something else for me.'

Chapter Nineteen

Matt leaned back against the pillows and closed his eyes. The day was well advanced but the sun was still high, turning his room into a furnace. He had thrown back the covers and was naked, apart from the bandage on his arm, but there was little air coming in through the open window to cool his skin.

The groom had returned from Whilton some time ago with Matt's portmanteau, but although he had pulled out the book he had been reading it was still on the table, unopened. Matt had other things to occupy his mind.

What he had discovered from Jepps about the Viscount was interesting and he wished he could have learned more details, but by the time the sawbones had finished with him, the afternoon stage had come and gone, taking the ex-soldier with it.

Since then, Matt had divided his time between lying on the bed and pottering around the room, testing his leg a little more each time, and finally concluding that the doctor was right; it was bruised, but he had done no lasting damage. His arm was also healing well. He had removed the sling and was very hopeful that by the morning he would be able to ride.

He was dozing when there was a soft knock and the door opened.

'I hope I am not disturbing you?'

'Flora!' His eyes flew open and he quickly flicked the sheet over his body.

'I came to see how you go on,' she said, coming in and closing the door quietly behind her.

'You should not be here.'

She was removing her hat and pointed to the lace draped over it. 'I wore a veil, no one here knows who I am. You are looking better today.'

'Thank you, I feel much better.'

'And you have seen a doctor?'

'Yes. He was fetched out last night and returned earlier today. I was fortunate, it was only a flesh wound. He rebandaged it again and thinks there is little risk of infection. As for the bruise on my head, that will heal by itself in a few days.'

'And your leg?'

'It will be painful for a while but nothing more serious.'

'I am glad,' said Flora, gazing at his naked torso and thinking that the real flesh was so much more impressive than a stone statue.

'You are staring.'

She blushed. 'I beg your pardon. I have never seen—that is…'

'My nightshirt is over the back of that chair. If you will bring it over, I will put it on.'

'No, no, you will be cooler without it.' She felt overdressed in her cotton riding habit.

Observing Matt's grin, she blushed even more. 'It is very hot. Shall I go and order refreshments for us?'

'There is a bell pull by the fireplace.'

She felt Matt's eyes on her as she moved across the room to ring for a servant. They were silent until he had given his orders to the man who hurried in, then he invited Flora to come and talk to him.

'I have been alone here since Jepps left this afternoon,' he said.

'You have sent him to Bellemonte?'

'Aye. He caught the stage to Banbury earlier today.'

She pulled a chair beside the bed and sat down. 'I hope he is safe, then. Lord Whilton is searching locally for him. And for you. He knows now that you are alive.'

'Does he know your part in my rescue?'

'No. Although he suspects you might try to contact me. He is sending over one of his footmen tomorrow, my personal escort until the wedding. That is why I had to come now, before my every action is watched—'

She broke off as a servant entered with a tray. Matt ordered him to leave it on the side table and when they were alone again he went on.

'So, no one knows where you are?'

'No.'

'Is your maid not waiting downstairs?'

She shook her head. 'I took to my bed after the Viscount left, pleading a headache and saying I did not want to be disturbed. Then I slipped out and rode over here.'

'But surely the grooms will know where you have gone!'

'I had a quiet word with John Coachman and he arranged for everyone to be busy elsewhere for a half-hour. I would not have any of them reprimanded for allowing me to go out alone.'

'Are you telling me you saddled your own horse?'

She opened her eyes wide at him. 'Of course, and I used the mounting block in the stable yard. I am not completely without accomplishments, Mr Talacre.'

'I am beginning to realise that! You should not be here.'

'I had to see you. Our parting last night was too sudden.'

'Yes. We need to talk.'

He held out his hand to her, but she ignored it and stared at her own hands, firmly clasped in her lap.

'That is not why I came,' she said quietly. 'My situation has not changed, but I wanted to see you, to say goodbye properly.'

She looked up to find his eyes fixed on her. What she read in them made her heart race and she quickly got up from her chair.

'Let me pour something for us to drink. Let me see...what will you have, sir?'

By the time she had poured beer for Matt and a glass of lemonade for herself she had regained her equilibrium.

'I hope Jepps will settle at Bellemonte,' she said, sitting down again. 'It was kind of you to protect him and find him work.'

'Would you have him charged, possibly hanged, for the Viscount's crime?' he asked, watching her face. 'No, I thought not. Actually, I believe he will do very well. He is no simpleton, but the Viscount bullied and browbeat him, deriding him as a cripple. I know how that feels.'

'Because of your own leg wound?'

'Yes. I was left for dead at Waterloo and Lord Dallamire—Major Mortlake as he was then—came looking for me. When the war was over, Conham took me on as his aide-de-camp and we became more friends than master and servant. He believed in me, you see,' he said, simply. 'Without him, if I had survived at all, I could have ended up a beggar, like Jepps.'

Looking at Matt's charming smile and his eyes shining with energy, Flora doubted that, very much. He was too spirited, too full of life to let circumstances grind him down. He would have survived, just as he would survive this. And she would, too. She would marry the Viscount and Matt would return to Bellemonte and one day meet the woman who would be fortunate enough to become his wife. To wake up and see his ruggedly handsome face on the pillow every morning. To have his naked body next to hers...

Stop it, Flora!

She shifted in her seat, batting away thoughts that made her want to blush. 'And how did you become a co-owner of Bellemonte?'

He grinned. 'Conham inherited the gardens, along with the hotel and the pleasure baths. It was all very run down and he was minded to sell it, to settle some of his debts, but Rosina—who is now his Countess— persuaded him to keep it on.

'I had sold my captaincy and I invested the money in the gardens, as well as every penny I have saved since then. Conham, Rosina and I now own Bellemonte between us and it is thriving, although there is still much to do.'

She could not help but smile at his enthusiasm. 'You appear to have achieved a great deal already.'

'Yes, and I cannot wait to get back to work there. Another day or two resting...' He looked up suddenly. 'Have you dined? No, you left Birchwood House far too early. Very well, ring the bell again, we will have dinner sent up to us!'

Flora intended to refuse, now she had assured herself Matt was going on well and she should take her leave. But somehow the temptation to stay with him a little longer was too great. Although there was one problem...

She cleared her throat. 'You will need to dress, if we are to dine at the table.'

'Ah.' His eyes twinkled mischievously. 'I was not prepared for company,' he said.

He sat up and put the sling over his head, then slipped his bandaged arm back into it. Then he looked across at Flora.

'Perhaps you would care to turn your back while I put something else on.'

Flora obliged, trying not to listen to Matt moving around, gathering together the various items of clothing. She heard a hiss of pain as he jarred his arm trying to dress himself and after a few more minutes listening to his muttered curses, she gave up.

'You are clearly having difficulty with only one arm. Let me help you!'

She turned and was relieved to see that he was at least wearing his drawers. She picked up a stocking and began to gather it up.

He sat on the edge of the bed as she rolled on one stocking, then the other, before fetching his breeches.

She tried not to blush as he stepped into them, and pulling them up required her to stand even closer. There were several jagged scars on his body, old wounds, she guessed. Better to concentrate on the battles he had fought and survived than think of his muscular thighs or…

'Just deal with the waist buttons,' Matt said hastily, lifting the front flap of the breeches and holding it in place.

Flora realised he was on edge, which settled her own nerves a little, and she managed to fasten the buttons before moving on to the next problem: hiding that broad chest with its shadow of crisp, dark hair that tapered down his body like a shield.

'I am sorry, but we are going to have to disturb your arm again,' she warned him.

'I could put on my banyan,' he suggested, nodding towards the colourful silk robe at the bottom of the bed.

'Oh. Yes. Of course.'

She quickly helped him slip his good arm into the silk sleeve and draped the other side over the sling.

'I'm afraid I must ask you to tie it for me,' he said, his voice husky.

Flora stepped closer and reached around him to pick up each end of the silk belt. Her cheek was almost touching his chest and she tried not to think of the muscled contours beneath the silk.

She started when his good arm came down around her waist, pulling her close in to his side. With a gasp she looked up into his eyes. They were warm as melted chocolate and oh, so inviting, and the half-hearted protest died away. She stretched up, her senses reeling as their lips met. She closed her eyes, putting one hand up to his cheek as she responded eagerly to the demands of his mouth on hers.

He deepened the kiss, drawing up an ache from somewhere deep inside. It was in equal parts frightening and exhilarating. Her very bones were melting beneath the explosion of desire unleashed inside her.

With an immense effort Matt broke off the kiss and raised his head, trying to damp down the fire raging within him. It burned even fiercer when he heard Flora's soft sigh.

'Oh,' she breathed. 'Oh, Matt!'

She buried her face in his shoulder and his arm tightened.

'Forgive me.' Matt closed his eyes, fighting to keep control. 'I should not have done that.'

'I *wanted* you to kiss me.' She looked up, her eyes bright with unshed tears. 'I know I shouldn't have come, but I had to see you, just once more. It will be the last time. When I am married…'

He said quickly, 'Let us not think of that.'

'No.' With a sigh she took up the ends of the belt and fastened them around the banyan.

'It's the first time a lady has ever helped me *into* my clothes,' he quipped.

He was trying to lighten the mood and she followed his lead.

'I am sure it won't be the last!'

He saw her blush when she realised how this might be misconstrued and she hurried to the door, saying she would go down and order dinner.

Matt sank back on to the side of the bed and rubbed a hand over his eyes. What the devil should he do now? He cursed silently. He knew exactly what he *should* do. He should send Flora home. Immediately.

'No,' he said aloud to the empty room. 'We shall dine first. Then we will kiss and go our separate ways.'

But heaven only knew if he'd have the strength to send her away.

Chapter Twenty

The stifling heat had abated by the time dinner was served. They sat each side of the little table by the window, where a gentle breeze occasionally drifted in. Flora had thought she would feel awkward, dining alone with Matt, but any tension between them quickly dissipated as the meal progressed. Matt insisted on pouring the wine while Flora served him from the selection of dishes and cut up his meat.

When they had finished, he sat back in the chair and closed his eyes, a faint crease in his brow.

She said quickly, 'Is anything wrong, are you in pain?'

'Between my blasted leg and this arm, I feel as if I had been in the ring with Gentleman Jackson.'

'Is that a reference to the art of boxing?' She wrinkled her nose. 'I suppose you mean to say you feel bruised and battered.'

'It could hardly be otherwise if I had been sparring with the great man himself.'

'You have spent too long on your feet,' declared Flora. 'You should have been resting in bed today.'

'Nonsense. I intend to head back to Bellemonte tomorrow.'

She saw the furrow deepen in his brow and put down her glass.

'Enough pretending, Matt. You must go back to bed. Immediately.'

The fact that he did not refuse outright told her he was in some pain. Although he did make a half-hearted protest.

'But we have not yet finished our wine.'

'You can drink it in bed and I will sit with you.'

'You will not leave?'

She smiled. 'No. I will not leave. Not yet.'

She went over to the bed and began plumping and turning the pillows and straightening the covers.

'I will help you undress, too. As long as you do not make any teasing remarks!'

Ten minutes later Matt was back in his bed, naked save for the bandage on his arm and feeling much more comfortable. He lay back against the pillows and closed his eyes for a moment.

'Thank you,' he said. 'That is better.'

'Truly?'

'All I need now is my wine,' he murmured.

Through half-closed eyes he watched Flora refill

the glasses and carry them across. She moved with such grace and looked beautiful, even when she was pretending to be cross with him, as she was now, narrowing her eyes and frowning at him.

'You cannot help being provocative, can you, Matt Talacre?'

He looked at her innocently. 'You insisted I should tell you if I needed anything.'

She handed him a glass and sat down beside the bed. 'What you *need*, sir, is a servant! You should pay the landlord to have one of his people wait upon you for the remainder of your stay.'

He laughed. 'It is my intention to leave in the morning. Magpie is very biddable; I shall be able to manage her with one hand.'

'But your leg, you have just said it is still paining you.'

'It is not so very bad. And my route has plenty of posting inns. I can travel in stages.' He added, seriously, 'I must go, Flora, before the Viscount discovers me.'

'Yes,' she said woodenly. 'You must go and I must marry him.'

Matt's heart went out to her. It was useless to suggest she should cry off and weather the storm. A scandal like that, where Farnleigh had been complicit in covering it up, would ruin the family. He could offer her his hand, but she would refuse. They both knew that a notorious wife would ruin him, too.

For the past two years he had built up Bellemonte to be a respectable venue not only for the highest Society but for the wealthy tradesmen of Bristol, whose morals were far stricter than those of the aristocracy. Its success depended upon him keeping his reputation as a fair and honest man. If Whilton made it known that Matt had stolen Flora away from him, it would put paid to his ambitious plans for Bellemonte.

And yet I would give all that up if I could be sure she loved me!

Aye, there's the rub, thought Matt. We have neither of us mentioned love. I am a tradesman and almost a cripple. If Flora was free of scandal as well as the Viscount, would she still look at me?

'But let us not talk of tomorrow,' said Flora, breaking into his thoughts. 'Tell me how you are going on with the improvements at Bellemonte.'

He grabbed at the chance to talk of something else. As the sun moved lower in the sky they talked of his progress with the new stables, his ideas for adding a new wing to the hotel and building a private swimming pool for ladies next to the existing baths.

They finished the wine and broached a second bottle. Dusk fell and still Flora remained in her chair. Matt knew he would have searched for more subjects to discuss, if there had been a lull in the conversation, but there was not. Neither of them was in any hurry to bring the evening to an end.

'Ow!' Matt shifted suddenly, his hand going to his weak leg.

'What is it?' asked Flora.

'Cramp in my calf. Nothing serious.'

'Let me help.'

Matt made a grab for the sheet covering his hips as she uncovered his feet and perched on the side of the bed, pulling his leg on to her lap. He tensed, almost holding his breath as he watched her gently rubbing the calf.

As the stiffness lessened, Matt closed his eyes and sank back against the pillows.

'There,' she said. 'How is that?'

'Exquisite torture,' he muttered, trying not to groan. The cramp might be easing, but the rest of his body was reacting to her touch. 'It's passed now, you can stop,' he muttered, trying not to sound desperate.

He was thankful the sheet was bunched up across his thighs, hiding any tell-tale signs of his true feelings. Flora gently placed his leg back on the mattress and slipped gently off the bed, but she did not move away.

'Is anything wrong. Flora?'

'Those scars,' she murmured, her eyes fixed on his naked chest. 'How did you get them?'

'Old battle wounds from my time in the Peninsula.'

He glanced down. 'That one, on my ribs, for example, was caused by a French Chasseur's sabre at Sahagún.'

'Did it hurt?'

She touched the thin line and set his heart pumping hard against his ribs.

'Not so much at the time. Hardly a scratch really. I didn't notice I had taken a hit, until after. There's another one, on my shoulder. That was a slash from another sabre. This time at Salamanca. I was fortunate there; another inch and the slash might have taken off my sword arm.'

'And this one?'

'Sniper.' It was as much as he could do not to flinch as her finger grazed his breast. 'At Almeida.'

'It is so close to the heart.' She was looking at him, those hazel eyes dark with concern. 'How did you survive?'

'It was deflected and had lost most of its power, so it didn't go very deep.' He dragged in a breath as she rested her hand over the scar. 'The surgeon dug it out easily enough.'

She shuddered, then slowly lowered her head and planted a kiss on the small round welt.

He clenched his fist, hard. 'Flora, don't!'

She looked at him, her eyes swimming with tears.

'Any one of these could have been fatal and I would never have known you.'

Flora lifted her skirts so she could sit on the bed beside him. She leaned down and gently kissed the scar on his shoulder. As her lips touched the rough skin he let out a shuddering sigh. Emboldened by his reaction, she slid her hand across his chest, feeling the dark hairs crisp between her fingers. Her body was tingling, she felt so alive, every sense heightened.

She stretched herself alongside him on the bed, aware that there was only the thin cotton of her riding habit between them. He groaned as she trailed kisses over the stubble of his jaw.

'Flora, please, don't do this.'

'Let me stay with you tonight,' she whispered, her lips grazing his cheek. 'Don't send me away yet.'

She raised herself up and gazed down at his dear face. He was frowning and suddenly she felt a jolt of uncertainty.

'Don't you want me?'

'Want you—?'

One moment those dark eyes were burning into her and the next he had hooked his hand behind her head and pulled her close, answering her with a kiss so fierce, so strong that her bones melted. She collapsed against him and his good arm came around her, pinning her there while he kissed her, long and deep. Desire blazed through Flora, burning her up and filling her with a force so powerful, it left her dazed and weak.

She broke away while she was still capable of thought.

'We should stop now,' she muttered. 'Your arm. The wound will start bleeding again.'

'I'd take that chance, but if you stay any longer, I won't be responsible for the consequences.' He closed his eyes, then, 'Are you sure you want to do this, Flora?'

'I want you too much to stop now,' she told him. 'I am not a child, Matt. I know what is at stake. I shall belong to the Viscount for the rest of my life, but now, tonight... I want to do this!'

The way his eyes blazed sent her heart leaping.

'Go and lock the door, sweetheart. Then we will have to get you out of those clothes.'

In the fading light Flora quickly removed her riding habit, petticoats and shirt. It took Matt some time to release her stays but at last she was free and dressed only in her shift. She carried all the discarded clothes over to a chair in the corner and hastily arranged them, conscious that she would need to wear them again later.

It was only when she turned that she found Matt had slipped out of bed and followed her. She suddenly felt very shy and stepped back until she felt the solid wall at her back. He cupped her cheek.

'Nervous?'

She shook her head and he kissed her gently.

'I'm afraid you'll have to help me remove your chemise, love,' he murmured.

Flora grasped the thin linen and swiftly lifted it up over her head. Before she could pull off the shift, Matt caught her hands in the material and held them against the wall. She was a prisoner, the shift still covering her face, and she gasped when she felt his lips close on one breast. Flora moaned, almost swooning as his tongue teased the nub, slowly circling, while his fingers worked a similar magic on the other breast and drawing an unbearably delicious ache from somewhere deep between her thighs.

She almost cried out in despair when he stopped, but as soon as she was free of the shift he captured her mouth in a kiss that was slow and deep, drawing up the fire he had kindled and she responded, her mouth open against his, their tongues tangling in a dance as old as time.

She slipped her arms around his neck and plunged her fingers into his silky curls. His hand caressed her neck while he covered her face in hot kisses. She threw back her head, eyes closed as his lips travelled on, leaving a heated trail on her neck to fix again on her breast, licking and sucking until the breath caught in her throat and she was arching against him.

Still he did not stop and she shifted as the relentless pleasuring continued. His hand caressed her waist and then her stomach, gently moving lower until she was trembling, almost swooning as his fingers slipped between her thighs.

He was stroking her, slow rhythmic movements that sent bolts of pleasure coursing through her, one after the other. She felt herself opening, pushing against his fingers. A moan broke from him and a sudden anxiety for his injured arm made her think they should stop, but even as the thought occurred it was blown away by the relentless movement of his fingers, which caused her body to convulse. She cried out and clung tightly to Matt as her body shuddered out of control.

At last the juddering convulsions eased and she became aware of the hard, aroused body pressed against her. She slipped her hand down between them.

'Careful, I am not yet done!'

'I know.'

Matt sucked in a breath when she gently touched his arousal. As her fingers explored, his good arm tightened around her until, shuddering, he released his seed against the soft swell of her belly.

With a groan he lowered his head, resting his cheek against her hair as they held one another. After a few moments Flora stirred.

'Why did you not…?' Her words trailed away.

He growled. 'Do you think I would risk giving you a child for Whilton to call his own?'

'No.' She cupped his face with her hands and smiled

up at him. 'Thank you,' she said, kissing him. 'And thank you for making me feel so...*alive*!"

Matt hugged her against him, marvelling at the passion he had aroused in her. It was far more than his clumsy caresses deserved.

'Did I hurt you?' he asked.

'No, you didn't hurt me.' She nuzzled into his neck and said shyly, 'Oh, Matt, I have never felt anything like that before.'

The awe and wonder in her voice made his heart swell. For a moment he felt almost tearful, but he concealed the unfamiliar emotions with a light quip.

'I should hope not.'

Flora saw his crooked smile, heard the amusement in his voice, but she was not deceived. His eyes glowed with a silent message that made her heart ache. There was so much she wanted to say, but could not.

Instead, she became practical.

'I need to wash before I dress.' She walked across to the stand and touched the jug. 'It's warm enough.'

She used the water to clean herself before putting on her shift. When she looked around, she saw Matt sitting on the edge of the bed, his arm back in its sling.

'Is it hurting? I hope we have not done more damage.'

'No, it aches a little, that is all.' He grinned. 'It was distracting, keeping it out of the way. Next time will be different.'

Her attempt at a smile failed. She said, 'I pray every day for a miracle that will allow us a next time.'

'Prayer and miracles!'' He scoffed. 'Two things I do not believe in.'

His bleak tone caught at her heart.

'You should rest now, Matt.'

'Will you come and join me?'

That teasing note was back in his voice, but she shook her head.

'You know I must get back.'

'Yes, you must.'

His sigh was even harder to resist, but Flora resolutely turned away and began to dress. When it came to her stays, she was obliged to ask for his help again. She walked over and stood with her back to him while he tightened the laces.

'What did you mean?' she asked him. 'About not believing in prayers and miracles?'

'They are lies, peddled by the church, which tells you to have faith and all will be well.' He sounded so bitter that she looked at him with concern.

'Is this about your experience in the army?'

'In part. But it goes back a long way before that. My mother was a pious woman and little good it did her!'

'Will you tell me?'

'It is not an edifying story.'

He had somehow managed to fasten the stays, but

instead of pulling on her skirts she sat down on the bed beside him and took his hand.

'But it is about you,' she said softly. 'And I should like to know as much as I can about you.'

Before it is too late, she added silently, knowing they would soon say goodbye for ever.

For a while she thought he would say no more. Then she heard him sigh.

'My parents were both God-fearing people and they dragged me to church every Sunday and holiday. But despite his faith, my father was a gambler. He ran up huge gaming debts, although my mother and I knew nothing of it until he blew his brains out.'

'Oh, Matt!'

'Our priest was reluctant to bury him, even though the magistrate decreed it was not suicide. The fact that my parents had rarely missed a Sunday service since they were married counted for nought.'

He fell silent and Flora waited, clasping his hand between both of hers, and at last he continued.

'We persevered and with the support of the squire my father was finally buried in the local churchyard. But his debts left us all but destitute. It was too much for my mother, she joined him in the ground a few months later.'

She rested her head on his shoulder and closed her eyes, imagining the horror of those dark times. 'I am so sorry.'

'Don't be. It was a long time ago. I took the King's shilling and have not done too badly for myself.'

'But it still hurts you and I am sorry for that.'

'Yes, it still hurts.'

Flora sat with him as long as she dared, trying to comfort him with her presence, but at length she knew she must leave. Giving his hand a final squeeze, she went off to finish dressing in what was left of the twilight. She was fastening her skirts when he spoke again.

'I haven't told anyone about my father, other than you and Conham.'

'I shall not divulge it to another soul, Matt, I promise you.'

'No, no, that's not why I mentioned it. I mean I feel better for talking about it.'

'I am glad.' She buttoned her jacket and walked back to him. 'I must go now. I hope I do not look too disreputable.'

'You look adorable.'

She averted her eyes, unwilling to let him see how much she wanted to stay.

'Betty will not be fooled,' she said, with forced cheerfulness. 'But she is well rewarded for her loyalty. With the extra I have been paying her since I met you, she will soon be a woman of means!'

He reached for her hand and pulled her closer.

'Have I been a bad influence on you?' he asked, kissing her.

Flora closed her eyes, savouring the taste of his lips, but broke off quickly, while she still could.

'Shameful!' she said brightly. 'Now you must go back to bed and let me finish dressing.'

Matt remained sitting on the edge of the bed. The sun had already set and the room was full of shadows. He could not see her clearly until she walked over to the mirror and fixed her curly brimmed hat atop her burnished curls.

'There, will I pass muster?' she asked, turning towards him.

'You look beautiful.'

Her smile was strained. He put out his hand and when she took it, he rose and pulled her closer. Sadness hung around her, palpable as a cloak.

'Come with me,' he said urgently. 'Come back to Bellemonte with me and we will find a way through this!'

She lifted his hand and pressed the back of it to her cheek. 'Oh, Matt, if only there *was* a way, but I have thought and thought about it. Too many people will suffer if I do not go back. Not only my aunt and uncle. Quentin will make sure my parents' treachery is known by everyone and not just in Whilton. Not only would I be a traitor's daughter, but a jilt, too. Quite beyond redemption. That is why I cannot come to Bellemonte with you. We both know your respectable investors and patrons would turn their backs on you.'

He wanted to deny it, but the truth of what she was saying held him silent for a heartbeat too long. She sighed.

'It was madness for me to come here. But I had to see you. I could not help myself.'

'You regret it, then?'

'No, not for myself. Never!' Even in the deepening gloom he could see her eyes shining, glistening with unshed tears. 'I shall remember this for ever.'

'But if Whilton finds out—'

'He won't. Those who know of my indiscretions are very loyal. They have been keeping my secrets since I was a girl.'

'And you are still going to marry him, even though he is such a monster.'

'Yes, I shall marry him.'

Matt clung to her hand, silently willing her to stay.

'Let me go, Matt.' She reached up to give him one final kiss, then gently freed her hand.

'There is four weeks yet until the wedding,' she said, pulling the veil down over her face, 'Who knows what might happen? We—*I*—will pray for a miracle.'

With that she turned away, picked up her gloves and riding crop from the side table and left the room.

Matt listened to her footsteps growing fainter. He strained his ears until there were only the usual sounds, the muffled laughter from the taproom below, the creak of the walls as the building cooled down. His room overlooked the fields to one side of the inn with no view of the road so there was no point going to the window to see her ride away.

She was gone and they would not meet again.

Chapter Twenty-One

Matt tried to sleep once Flora had left, but the events of the past few days disturbed his rest. As did Flora. Her joyous laugh, the way her eyes sparkled when she was happy, the feel of her in his arms, her body against his. The look on her face when she had left him for the last time would haunt him for ever.

After a night spent tossing and turning, Matt left the King's Head, eager to return to Bellemonte. The journey was slow and painful, his injured arm was practically useless and his weak leg suffered from hours in the saddle, but he made the journey in three days.

He had a brief meeting with his manager and then returned to his apartment at Bellemonte House, where he allowed his valet to fuss over him, putting a fresh bandage on his arm, helping him to change into clean clothes and finally serving him an elegant dinner.

However, when he wanted to help his master to bed, Matt had other ideas. He sent his man off on an errand to the pleasure gardens.

It was not long before there was a quiet knock on the door and Jepps looked in.

'You sent for me, Mr Talacre?'

'Yes, come in, man.' Jepps walked across the room with his irregular, halting gait. He glanced at Matt's own leg, resting on a low stool, but said nothing. Matt went on. 'No trouble getting here, I hope?'

'No, sir, I arrived yesterday. Gave your letter to Mr Cripps, as you ordered, and he set me on. I'm using my mother's name now, though. Miller.'

'Yes, Cripps told me. He says from what he's seen of you so far you are a good worker.'

The man brightened a little at that. 'I does me best, sir. Trying to put the past behind me, now.'

'Aye, well, before you do that completely, I'd like to know everything you can tell me about the Viscount. Not the recent history, but what you know of Captain Gask. His regiment, the names of the troopers who served under him, any dates, places they mentioned—I want a note of all of it.'

Jepps looked anxious. 'That'd take me a while, sir. I'm awful slow at writing.'

'No matter, I will do that for you. Bring that small table over here, if you will, and the campaign box. I will write everything down for you and you can sign it when you are finished. Will you do that?'

'Aye, I will, sir. After what you've done for me, I'll do that gladly!'

It was near midnight and the candles were guttering when Jepps had finally finished his tale. Matt thanked him and sent him away. He picked up the paper from the writing slope of his campaign box and waved it slowly, making sure the ink was dry before he folded it. He did some calculations and concluded there was not a moment to lose. He would spend the morning making his arrangements, but by tomorrow evening he must be on his way to Dallamire. He hoped Conham would be at home, because he needed help to carry out his plan.

He had told Flora he didn't believe in miracles, but he did believe in chance and good fortune. It was possible that all was not yet lost.

Flora's return to Birchwood House went unnoticed, except for the three loyal family retainers who had seen her off. Amos and John Coachman might guess she had been to the King's Head, but they would say nothing, and Betty asked no questions. With the prospect of being dresser to a viscountess ahead of her, the maid preferred not to know too much about her mistress's actions these past few weeks.

Life settled down into its usual uneventful pattern for Flora, very much as it had been before Matt Talacre had come into her world. But it was not quite the same: she was accompanied everywhere now by the large and taciturn footman sent over by Lord Whilton and she missed Matt so badly it was like a constant, physical ache.

There had been no word, but she heard no gossip about him either. There were rumours about Jepps, though. It was widely reported that he was Matt's attacker and had run away to avoid arrest. Flora could only hope they were both now at Bellemonte, safe and well.

It took Matt two days to reach Dallamire and he limped into the house, his leg stiff from sitting hours in the post chaise and with his arm still supported in a sling.

'What the devil!' Conham took one look at him and hurried forward. 'By heaven, man, what have you been doing to yourself? Let's get you inside!'

Matt batted away the Earl's attempts to help him. 'I can walk well enough, thank you,' he muttered as he accompanied his host into the house and through the marbled hall to the drawing room.

Lady Dallamire was waiting there and she gave a gasp of dismay at the sight of him.

'Matt, you are as white as a sheet! Come and sit down—'

'Oh, no, Rosina, not before you have greeted me properly!' He put his good arm around her and pulled her close.

Laughing, she kissed his cheek, but then insisted on guiding him to a sofa.

'You must sit, too,' he said, pulling her down beside him. 'It is only, what, four weeks since your lying in. By the bye, when will I meet my godson?'

'You may see Little Matthew tomorrow. He is sleeping now and I will not have him disturbed.'

'Of course not.' He cast an admiring glance at her. 'Motherhood suits you, Rosina. You look very well. Blooming, in fact.'

'Flatterer!' she scolded him, blushing at the same time and clearly mightily pleased with his compliment.

'Now then,' said Conham, watching this exchange with a mock frown. 'When you have finished flirting with my wife perhaps you will tell me what has happened to you.'

'A slight altercation with a rifleman,' said Matt.

'Not a very good one, if you are still alive,' observed the Earl, handing him a glass of wine.

'Conham, do not be so unfeeling!' Rosina protested.

'No, he's right. The man hadn't fired a gun in anger for ten years and was…er…out of practice.'

'You mean he intended to kill you?'

'He was ordered to do so, certainly.'

A momentary silence met his statement.

'And do you know who ordered him?'

'Yes. Viscount Whilton. The man who currently possesses my—our—Rysbrack statue.'

'I think you had best tell us the whole,' said the Earl, refilling his own wineglass and sitting down.

Matt obliged, although he did not tell them everything. It was necessary to mention Flora, of course, but he tried to concentrate on his dispute with the Viscount over the ownership of the statue.

When he had finished, Rosina laughed.

'And you have put your would-be assassin to work at Bellemonte? If that isn't just like you, Matt Talacre!'

'What else could I do with the fellow? He hadn't wanted to kill me. He is an ex-soldier and has been working as a groundsman at Whilton Hall. I thought he might do well in the gardens.'

'And what of the Viscount?'

'Ah.' Matt hesitated. 'Well, that's where I need your help, Conham.'

Once he had told them his plan, the Earl was only too eager to help him. It was Rosina who picked up on something Matt would rather have left unexplained.

'It seems to me you are going to extraordinary lengths over a statue, Matt,' she remarked.

'It's a matter of principle.'

'But why the urgency, why must you challenge the man with all this evidence before his wedding?' She waited, watching Matt as he struggled to find a satisfactory answer. Then she smiled knowingly. 'Could it be that you have an interest in the bride?'

'She deserves better.'

Matt felt his cheeks growing warm, for now Conham was watching him, too.

'I want to save the lady from making an error,' he went on. 'I cannot think any woman would want to marry such a man.'

'And do you think she would rather marry you?' asked Conham. He laughed. 'Oho, it's a Case! Look at him, Rosina. I never thought I would see Matt Talacre lose his head over a woman, but I am pretty sure it has happened.'

Matt fought with himself. He considered trying to laugh it off, but the Earl was an old friend. And Rosina was too shrewd to be taken in by a fudge.

'Aye, well, there is a little more to it than I have told you.'

'Then tell us now,' she invited him.

'It involves the lady's history. It is not really my secret to share,' he demurred.

Rosina leaned forward in her seat. 'Then keep your secrets, by all means, Matt, we will still do what we can to help. But heaven knows we have been through enough together for you to trust us.'

'Rosina's right.' Conham pulled his chair closer. 'If this lady means so much to you, old friend, then tell us everything. We won't judge her, or you.'

Chapter Twenty-Two

'Good morning, Flora. Your last as Miss Warenne! Tomorrow you will become Lady Whilton—are you not pleased the day has come?'

Flora smiled dutifully at her uncle's cheerful greeting as she took her seat at the breakfast table. It was four weeks since she had last seen Matt Talacre and pleased was not how she would have described her feelings this morning. Four weeks of pretending to her aunt and uncle that she was not averse to marrying Quentin Gask.

'I hope you haven't forgotten we are joining Lord Whilton at the hall for dinner tonight,' Aunt Farnleigh reminded her.

'Of course she hasn't forgotten,' said Mr Farnleigh a little testily. 'It was in His Lordship's letter to me yesterday, informing us that he and Mrs Gask had returned. Do you not recall? I read the whole to you both.'

'Oh, yes, of course. Silly me. The older I get the more forgetful I become.'

'Yes, yes, well, we are both growing older, my dear,' replied her fond spouse. 'That is why it is so very comforting to know that our niece's future is secure.'

Flora kept her eyes on her plate, fighting down her frustration. It was as if they had forgotten that she was being coerced into this marriage, that Quentin had put a servant into their house to spy upon her.

She glanced up, feeling a rush of affection when she saw her uncle reach across to squeeze his wife's hand. They were powerless to change the situation. Was it any wonder they preferred to think it was all for the best? They would have been distraught if they knew how she really felt about the forthcoming marriage.

Matt opened his eyes and stared up at the unfamiliar carving on the tester. He had been travelling so much recently that for a few moments he had no idea where he was. But memory soon returned.

Aylesbury. Some fifty miles from Whilton. That should be an easy day's journey in the Earl's travelling carriage, but Matt was anxious to be going. The greyish light outside his window told him it was close to dawn. Conham would not thank him for waking him this early. He must give his friend another hour at least.

He put his hands behind his head and closed his eyes, recalling the look on the Earl's face when he had arrived at Dallamire just over three weeks ago. He remembered that night so well, the shared confidences, the love and support he had received from both the Earl and his wife. It had helped him, knowing that whatever the outcome, he was not alone now.

He dozed for another hour or so then looked at his pocket watch. Seven o'clock. He would wash and dress and if Conham wasn't up, he would damn well wake him!

He had only fulfilled part of his plan when the Earl knocked and walked in, dressed and eager to be moving.

'Come along, Talacre, you sluggard. Time to finish this business!'

Whilton Hall was glowing in the sunlight when the party from Birchwood House arrived. They were shown into the drawing room where Mrs Gask was waiting to greet them. Flora thought she looked smaller and more anxious than ever. She was very conscious of her duties as hostess and bustled around them endlessly.

'The Viscount has been delayed… Will you not sit down? Oh, but perhaps, Mr Farnleigh, you would like to pour the ladies some refreshment? We do not stand upon ceremony here tonight and you will find the tray on the sideboard. Tomorrow, though, tomorrow is such a big day…'

She twittered on like an agitated sparrow until the Viscount came in, apologising for not being there to greet them.

'The new carving for the overmantel has arrived,' he explained, indicating the servants following him into the room.

They were carrying a large object covered with a cloth, which they proceeded to place on a stand set up in the window embrasure beside the fireplace. The Viscount was more animated than Flora had ever known him, pacing back and forth until the servants had finished, then he waved them away.

'The arms of Warenne, impaled with those of Gask,' he said, as the door closed behind the last of the footmen. 'Come, come and see it for yourselves.'

Obediently, everyone rose and moved closer to the stand. The Viscount whipped away the cover with a flourish, revealing a large oak shield, intricately carved and painted.

'There!' he cried, 'Is that not magnificent? It will be installed in the chimney piece tomorrow, replacing the arms carved for my father.'

He was beaming at them, waiting for a response. Flora heard her uncle clear his throat.

'It's very impressive,' he said. 'I do not ever recall seeing the Warenne coat of arms before.' He glanced anxiously at his wife, who shook her head.

'Neither Father nor my brother Charles had much interest in ancestry,' she said, uncertainly.

But the Viscount ignored her and was already addressing Flora.

'Look, do you see? Two lions passant. The arms of William the Conqueror!'

His reverential tone made Flora want to mock him, but she fought down the impulse and said merely, 'I did not think he was one of my ancestors.'

'No, no, most likely not,' he went on, looking intently at his new acquisition. 'The lions are also the symbol of Normandy; a fitting match for the lion rampant of the Gasks, my dear.'

An awkward silence fell, ending only when the butler came in and Mrs Gask raised her querulous voice to say, 'Shall we all go in to dinner?'

Flora was grateful for her aunt and uncle's efforts to make conversation in the dining room. For her own part, she was glad to be sitting close enough to Mrs Gask to talk to her. She felt sorry for the poor lady, brought to Whilton whenever Quentin needed a hostess. She knew the widow had rooms in the Viscount's house in Ipswich and, from the little conversation they had, she was able to glean that Mrs Gask enjoyed the town far more than the country.

'I hope you will come to stay with us when we are in London,' said Flora. 'We could visit the theatre together.'

'London!' The lady looked startled. 'Oh, no—you will be making your curtsy at Court.'

'Yes, but when the Viscount and I visit the capital after that, I should very much like to have your company.'

'But you will not be going to—that is, I mean, I will gladly join you here at Whilton, if you wish. My cousin intends that you should make your home here.'

'Of course, but I shall not be here all the time! I must acquaint myself with the Viscount's other properties and naturally, we will go to London to enjoy the entertainments there.' She laughed. 'I am looking forward to visiting the museums and theatres as much as shopping and going to balls.'

Mrs Gask continued to look horrified and Flora's nerves prickled uneasily. She glanced towards the head of the table, where Quentin was engaged in conversation with her uncle, then turned back to Mrs Gask.

'Does Quentin plan to keep me prisoner here?' she asked her, bluntly.

'A prisoner? Dear me, no.' The widow's laugh was unconvincing and she was almost squirming in her chair. 'How ridiculous, Miss Warenne!'

The widow jumped as the Viscount suddenly rapped on the table. 'What are you saying to Miss Warenne, Cousin? Pray tell us all.'

'We were talking of London, my lord,' said Flora. 'I have invited Mrs Gask to join us there for a few weeks, to relieve you from the tedium of accompanying me to all the museums and galleries I intend to see.'

She watched him carefully and observed the faint signs of annoyance flicker across his countenance.

'My dear Flora, there will be plenty of time to make plans once we are wed. Now, I believe my cousin is about to carry you ladies away to the drawing room.'

'Oh, yes, yes, of course.' Mrs Gask rose hurriedly. 'Mrs Farnleigh, Miss Warenne…?'

The ladies followed their hostess to the door, but as Flora passed the Viscount's chair, he put out his hand and caught her wrist.

'We will talk about future plans later,' he said softly. 'Between ourselves. It is not something to be discussed with my cousin.'

He was smiling, but his eyes were ice-cold. Flora felt again the familiar chill trickle down her spine. She breathed slowly, schooling herself to speak calmly.

'As you wish, Quentin.'

Satisfied she had understood him, he released her. By the time Flora reached the door the other ladies were already disappearing into the drawing room and as she walked across the hall to join them, she saw a fair-haired figure hovering in the shadow of the staircase.

'Mrs Goole.' She stopped and waited.

The housekeeper hesitated, then came closer, hands folded before her.

'Yes, ma'am? Is there anything you want?'

The light from the windows was sufficient to see that the woman was nervous, but she glared defiantly at Flora, who sighed.

'Mrs Goole, I don't think this is what either of us *want*, but—'

The woman's hands clenched into fists and she took a step forward until she was only inches from Flora, her face red and blotched from crying.

'You know nothing!' she hissed. 'He promised me I'd be mistress here. Swore he would marry me. Now I'm to be sent off to one of his other houses in the north!'

'I am very sorry for you—'

'I don't want your pity!' she spat. 'I just want you gone!'

To Flora's surprise, the housekeeper threw up her apron, covering her face. Flora watched her using it to wipe her eyes and she sighed, sympathy overriding every other feeling. She reached out and touched the woman's arm.

'Believe me,' she said quietly, 'I would not be here if I had any other choice.'

And with that she walked on to the drawing room with never a backward glance.

The first thing Flora saw when she entered the drawing room was the shield on its stand. It reminded her of the forthcoming ceremony tomorrow, which would bind her to a man she did not love. Neither did Quentin love her, she knew that: those gaudy images on the shield were the reason he was marrying her. Flora shuddered. He wanted her for her ancestry, her bloodline. If she could not give him an heir, he would have no further use for her. Would he then try to dispose of her? She thought it very likely.

Flora chose to sit with her back to the shield, telling herself she was being far too despondent. They were not living in the dark ages; many women were trapped in loveless marriages and they survived. Many lived reasonably happy lives. She knew she would be envied by many. Her husband was rich, titled and she would have so many advantages. That was what she must think of now, the good she could do in her new, elevated position.

The thought lifted her spirits and she was able to join in the conversation with her aunt and Mrs Gask until the tea tray was brought in, almost immediately followed by the gentlemen. Flora raised her eyes to watch her fiancé, trying to bring back even a little of the liking or affection she had once felt for the man. He was looking cool and immaculate in his dark evening dress, but she felt nothing but loathing for him now. He had treated her abominably and she could not forget it.

Her right hand covered the diamond ring on her marriage finger. She longed to snatch it off and throw it into Quentin's cold, handsome face, but at that moment her eyes went to her uncle, following his host into the room. He was perspiring a little in the heat and his shirt points had begun to wilt. He was looking tired, too, and she realised how much this recent worry over her marriage had aged him.

The little spurt of rebellion in her soul faded. The chains binding her into this marriage were as strong as ever, however bleak and dark the future.

It was late when Lord Dallamire's travelling carriage eventually reached the gates of Whilton Hall. A series of small mishaps had delayed their journey, and the Earl pulled out his pocket watch and held it close to the window, where the full moon provided enough light for him to see the face.

'Nearly ten o'clock. My apologies, Matt, we are much later than anticipated.'

'Couldn't be helped, Conham. You weren't to know there'd be an overturned carriage blocking the road, or about that collapsed bridge taking us miles out of our way.'

The coach pulled up in front of the house and they jumped out. Light shone from the windows of the house, but the big wooden doors in the gatehouse arch were firmly closed.

'Positively medieval,' drawled Conham as they walked across the bridge.

'Aye.' Matt gave a short laugh. 'Whilton was born several hundred years too late!'

They reached the doors and he rapped on the wood, his fist making no more than a dull thud on the thick planks.

'I think this might work better.' Conham reached out and pulled on the rope hanging against the shadowed wall. A bell pealed, somewhere on the other side of the door.

'Damme, I should have seen that,' Matt exclaimed.

Conham grinned. 'That's why I was a major and you a lowly captain, my friend.'

A thin strip of light appeared in the narrow gap between the doors and a voice demanded to know who was there.

'Lord Dallamire and Mr Talacre, to see the Viscount. Open the door,' Matt replied.

'Beg your pardon, my lord, but Lord Whilton has given instructions that no one is to come in tonight.'

'I know it's late, man, but I am the Earl of Dallamire,' said Conham at his most commanding. 'His Lordship will see us.'

'No, he won't, not tonight. Come back in the morning.'

Matt took out his purse and shook it, making the coins jingle. 'I will make it worth your while.'

There was a pause, and for a moment his hopes rose, then,

'Beggin' your pardon, sirs, but 'tis more than my life's worth to go against His Lordship's orders. You must come back tomorrow.'

The light disappeared. Conham stepped back and looked up, surveying the front of the building.

'Well, what now?' he said. 'Is there another door or must we lay siege to this place?'

'I don't know of another way to get in, short of finding a boat,' said Matt. 'Confound it, we shall have to come back in the morning.'

They had almost recrossed the bridge when Matt heard a noise behind him. He stopped and turned.

'By heaven, the wicket is open. Come on, Conham!'

They hurried back to find a buxom, fair-haired woman standing in the opening.

'Mrs… Goole, isn't it?' said Matt, recognising the housekeeper.

'You wanted to see Lord Whilton.'

'Yes. We thought he had retired.'

'No. Not yet.' She stood back. 'Come in, I will take you to him.'

Refreshments had been brought in and Mrs Gask was busy serving tea to her guests. Flora collected a cup and went to stand beside her aunt.

'We should not stay too much longer,' she murmured.

'No, no, of course not,' agreed Aunt Farnleigh. 'You need to be rested for tomorrow, my dear.'

'What is this?' asked the Viscount, coming up 'You are not thinking of leaving us yet, I hope?'

'I think we must,' Flora answered him coolly. 'We all have a busy day ahead of us.'

'I will not hear of it,' he said, guiding her to a settee and sitting down with her. 'We have hardly spoken three words together. I shall think you are avoiding me!'

Flora tried to make light of the idea. 'Good heavens, what a nonsensical thought!'

'Is it?' Quentin laughed, but he went on softly, 'You will not be able to avoid me tomorrow night, my love.'

He stroked the back of one finger down her cheek and an icy shiver ran through Flora. She closed her eyes, willing herself not to flinch.

'The Lord Dallamire and Mr Talacre, my lord!'

Chapter Twenty-Three

At the servant's unexpected announcement Flora's eyes flew open, but still she could not believe what she was seeing. Matt was here, in the room, with a tall stranger at his shoulder. As if fearing his master's wrath, the footman had quickly retired and shut the door. She felt a surge of elation. Matt met her eyes and they shared a look and a quick smile before his gaze moved on, sweeping over the rest of the company.

The Viscount was on his feet, glaring at the two new visitors.

'What the devil is the meaning of this?' he demanded.

Matt bowed with exaggerated politeness. 'I beg your pardon—are we de trop?'

Flora tried to rise, but Quentin put a hand on her shoulder, keeping her in her seat.

'You are interrupting a private dinner,' he said coldly. 'I ask you to leave, before I have you thrown out.'

'Oh, I don't think that would be wise, Lord Whilton,' said the stranger. 'Not before you have heard what we have to say. But where are my manners?' He pulled the hat off his auburn hair and bowed. 'The Earl of Dallamire, at your service!'

So, this was Matt's friend and patron of Bellemonte, thought Flora, momentarily distracted from the immediate drama. Quentin's next outburst brought her back to the present.

'I don't care who you are,' he raged. 'I gave orders that I was not to be interrupted tonight. You have no right to enter my house by force!'

'Oh, we didn't, we were invited,' replied Matt, stripping off his gloves. 'By your housekeeper.'

Flora was surprised to hear that and she glanced up at Quentin. He was looking stunned, but recovered quickly and said, coldly, 'Very well, you had best tell me why you are here.'

'A little matter has come to our attention that we wish to discuss with you,' the Earl replied. 'Concerning your military career.'

'My what?'

'The Light Dragoons, I believe,' said Matt. 'You were a captain.'

Flora blinked. She was at a loss to know where all this was leading, but she did notice how the Viscount's manner changed. The bristling animosity had disappeared and he was at his most urbane when he responded.

'Indeed? Very well, we can discuss this after my guests have left. I was about to send for their carriage.'

'No, I think they should hear it.' Matt stepped quickly between Quentin and the bell pull.

Tension crackled in the room as the two men faced each other. The Farnleighs had been silent thus far, Flora's uncle standing behind his wife's chair. Now he took a step forward, looking uncomfortable.

'Yes, yes, we should be going, we would be very much in the way—'

'No, sir, you should stay,' Matt told him. 'You will be interested in what we have to say. After all, tomorrow you will be related by marriage to Lord Whilton, will you not?'

'They should go,' snapped the Viscount. 'Their presence is not necessary.'

Flora rose to her feet. Quentin was rattled and she was determined to know why.

'Oh, but I should like to hear it,' she declared.

The Viscount turned to frown at her. 'Sit down, madam. This does not concern you.'

She ignored him and walked over to the side table, where the wines and decanters from earlier in the evening were still laid out. Strangely, she was no longer afraid of offending her fiancé.

She said, 'Uncle, do sit down and I will bring you another glass of wine. And more ratafia, for you, Aunt?'

'It is very foolish of you to disobey me, my dear,' drawled the Viscount.

His icy tone had no effect on Flora. She merely smiled at him before addressing the Earl.

'May I pour you a glass of wine, my lord? I believe the claret is very good.'

Lord Dallamire's nod and smile was all the encouragement she needed to continue.

'Flora!'

Quentin's voice cracked like a whip and she turned to face him.

'My dear Quentin, your cousin Almeria is quite overcome.' She paused to glance at Mrs Gask. The widow was cowering in her chair with a handkerchief pressed to her lips. 'As your fiancée, it behoves me to step in and play hostess.'

She smiled, completely unmoved by his scowl, or the way his hands were clenching and unclenching at his sides. He no longer had any power over her. She did not know quite what the outcome of this night would be, but it would not result in their marriage and for now, that was quite enough.

Mrs Gask rose to her feet.

'I am feeling quite unwell,' she said, dragging her handkerchief between her nervous fingers. 'If you will excuse me, I think I shall retire.'

'A very good idea,' said Flora, accompanying her to the door. 'Go and rest, I will look after our guests.'

Ignoring the muttered curses from her fiancé, Flora shut the door upon the hapless widow and went back to the side table to continue pouring out the wine. The Earl thanked Flora as she handed him his glass, but Matt took his with barely a word. He did not even look at her and for a moment she was overcome with doubt.

When he and Lord Dallamire had first entered the room Flora thought they had come to rescue her, but after that first look, Matt had given no sign, as though she was no more than a brief acquaintance. Could she have imagined it? Perhaps she was mistaken and she was only a secondary consideration in his plans.

She refused to dwell on the idea and concentrated on playing hostess. She poured two glasses of wine, one each for herself and the Viscount, and carried his across to him, careful to keep at arm's length in case his barely contained anger should spill over.

'Now, I think you may begin, Mr Talacre,' she said, sitting down on an empty chair.

Matt inclined his head, unsmiling. He was filled with admiration for Flora. She was so calm, so assured, but he dared not show it. He could not risk Whilton suspecting there was anything between them.

'Very well.' Lord Whilton walked over to his usual highbacked chair and sat down. 'It seems—for now—I must acquiesce to my fiancée's wishes. Say what you have to say, Mr Talacre, and let us be done with this charade.'

He sat back and crossed one elegantly clad leg over the other, a sneer marring his handsome features. Matt went over to join Conham in front of the elaborate chimneypiece, where they had sight of everyone in the room. He did not trust himself to look at Flora again. He knew she had read the message in his eyes when he walked in and she trusted him now to rescue her. He only hoped he would not let her down.

He said, 'It is not a charade we have for you but a story, my lord, a true tale.'

'An unedifying one, I am sorry to say,' added Conham. 'We start in the autumn of '08, when General Sir John Moore took command of the British forces in Portugal, with thirty thousand men and the intention of marching into Spain and supporting their army in the fight against Napoleon. I will not bore you with detail, but after an initial victory at Sahagún, the British found themselves deep into Spanish territory with little hope of support from the Spanish. Napoleon already controlled Madrid and his army vastly outnumbered the British.

'Moore had only one option, to escape or risk the British army being totally annihilated. Thus began one of the most hazardous episodes of the Peninsular War, the retreat to Corunna. It was a time when the army needed all its officers to maintain order and help the men through the ordeal. With increasingly bad weather and the French close behind, discipline in some of the British ranks began to break down. Spanish villages were looted and many of the soldiers became so drunk on stolen wine that they were left behind, to be killed by the weather or the French.'

'And those who made it to Corunna found no ships waiting to carry them safely back to England,' added Matt. 'They had to wait and fight to secure the bay long enough for the ships to come in and evacuate them.'

He paused, recalling those the dark days, the exhausted troops, those too sick to embark being left behind. Even now the thought of it turned his stomach.

'But this all happened nearly ten years ago,' spluttered Farnleigh. 'What possible bearing can it have on us?'

'The fact that your host was a captain with the cavalry at the time,' replied Conham. 'It was assumed he had been killed or captured by the French after one of the many skirmishes, but the truth was that he deserted his post. Left his men to their fate and saved himself.'

'Now there, my lord, you are mistaken,' drawled the Viscount. 'I lost my memory, after being attacked and left for dead. I explained it all at Horse Guards when I returned.'

'Yes, you did.' Lord Dallamire nodded.

Flora's heart sank when she saw the look of triumph on Quentin's face. He sat up straighter in his chair.

'If that is all, gentleman, then you can take your leave,' he said imperiously. 'My guests have endured enough of your nonsense. Your scurrilous attempts to discredit me. Perhaps my *fiancée* would be good enough to ring the bell.'

There was no mistaking the menace in his tone now. Flora's rebellious spirit wavered and she glanced at Matt, but he was not looking at her. Unlike her aunt and uncle. Their whole attention was upon her, knowing their future happiness depended upon what she did next. Her blood ran cold. Had she gone too far, or would Quentin still honour their bargain if she obeyed him now?

'I am waiting, my dear,' purred the Viscount. 'Or shall we have more revelations?'

'Oh, we shall have more, Whilton,' barked Lord Dallamire. 'We haven't finished your story yet.'

Quentin swore. 'I was exonerated of all blame! It is all in the records.' He jumped up and stalked across to the door. 'Now get out of my house!'

'But the records aren't true, are they, Whilton?' Matt's voice cracked like a rifle shot across the room, stopping the Viscount even as he reached for the door handle. 'They only have your word for it. Others tell a different tale.'

'Hah! Who dares say that? And why have they never come forward?'

It was the Earl who answered.

'Men who survived one particular battle say it. At the time they were only too glad to be rid of you, although some of them did try to take their revenge, did they not? They saw you in Portsmouth and set upon you.'

'Jepps!' Flora shuddered at the venom in the Viscount's voice as he spat out the name. 'He told you this, this taradiddle!'

'Do you mean that groundsman of yours?' exclaimed Mr Farnleigh. 'He attacked you?'

'On the contrary,' said Matt. 'It was Jepps who found *Captain Gask*, as he was then, after his troopers had given him a beating.'

'Ha! He told you that, did he?' scoffed the Viscount. 'Where is the villain?'

'Safe from you, now,' Matt told him. 'He told me that you ordered him to kill me and I have his deposition to that effect, signed and witnessed.'

'And do you think anyone will believe his word against mine?'

'I believed him,' said Matt. 'Are you willing to risk facing him in a court martial? And the others, of course. Think of the scandal, Lord Whilton. The disgrace.'

Flora held her breath. Quentin was very pale and

she knew how much he valued his reputation, his good name. She thought bitterly that her reputation mattered little to him. He needed her only to provide him with his heirs.

'What is it you want?' he said at last. 'Is it that confounded statue?'

'Of course,' said Matt.

Flora's nerves were so on edge that she could not sit still. She jumped up and walked across to one of the windows overlooking the courtyard. It seemed to her now that Matt had come here with Lord Dallamire merely to retrieve the statue. Had she misunderstood everything? If so, her position now was precarious.

She gazed at the window, but it was too dark outside to see anything but distorted reflections of the room. Her aunt and uncle were sitting silently in one corner while Matt and the Viscount faced one another in the centre of the room. Flora crossed her arms, feeling slightly sick. Quentin only valued her for her lineage. She thought it perfectly possible that Matt had seen her only as a useful tool to help him recover his property. The certainty she had felt earlier faded. Her spirits now swung wildly between hope and despair at ever being free of her past.

The reflections shifted. She saw Lord Dallamire step up beside his friend.

'Our case on the ownership of the Rysbrack is solid,' he informed the Viscount. 'It would be in your interests to let Talacre buy it back from you. If the offer still stands?'

He looked a question at Matt, who nodded. 'Yes, it still stands. But first, Lord Whilton, you will release Miss Warenne from her betrothal to you.'

Flora swung around, her heart hammering against her ribs. It was what she wanted, what she had hoped to hear, but surely the Viscount would refuse. And yet, Matt looked so calm, so confident. How could he think Quentin would release her, merely for the asking?

'Miss Warenne is perfectly free to cry off if she wishes.' Quentin turned towards her, a horrid little smile playing around his mouth. 'Well, Flora, are a few unfounded rumours about me sufficient for you to make you break off our engagement?'

Silence fell over the drawing room. Matt saw that the Farnleighs were watching, horrified, and Flora was deathly pale. Whilton's confidence that she would not defy him was as yet undented and Matt knew he needed to bring this to a head.

He said, 'I think we have a little misunderstanding here, my lord. It is *you* who will cry off, although I am sure everyone would understand Flora's doing so, once the truth about you is known. You see, these are not unfounded rumours. We have signed depositions from Troopers Coupe, Yardley and Purvis. They make interesting reading. Not only did you abandon your men, you also deserted your mistress. Did you know she was among those who perished as they crossed the mountains?'

'A camp follower.' Whilton dismissed this with a wave of his hand. 'She was of no importance.'

The disgust Matt felt was reflected in Conham's frowning face.

'We have other names, too,' said the Earl. 'We have not yet found these men, but I have no doubt their testimony will be no less damning for you. However, if you release Miss Warenne from her engagement, and return her mother's letters, we *might* be persuaded to allow the matter to drop.'

'Air dreaming, my lord!' exclaimed Whilton. 'Do you think anyone is interested in what happened ten years ago?'

The Viscount was still blustering, but he sounded a little less confident now.

'Oh, they will be,' said Matt. 'You see, Lord Dallamire and I remained with the army until Waterloo. We still have a number of acquaintances at Horse Guards. They will most certainly be interested in what we have to tell them.'

'Well, sir, what is it to be?' Conham demanded. 'Will you risk a court martial and see the noble name of Gask brought into disrepute, or will you agree to our terms?' He waited for a moment, then said impatiently, 'Hurry, man, make your choice. It grows late and I have had enough of this now.'

Matt watched as Whilton stood in silence, considering his options. At last he nodded.

'Very well, I agree.'

Almost trembling with relief, Flora pulled the diamond ring from her finger.

'And my mother's letters?' she asked, handing the ring to the Viscount.

He studied the ring for a moment, then looked down his nose at her. 'They are not here. I sent them to my bank for safe keeping.'

'Now that I know is untrue!' exclaimed Matt, as she recoiled in dismay.

He went across and tugged the bell pull. Flora stared in surprise when the housekeeper came in.

'Ah, Mrs Goole,' said Matt. 'Perhaps you would fetch the letters we talked of earlier.'

'No need, sir, I have them right here.' She disappeared back into the hall, returning, moments later, carrying a leather document wallet. 'I fetched it just after I heard he'd left his mistress and his men behind to die—begging your pardon for listening at the door.' She handed the wallet to Matt. 'There you are, it was in his desk, just as I thought. He keeps the study locked, but I have a key, of course.'

She patted the chatelaine hanging around her waist.

'Why, you—!' Whilton started forward, but the Earl

was quicker, blocking his way. 'What the devil do you think you are doing, woman?'

The housekeeper glowered at him.

'I am giving you your own again!' she raged. 'You are so puffed up in your own conceit you thought you could install your wife here and still have me to warm your bed whenever it suited you! Did you really think I would stay, once you brought another woman into my house? Acting as if that title of yours had made you some sort of god, ordering things as you please! Well, you had the wrong sow by the ear this time, *my lord*. I am no mutton-headed doxy, waiting around for your pleasure. I'll be off from here in the morning and we'll see how you like that!'

'You can't!' he screamed at her. 'I won't let you.'

'Oh, yes, you will and you'll leave me in peace, too, or there's tales I can spread about you, sir, that will shock your fine neighbours!'

Matt grinned, impressed at this interchange.

'Bravo, Mrs Goole,' he murmured, 'That's telling him!'

She sniffed. 'I believe in pound-dealing, sir, and it took me a long while to realise that His Lordship don't. And his forcing Miss Warenne to marry him is something I don't hold with,' she ended, giving Flora a look that might have been an apology.

'No, neither do we,' said Conham. 'Thank you for your assistance, Mrs Goole. Now, if you would like to pack your bags, I shall hire a coach to call here in the morning and take you wherever you wish to go.'

He walked with her to the door and ushered her out of the room.

'By heaven, you have a nerve, sir,' exclaimed the Viscount with a savage laugh. 'You treat a servant as if she were a duchess.'

'Her bloodline may well be as noble as yours,' Conham replied, his own lip curling in contempt. 'In the course of our investigations we have discovered that your claim to that red lion rampant is dubious, to say the least. It is far more likely your family came originally from a small place in Scotland. Near Perth, I believe.'

The Viscount glared at him, his face blotched with suppressed fury, and Matt hoped the Earl had not gone too far. They had yet to agree a deal on the statue.

'Now, let us finish this business and we will be on our way,' said Conham, as if reading his mind. He drew a thick wad of notes from his coat. 'I have the sum agreed here, plus papers that require your signature.'

Whilton scowled. 'Yes, yes, if that is what it will take to get you out of my damned house, then let us do it now.'

Matt released the breath he had not realised he was holding before sharing with his friend a swift look of satisfaction.

Conham nodded. 'Very well, you and I will go to your study and conclude the deal.' His gaze rested thoughtfully on Flora, who was clearly labouring under some strong emotion, then he turned and looked at Matt. 'No need for all three of us to go, my friend.'

Matt watched the two men walk out of the room and for a moment there was silence. He was wondering how to get Flora alone when Mrs Farnleigh threw up her hands and gave a little cry.

'Oh, heavens, I was never so shocked in all my life!' she cried, her voice wavering uncertainly.

'There, there, my dear,' said her husband, awkwardly patting her shoulder. 'All's well that ends well, eh?'

'Perhaps, sir, you should order your carriage and take Mrs Farnleigh home now,' Matt suggested. 'His Lordship and I will convey Miss Warenne to Birchwood House once our business here is concluded.' He walked across to Flora, smiling. 'Well, my love, what do you say?'

'Your love?' She regarded him, her face unreadable, then her eyes blazed with fury. 'Your *love*? How *dare* you?'

And with that she launched herself at him like a wildcat.

Chapter Twenty-Four

Flora pummelled Matt's his chest with her fists. Hard. He caught her shoulders and held her off. Farnleigh was staring in astonishment and Matt jerked his head towards the door. He paused only long enough to see the man help his wife to her feet and lead her out of the room before addressing the termagant who was striving to attack him.

'Flora, Flora, what have I done?'

'Done? You odious, *odious* creature!' she cried, struggling against his hold. 'After weeks of silence, you arrive without a word of warning, denounce my fiancé and convince me you are here only to take back your precious statue! And if that was not enough, you h-have the audacity to call me *l-love!*'

Matt almost laughed with relief. He pulled her into his arms, ignoring her half-hearted attempts to resist him, and after a few moments she collapsed against him, weeping into his shoulder.

'And what should I call you?' he murmured, resting his cheek against her hair.

'W-we never s-spoke of love,' she sobbed, her voice muffled against his coat.

He put his fingers beneath her chin and turned her face up towards him.

'Ah. Well, that was a monstrous error, because you are my world. My life.' He placed a gentle kiss on her lips. 'My one and only love.'

For a moment she was motionless, then with a little cry she threw her arms around his neck.

'Oh, Matt...' She sighed, her eyes shining. 'I do love you so!'

She stretched up, meeting his lips with her own in a kiss that expressed all the passion and pent-up emotions of the past few weeks.

'So, do you believe now that I love you?' asked Matt.

He was sitting on the settee with Flora on his lap. She was resting her head against his shoulder and gazing up at him with such a glowing look that he thought he might burst with happiness.

She gave an ecstatic sigh. 'I do, my dearest darling. I should never have doubted you.'

He kissed her again, then settled her more comfortably against him.

'I wish I could have told you, but there was no time to explain. Conham and I were obliged to find the survivors from Whilton's troop, obtain their depositions and get back here in time to stop the wedding. And even then, we did not know if we could pull this off. If Whilton had called our bluff, we could not be sure the army would wish to prosecute after all this time.'

She said in a small voice, 'I thought I did not matter to you. I thought you had come back just for the Rysbrack.'

That was so far from the truth that a laugh escaped him.

'Oh, sweetheart, how could you think I would prize a lump of stone above you?' he said, hugging her closer. 'But I confess that is what I wanted the Viscount to believe. I couldn't look at you because I was afraid he would see how desperately I love you and decide that punishing us both was worth the risk.'

'Yes, I can believe he might well have done that,' said Flora, shuddering.

For a few moments she remained silent, enjoying the comfort of Matt's arms around her, then she raised her head to voice the question that could no longer be ignored.

'Matt, how *can* you love me, knowing that my mother…?'

'That your mother spied for the French? How can you love *me*, knowing my father was an inveterate gambler who left his family penniless?'

She shook her head. 'That is not the same. And

now you run a successful business, you should marry a woman with a good dowry.'

'You have a dowry.'

'A few hundred a year.' She sighed. 'My uncle told me it should have been more, but he was obliged to use most of the money my father left to hush up the scandal.'

'Your money is not important to me, my love. I am not rich, but Bellemonte is flourishing and with your help I am sure we can make it even more successful.' He took her face in his hands. 'Neither of us can change our past, Flora. It is you I love, you I want by my side, now and in the future. As my wife, my partner. For ever.'

'Oh, Matt!'

She slipped her arms about his neck and kissed him, giving herself up to the desire he was rousing in her, until they were interrupted by the sound of voices at the door. She quickly slipped off his lap as Lord Dallamire came in.

'Where is Lord Whilton?' she asked, as he closed the door behind him.

'He has retired, leaving his man in the hall to see us out.'

'But he has signed the deal for the Rysbrack, all right and tight?' asked Matt.

'Oh, yes. You can arrange for your men to collect it and take it back to Bellemonte whenever you wish.'

The Earl grinned. 'He was most affronted when I informed him that duplicates of all those depositions against him are lodged with my lawyers, in case he should go back on his word. He had not thought to make copies of Mrs Warenne's correspondence.'

'Yes, that would be why he wanted to delay handing them over,' she said, nodding. 'He wanted to do the same! Thank goodness Mrs Goole knew where to find them for you.'

Matt's arm tightened around her. 'Aye, she has proved herself very useful this evening.'

'A woman scorned,' murmured the Earl, 'but possibly not for long. When I parted with the Viscount he went off in search of her. I am sorry to pain you, Miss Warenne, but I fear he is more enamoured of his housekeeper than he ever was of you.'

'I cannot be sorry for that, my lord,' she told him, 'Although I am a little sorry for her, if she decides to stay with such a man.'

A sigh escaped her, and Matt kissed her cheek. 'Enough of this. It is time I took you away from here.'

They collected their cloaks and coats and were soon seated in the Earl's carriage and bowling along lanes illuminated by the moonlight. Flora sat in the corner, her hand held snug in Matt's warm grasp.

She said, shyly, 'You must be eager to return to

Bellemonte, but I hope you will call on me before you leave.'

'I am not leaving you at Birchwood House,' Matt told her. 'You are not spending another night without my protection. I have no intention of losing you now. We will call there to collect your maid, if she is willing to come with you. Then, my dear heart, you are coming to the Whilton Arms with Conham and me. From there we will make our way back to Dallamire where we will be married just as soon as it can be arranged.'

'You must forgive my friend, Miss Warenne,' murmured the Earl, the faintest trace of laughter in his voice. 'He is behaving like a tyrant.'

'Nothing of the sort,' exclaimed Matt. 'You don't want to remain with your aunt and uncle, do you, Flora? They were prepared to let you marry that monster to secure their own comfort.'

'No, I do not wish to stay with them indefinitely, after all that has happened. But to desert them, leave them to face all the gossip that is bound to erupt tomorrow, when it becomes known the wedding is cancelled—'

'No one will be surprised to find you have accepted Lady Dallamire's invitation to go and stay for a while, until the dust has settled,' said the Earl. 'However, what you do after that is entirely up to you. You must not let Talacre bully you into marrying him. He has very little to recommend him, you know. No fortune to speak of and a lifetime of hard work ahead of him.'

'That sounds very much like you when Rosina took pity on you,' retorted Matt.

'Ah, but *I* had the advantage of a title.'

Flora laughed and threw up her hands.

'Stop!' she cried. 'Stop funning, both of you! First of all, I would very much like to accept Lady Dallamire's kind invitation, my lord, thank you. As for marrying Matt…'

'Yes?' he prompted, sitting tense and upright beside her.

Flora turned to look at him and said, softly, 'There is nothing I would like more than to spend the rest of my life with him.'

'Thank heaven for that!' exclaimed Matt, taking her in his arms. 'Oh, my dearest love, you have made me the happiest man in the world!'

The Earl watched as Flora melted against Matt and eagerly returned his kiss.

'Well, there seems very little doubt about that,' he muttered, settling himself into his corner and pulling his hat down over his eyes. 'A wedding it is, then, and as soon as may be!'

Epilogue

Summer was in full bloom when Matt and Flora drove into Bellemonte. From the carriage windows they could see the colourful flowers and the first berries adorning the hedgerows.

Matt reached for Flora's hand. She was not wearing gloves and he raised it to his lips.

'My wife.' He pressed a kiss on the gold band adorning her third finger. 'Happy?'

'Oh, yes.' She smiled and rested her head against his shoulder.

It was a full month since Matt had carried her away from Whilton Hall to live as a guest of Lord and Lady Dallamire. A month of busy days arranging her new life and blissful nights with Matt, when he had taken her to heaven and beyond.

The wedding had taken place two weeks ago, with only her aunt and uncle joining the Earl and Countess as witnesses.

'It was very good of Rosina and Conham to allow

us to be married at Dallamire,' she said, 'especially with such a new baby in the house. I enjoyed their company, but I confess I am now impatient to see my new home.'

'And I am impatient to introduce my new bride to Bellemonte,' said Matt, pulling her into his arms. 'I know everyone will love you, as I do!'

She melted into his embrace for another kiss, which lasted until the carriage slowed and began to turn off the highway.

Matt raised his head. 'Ah, we have arrived.'

Flora sat up quickly and straightened her bonnet.

'Oh, dear,' she muttered. 'I must look thoroughly ravaged.'

Matt laughed. 'You look ravishing!'

The carriage slowly moved around the square, passing the gardens where the black railings had been decorated with ribbons and bunches of flowers.

'Oh, how pretty!' exclaimed Flora. 'Did you arrange this, Matt?'

'I told them the date of our expected return, that was all.'

The chaise stopped outside the hotel, where several maids and footmen were hastily lining up along the path.

'Welcome to your new home,' said Matt, jumping down.

They had barely stepped through the gate when the manager hurried out to greet them.

'Welcome home, sir, welcome, madam! I am sorry there aren't more of our people here to greet you, but August is always a busy month and they cannot be spared.'

'No need to explain, Mr Cripps, I am only too pleased to see Bellemonte is so full.'

Flora smiled at the assembled maids and footmen as she accompanied Matt into the hotel.

'I see our baggage coach has arrived,' he said, looking back. 'Shall we let your maid and my man unpack everything before we go upstairs? We might take some refreshments in the morning room while we wait.'

Flora hesitated. 'We have been sitting down for so long that what I should really like is to take a stroll in the gardens.'

'A woman after my own heart,' Matt declared. 'How did you know that is just what I would like to do!'

She looked up at him with a twinkle in her eye. 'I saw you looking longingly towards the gates when we arrived!'

It was deliciously cool under the trees. Matt felt a vast sense of pride as he walked along the winding paths with his new bride on his arm. They went up to the viewing terrace, from where it was easy to look down over the gardens and see how the new plantings were progressing, and he could point out the changes that had occurred since she had last seen the gardens.

Flora was the perfect companion, attentive, interested, eager to discuss future plans and put forward her own suggestions.

The afternoon was well advanced by the time they strolled back down to the main path, which was noticeably quieter now.

Flora said, suddenly, 'This is where we first kissed.'

'Aye. That was when I realised how much I wanted you.'

'And I knew I couldn't have you,' she replied, wistfully.

Matt stopped and drew her into his arms. 'You have me now, my love.'

Flora turned her face up for him to kiss her, clinging tight as the now-familiar desire began to unfurl deep inside.

'We should get back,' she said, between kisses. 'Dinner will be waiting.'

'And after that, bed,' he muttered.

Excitement shivered through Flora at the promise contained in Matt's words and the kisses he trailed along her jaw and over her neck. He raised his head and she heard him drag in a resolute breath.

'You are right,' he said, pulling her hand back on to his arm. 'We must get back, but first, there is one more thing I want you to see.'

Her whole being ablaze with elation, Flora laughed

and shook her head at him. 'You are incorrigible! Very well, but let us be quick.'

They walked on a short way, then Matt stopped.

'Close your eyes,' he commanded.

Flora obeyed, clinging to his arm as he guided her onwards. Soon they turned on to a new path, where the fresh gravel scrunched beneath their feet. She guessed that the trees had been cut back here, because she was aware of the light on her eyelids and the air was fragrant with jasmine and honeysuckle. At last they stopped.

'You can open your eyes now.'

They were on the edge of a sunlit clearing and at its centre were two creamy stone figures, facing one another. Flora turned to Matt, smiling.

'Ares and Aphrodite!'

'Yes. Reunited at last.'

She went forward and rested her hand against the god she had last seen adorning the garden of Whilton Hall.

'You are right,' she agreed. 'He belongs here, with his lady.'

'As we belong here, together?' he asked her.

She heard the note of uncertainty in his voice and went over to put her arms around him.

'Very much so,' she said.

'I have so very little to offer you, Flora,' said Matt. 'There is only the apartment at the hotel for now, but

I shall build you a house, soon. It won't be as grand as Dallamire, but—'

She stopped his rush of words with a kiss.

'I don't want anything as grand as Dallamire,' she murmured, rubbing her cheek against his. 'I love Bellemonte and I am very happy to be living here. In fact,' she murmured, nibbling his ear, 'you promised to teach me to swim in the ladies' bathing pool.'

'Then I shall do so. Starting tomorrow, if you wish.' He stole another kiss before setting off back along the path. 'But there are a few other matters to be dealt with first.'

'Such as dinner, I suppose,' she murmured.

'*Not* dinner, my wicked torment,' he retorted. 'I was thinking more about taking you to bed.'

Flora blushed and laughed. 'That is what is on my mind, too. Perhaps we might walk a *little* faster...?'

* * * * *

*If you loved this story,
be sure to pick up one of
Sarah Mallory's
other charming historical reads*

The Duke's Family for Christmas
The Night She Met the Duke
Snowbound with the Brooding Lord
Wed in Haste to the Duke
The Earl's Marriage Dilemma

MILLS & BOON®

Coming next month

THE FORTUNE HUNTER'S GUIDE TO LOVE
Emma-Claire Sunday

'We're still in this together, right?' Sylvia quickened the pace of her handheld churn.

'Yes, but I assumed I'd be playing a more...advisory role.'

'But courting is...it's a whole production! Usually there's a *team* of people preparing a young lady to catch a husband. I'll need you for promenades, and dates, and hair and makeup of course—'

'I didn't realise your courtship rituals were so complicated.' Hannah finished filling her barrel, then gripped its handle and spun.

'Well, what about you?' Sylvia asked. 'What are your courtship rituals? If you don't care about appearances, how do you attract suitors?'

'Who says I don't care about appearances?' Hannah's face was serious.

'Oh—' Sylvia stopped churning, her hands now over her face. 'I'm so sorry, I didn't mean to imply— You just don't, you don't curl your hair or anything, but—but you are quite comely. Really beautiful, I think.'

Hannah held her expression for just a moment longer, then broke into a wide grin. 'Of course I don't care about *appearances*, Sylvia. But now I know the best way to get a compliment out of you is to just let you talk.'

Sylvia gasped, embarrassed but glad that she hadn't actually insulted Hannah. Still, she decided it was best to stop talking for now. She listened to the scrape of damp wood against the butter-making jug, the squish of cream going solid. Flecks of white splashed across her hands. Her armpits dampened with the sweat of hard work. She sighed.

'Do you actually like them?' Hannah eventually asked.

'Who?'

'The suitors. The men. Do they make you feel…*smitten*?'

'Of course they do,' Sylvia said, but her words were more automatic than genuine. She was becoming too exhausted to be anything other than honest. 'Or, they *will*. They'll make me feel smitten, enamoured, enchanted, all that…but no, not yet.'

'Why not?'

'I had no suitors while in mourning, and the year before I was too young to take the whole thing seriously. This year—this was supposed to be my year.'

Hannah nodded. 'The year of falling in love?'

'Exactly. The year of falling in love. But now…now it's the year of fortune-hunting.'

Continue reading

THE FORTUNE HUNTER'S GUIDE TO LOVE
Emma-Claire Sunday

Available next month
millsandboon.co.uk

Copyright © 2025 Emma-Claire Sunday

COMING SOON!

We really hope you enjoyed reading this book.
If you're looking for more romance
be sure to head to the shops when
new books are available on

Thursday 17th July

To see which titles are coming soon, please visit
millsandboon.co.uk/nextmonth

MILLS & BOON

FOUR BRAND NEW BOOKS FROM
MILLS & BOON MODERN

The same great stories you love, a stylish new look!

OUT NOW

Eight Modern stories published every month, find them all at:

millsandboon.co.uk

afterglow BOOKS

Afterglow Books is a trend-led, trope-filled list of books with diverse, authentic and relatable characters, a wide array of voices and representations, plus real world trials and tribulations. Featuring all the tropes you could possibly want (think small-town settings, fake relationships, grumpy vs sunshine, enemies to lovers) and all with a generous dose of spice in every story.

@millsandboonuk
@millsandboonuk
afterglowbooks.co.uk

#AfterglowBooks

For all the latest book news, exclusive content and giveaways scan the QR code below to sign up to the Afterglow newsletter:

SCAN ME

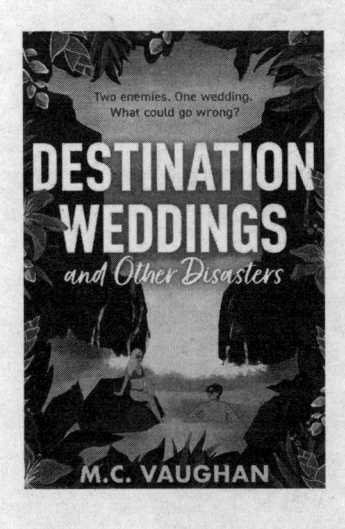

afterglow BOOKS

DESTINATION WEDDINGS and Other Disasters
Two enemies. One wedding. What could go wrong?
M.C. VAUGHAN

The Friends to Lovers Project
She has a plan. But he wasn't part of it...
PAULA OTTONI

- ✈ International
- ❤️‍🔥 Enemies to lovers
- (((♥))) Forced proximity

- 👬 Friends to lovers
- ✈ International
- △ Love triangle

OUT NOW

Two stories published every month. Discover more at:
Afterglowbooks.co.uk

OUT NOW!

Second Chance
HIS UNEXPECTED HEIR

3 BOOKS IN ONE

LOUISE FULLER · AMANDA CINELLI · HEIDI RICE

Available at
millsandboon.co.uk

MILLS & BOON